GUARDIAN

THE TIME HUNTERS

Berkley Sensation Titles by Angela Knight

Mageverse Series

MASTER OF THE NIGHT
MASTER OF THE MOON
MASTER OF WOLVES
MASTER OF SWORDS
MASTER OF DRAGONS

The Time Hunters Series

JANE'S WARLORD
WARRIOR
GUARDIAN

CAPTIVE DREAMS
(with Diane Whiteside)
MERCENARIES

Anthologies

HOT BLOODED
(with Christine Feehan, Maggie Shayne, and Emma Holly)

BITE
(with Laurell K. Hamilton, Charlaine Harris, MaryJanice Davidson, and Vickie Taylor)

KICK ASS
(with Maggie Shayne, MaryJanice Davidson, and Jacey Ford)

OVER THE MOON
(with MaryJanice Davidson, Virginia Kantra, and Sunny)

BEYOND THE DARK
(with Emma Holly, Lora Leigh, and Diane Whiteside)

SHIFTER
(with Lora Leigh, Alyssa Day, and Virginia Kantra)

GUARDIAN
THE TIME HUNTERS

Angela Knight

BERKLEY SENSATION, NEW YORK

THE BERKLEY PUBLISHING GROUP
Published by the Penguin Group
Penguin Group (USA) Inc.
375 Hudson Street, New York, New York 10014, USA
Penguin Group (Canada), 90 Eglinton Avenue East, Suite 700, Toronto, Ontario M4P 2Y3, Canada
(a division of Pearson Penguin Canada Inc.)
Penguin Books Ltd., 80 Strand, London WC2R 0RL, England
Penguin Group Ireland, 25 St. Stephen's Green, Dublin 2, Ireland (a division of Penguin Books Ltd.)
Penguin Group (Australia), 250 Camberwell Road, Camberwell, Victoria 3124, Australia
(a division of Pearson Australia Group Pty. Ltd.)
Penguin Books India Pvt. Ltd., 11 Community Centre, Panchsheel Park, New Delhi—110 017, India
Penguin Group (NZ), 67 Apollo Drive, Rosedale, North Shore 0632, New Zealand
(a division of Pearson New Zealand Ltd.)
Penguin Books (South Africa) (Pty.) Ltd., 24 Sturdee Avenue, Rosebank, Johannesburg 2196,
South Africa

Penguin Books Ltd., Registered Offices: 80 Strand, London WC2R 0RL, England

GUARDIAN

A Berkley Sensation Book / published by arrangement with the author

ISBN-13: 978-1-61523-072-3

BERKLEY® SENSATION
Berkley Sensation Books are published by The Berkley Publishing Group,
a division of Penguin Group (USA) Inc.,
375 Hudson Street, New York, New York 10014.
BERKLEY® SENSATION and the "B" design are trademarks of Penguin Group (USA) Inc.

PRINTED IN THE UNITED STATES OF AMERICA

As with all my books, I relied on my wonderful team of critique partners and readers to help me make *Guardian* as strong as possible. My dear friends Diane Whiteside and Margaret Riley were, as always, hugely helpful with plotting and brainstorming. Kate Douglas, a kind friend and outstanding writer, offered encouragement. Other readers include Linda Kusiolek and my wonderful Bookdragon, Virginia Ettel, who also moderates my Yahoo! Group with Diane's help. And then there's Roberta Brown, my personal agent goddess, who patiently read and commented on early drafts.

I also want to thank my computer genius brother-in-law, David Woodcock, who helped me speculate on future cybernetics. His knowledge of science and science fiction is invaluable.

My editor, Cindy Hwang, was, as always, both patient and encouraging. Her assistant, Leis Pederson, is always ready to help with anything I need, and I appreciate her deeply.

Most of all, I want to dedicate this book to my own personal hero, Mike Woodcock, husband extraordinaire, whose patience and love keeps me going.

Prologue

New York, 1993

Nick Wyatt lay sprawled across the twin bed, one
wiry arm flung over his tearstained face. He felt vaguely
ashamed. He was fourteen, dammit. He shouldn't be crying like a little girl.

But his mother was gone. For his entire life, she'd protected him, hidden him, run with him from the men . . .
no, *aliens* who sought to kill them both. He vividly remembered the way she'd looked the night they'd been cornered.
The Stone had burned on her upper arm, glowing like a
star as she'd punched and kicked, fighting off the six armored aliens like Jackie Chan.

She'd told him the Stone wouldn't allow its power to be
used in direct attacks. Which was stupid, if you asked him.
But she'd found it could be used to amplify physical strength
and protect fragile muscle and bone from impact with armored flesh.

They'd been so much bigger than she was in their red
and black scaled suits. When he was little, he'd called them

the Snake Men, but that sounded dumb to him now. And anyway, his mother said they weren't snakes. But they were strong, and they had swords that could cut through anything, kind of like light sabers. His mother had killed two of them with their own weapons, then grabbed him and run. They'd lost the aliens in back alleys of the city, as she carried him through the darkness in long, superhuman bounds. Her face above him had been set with a combination of fear and determination, her eyes hollow with a terrible *aloneness*.

"There's no one I can count on to help protect you," she'd told him once. "And protecting you is the only thing that matters."

She'd devoted her entire life to teaching him everything she knew about avoiding the aliens, fighting the aliens, hiding from the aliens. She was very good at fighting and running and hiding. But that hadn't saved her two days ago.

The question of how she'd died nagged at him like a deep, bleeding wound. All he knew was that he'd been playing Sonic the Hedgehog when the Stone had suddenly appeared around his upper arm. He'd heard his mother's dying voice coming from it, telling him she loved him and that he must survive.

And then there was nothing else.

He'd blown his Sega into a thousand ricocheting shards with a blast of light—and pure rage. He didn't care. Not about that stupid game, not about anything.

You must eat, the Stone said. It had taken to talking to him in the last day. He wasn't even sure if the deep, thrumming voice was real. *You haven't eaten in two days.*

"Fuck you," he snarled. "You didn't protect her. It was your job, *and you didn't protect her.*"

There were too many for her. And it was time for me to come to you.

Nick slammed his foot into the wall, leaving a deep dent in the plasterboard. "Fuck off."

The girl needs you. She is dying.

That was new. A girl? The Stone hadn't mentioned her before. Not that Nick gave a rat's ass. "I don't care about some stupid girl. I care about my mother, and you let her die!"

So you will let the girl die, too? There was disappointment in the deep, velvet voice. Almost like the father on a sitcom who'd caught his kid doing something wrong. Nick had never had a father like that. Heck, he didn't even know who his father was. *You could save her. You could keep her parents from grieving as you grieve. I could help you. Look . . .*

Suddenly he was in a dark room. The walls were strange, curving, dimly lit by a red light that seemed to have no source. And he was tied. Something cold and metallic circled his wrists and ankles, pinning him spread-eagle to a chilly, smooth surface. Jerking his head up, Nick saw strange symbols marked on the floor around him. *Like some kind of spell . . .*

His gaze fell on a statue at his feet. It was only about two feet high, but it looked like solid gold, except for black eyes that seemed to stare at Nick with hungry intensity. Two golden horns crowned its head, with a third protruding between them. It was naked, and its cock was huge. Nick recoiled at the sheer threatening *dirtiness* of it.

What the hell was going on? He was obviously having some kind of vision. His mother used to have those all the time. Her eyes would go out of focus, and her body would twitch as fear and worry chased each other across her face. Most of the visions were warnings from the Stone, some of which she told him about. Some she'd refused to describe at all.

"Let me go!" Nick screamed the words, but it wasn't

him screaming, and it wasn't his voice. It was a girl's. And
the words—whatever language she was speaking, it wasn't
English. He didn't know how he understood it. "My father's
going to kill you!" she yelled. "My wolf is going to rip out
your throat!"

My wolf?

A male voice laughed. "Oh, no doubt. No one escapes
the Death Lord and his dog." A man walked into her line
of vision. He was massive, with a ring of short silver horns
crowning his head. His eyes were red, slitted like a reptile's.
"But by then, you'll be dead. A sacrifice to the Victor."

That's how they look without their armor, the Stone
whispered.

That's *an alien*? Nick could believe it. Evil-looking bastard.

The man crouched at the girl's feet. "You know, I was
your age when your father killed mine. Just twelve years
old. Son of the great general Gavoni Jutka." His mouth
curled into a snarl of black rage. "Who was butchered by
the Death Lord, thus preventing the rightful conquest of
your stinking little planet!" His voice rose toward a roar.

"Jutka ordered the murder of my father's combat team!"
the girl snarled back. Nick had to admire her courage,
though he wished she had the sense to keep her mouth
shut. "He deserved exactly what he got!"

"So does yours, you bitch." Red eyes narrowed. "And I'm
going to make sure he gets it." He straightened to his full
height. "You're a little skinny, and a bit young for my taste,
but I could"—his hand descended to stroke his groin—
"ignore your flaws. If it meant seeing the look on Baran
Arvid's face when I tell him I took you before I slit your
throat and let you bleed out at the Victor's feet." His mouth
curled into a vicious grin. "A fitting sacrifice to our great
god." He turned and bowed deeply to the golden statue.

Nick could have cared less about the alien's god. He

was too busy trying to digest the horror of the bastard's threat. *Didn't he say she's only twelve? Jesus! I've got to do something! A blast . . .*

Would not work. They are too far away for even my power. But Baran, her father, searches for her. Reach for him. Show him where she is.

But I don't know where she is!

You must find out. Reach for them. Feel them.

How?

That is for you to determine. Your test.

He wanted to tell the Stone what it could do with its tests, but the alien was describing exactly what he intended to do to the little girl. The words were so filthy, she didn't entirely understand what he was saying, but Nick knew. He could feel it in the bastard's mind.

Had they done *that* to his mother? Had they . . . gloated like that?

Her father. He had to find this Baran Arvid. Nick could imagine him out there somewhere, thinking of her, panic clawing at his heart, the same sick, empty, helpless fear Nick felt. It was too easy to imagine how he'd feel if the alien carried out his threats on that helpless little girl.

There. Driving fear, somewhere in the distance, with a fierce, cold strength behind it. A grown man's mind, a warrior's intelligence. Nick reached for the Power of the Stone, flung himself for that distant point of will. He felt the rush of energy, a sense of speed, as that cool intelligence approached. He struck it hard . . .

And bounced.

Nick floated in darkness, stunned, blinking. It took him a moment to figure out what had just happened.

Baran's mind had blocked him out. It was as if the man's skull was enclosed in a solid steel bubble.

Like hell. Gritting his teeth, Nick gathered his power and drove against that shield again. And again, battering at

it, shouting, *screaming.* Baran strode on, unhearing, unaware of his desperate attempts.

He's too strong, too closed, the Stone said. *Try the other.*
What other?

There. Another point of desperation, trotting by the side
of the girl's father, nose to the ground, scenting, seeking.

Her wolf.

But this was no ordinary animal. The mind he touched
was a blend of instinct and computer intelligence. But there
was fear, too, and raw desperation. All of which left its
mind open to him. He shot inside, and was abruptly looking out of lupine eyes.

They strode along a strange street. People streamed by
dressed in strange, colorful robes, and odd craft zipped
through the sky overhead. Buildings towered to either side,
curving, pale shapes that looked like nothing he'd ever
seen before.

In one of them, a soaring needle brushing the sky ahead,
he could feel the girl. Feel her terror, feel the sick anticipation of her alien captor. Feel how little time was left.

Somehow—he never knew exactly how—he reached
out and planted that knowledge within the wolf.

"There!" the animal said—it *talked*?—in the same odd
language she'd used. "I know where she is!" He broke into
a run, his claws clicking on the cool, strangely smooth
walkway.

"What?" Baran demanded, sprinting after him, dodg-
ing pedestrians who ducked aside with indignant shouts.
"Frieka, where in the Seven Hells are you going?"

But the wolf didn't stop, driven by Nick's fear, Nick's
knowledge of just how little time they had. Baran charged
after him, winding through the crowd, ignoring the shouts
and stares.

The two were fast, and yet so horribly slow, reaching
the needle spire some endless time later. The doors snapped

open for them, and they charged inside. They ducked into some kind of tube thing that swept them upward on a column of invisible force.

Finally—finally!—they reached the right floor and exited into a long corridor, Nick/wolf leading the way. The hall was lined with doors, all in soft blues, all firmly closed.

"Riane!" the wolf bellowed, his voice ringing out.

"Frieka!" the girl screamed from behind one of the doors ahead. "Help me!"

The alien cursed. "Bitch!" Steel slithered, the sound of a knife being drawn.

Baran dove past the wolf in a furious, bull-like lunge, hitting the third door like a cannon blast. Either the door was thin or he was incredibly strong, because it caved in like a sheet of tinfoil. He didn't stop, blood flying in his wake as he charged for the alien. He'd cut himself breaking down that door.

With a startled shout, the kidnapper leaped to his feet and swung his knife at Baran's throat. Baran blocked the blade with one arm, ignoring the spray of blood as it connected with his wrist. His fist rammed into the alien's horned skull. And *through* it in a spray of gore and bone.

As the alien fell dead, the wolf licked the girl's face with joyous desperation. Nick had time to notice the red and blue tattoo that spilled down one side of her face before Baran broke her bonds and jerked her into his arms.

"Mother Goddess, Riane, I thought we had lost you!" he choked out.

She wrapped her thin arms around his massive neck and clung. "He was crazy, Daddy! He was going to sacrifice me to that sick god of theirs." She began to cry, great gulping sobs. "I didn't think you'd get to me in time . . ."

"Baby, don't cry. Frieka found you." He dropped a big hand to the wolf's head. "I don't know how."

"I don't either," the wolf said. "I'm just damned glad I did."

Nick opened his eyes. The familiar dingy beige of the ceiling lay over his head, with the same water spot he'd been staring at for the last two days. Yet he no longer felt such black despair.

He hadn't been able to save his mother, but he'd saved that girl. What was that name her father had called her? Diane? No, with an R . . . Riane.

Maybe he had a reason to go on after all. Maybe.

He'd still have to run, hide, as his mother had taught him. Avoiding the aliens had never been easy. It would be even harder for a fourteen-year-old kid alone. Though with the powers the Stone gave him, he could probably get people to help him or ignore him—or both—depending on what he needed.

And maybe he could save others as he had Riane. That had to be worth something. Didn't it?

Maybe he'd even see her again . . .

· 1 ·

Milltown, South Carolina, sixteen years later

The vision rolled over Nick Wyatt like a lush, erotic storm—the richly feminine scent of a woman, the intoxicating taste of an eager mouth, the feel of rose-petal skin, delicate over long, firm muscle. He did not know her, had never met her, yet the vision branded her on his consciousness with white-hot reality. His body leaped for hers, hardened in a burning rush.

Lips like distilled sin curled into a hot smile that flashed in his mind. Her eyes blazed at him through the darkness, feral scarlet light behind the fall of her fiery hair.

She is not human.

His mind whispered it at him, the warning almost enough to chill his heat. Almost.

Then he saw the curving line from breast to hip, the sweep of long leg, the feline shift of weight as she moved. And the heat rose again. His cock lengthened, stretching, aching, as his balls tightened between his thighs. In that moment, he didn't care whether she was human or not.

Her hair fell back, revealing her features, and he saw her clearly for the first time. An intricate tattoo in shades of red and blue curled along one side of her face.

He knew her after all. Hell, he'd never been able to forget her.

It was the girl. The girl he'd last seen when she was the twelve-year-old prisoner of a murderous alien. But like him, she was no child now.

He'd found her again.

Nick snapped out of the vision with a jerk, his body stiffening, his heart banging furiously. There was something cold and heavy in his hand. He looked down and saw the Glock. He'd been cleaning the big automatic when the vision hit. Feeling clumsy, disconnected, he put the .45 aside on the end table, barely noticing the stiff wire brush that fell from the fingers of his other hand. The air smelled of gun oil and the ghostly memory of her scent.

The Stone cast a soft green glow that danced around the room as he reeled to his feet. Its power heated the intricate silver setting that clasped his biceps like a hand. The heavily engraved metal felt almost hot enough to burn.

Definitely a vision then, not just a horny dream born of celibacy.

Sweat rolled down his naked torso into the waistband of his worn jeans as he padded barefoot across the little apartment. He heaved the window open despite the shriek of glass and the protesting creak of wood. His landlord had painted it shut. With his strength, Nick had scarcely noticed the resistance as paint ripped free.

He let his damp shoulder thump against the frame of the window as he stared out into the night, heart pounding. The headlights of passing cars swept past the apartment complex. Normal people, heading home to normal lives, never knowing what lay just beyond the edges of their worlds.

Here be monsters.

Nick knew all about monsters.

A welcome breeze poured into the room past the dingy curtains, drying the sweat that dewed his massive shoulders, the thick slabs of pecs and abdominals. The cool kiss of it drew his attention downward to his zipper, lying in an uncomfortable ridge over his aching erection.

Hunger growled through his blood, demanding release, ancient and animal. Shuddering at the touch on sensitized skin, Nick unzipped his jeans. His cock leaped out into his hand, hard and heavy.

Clenching his teeth on a rumble of hoarse need, he began to stroke the thick shaft.

Whether she'd be his destruction or his salvation, the girl—woman now—was coming. The only question was when she'd arrive.

He wished he could ask the Stone, but it no longer spoke to him with anything but visions and flashes of intuition. He suspected it had only spoken to him when he was a boy because it had known how close he was to ending his own life.

But now she was coming. At last.

He couldn't wait.

The planet Xer, in the future

Ivar Terje strutted along the Cathedral Fortress's dark corridors, pretending to ignore the Xerans' contemptuous glances at his hornless head. They made a big deal out of the horns they all wore; the pattern and shape and engraving translated into social status and religious accomplishment.

Which Ivar didn't have.

He ground his teeth in irritation. He'd sacrificed for these bastards, betrayed his own people to help the Xerans achieve their goals. You'd think that would earn him a little respect.

Now he'd been summoned like an errand boy. They'd even sent a cadre of guards to get him. All six strode along around him, impassive in their gaudy black and red armor.

Maybe they were going to give him another mission. He'd been cooling his heels here for two weeks, ever since they'd broken him out of the Outpost brig. He wanted *off* this planet of horned religious lunatics. Wanted it almost as much as he craved revenge on the Enforcers he'd once served beside.

Sanctimonious bastards. Especially Chief Alerio Dyami, who'd dared to lock him in that brig. Ivar was going to kill that son of a bitch first. Especially since Dyami was probably banging Ivar's ex-lover, Dona. The two had been rutting after each other for years. They just hadn't known *Ivar* knew it. But then, they hadn't known shit, not about his treason, not about anything. Until he'd damn near beaten Dona to death a couple of weeks ago.

It hadn't even been difficult to fool them all, because Ivar was very, very good at what he did. *Anything* he did. A neuronet computer wound through his cyborg brain, enhancing his reaction time just as countless nanobots reinforced every muscle fiber and bone cell in his cyborg body. All of which gave him enough strength to make him more than a match for even a Warlord like Dyami. He was looking forward to proving it by beating the fucker's face in.

He was still smiling at the thought of Dyami's bloody death when the guards escorted him into a room so cavernous, their armored footsteps echoed. There were no seats anywhere in the vast stone chamber—just black columns and red silk hangings. No windows either. Instead, the walls were inset with stone niches in which stood statues of people writhing in pain or ecstacy—could be both, knowing the Xerans.

Sick fucks.

One statue drew his attention: a shimmering figure of a huge man, apparently solid gold. One big foot was planted on the neck of a cowering figure who was obviously a Vardonese Warlord, judging by the long, beaded hair. Ivar grinned, reminded of Chief Dyami.

The Xerans had invaded Vardon forty years ago or so, occupying the planet for five years until the Warlords drove them off with a vicious guerrilla war. It was the first major defeat Xer had ever suffered.

Ivar wondered if the statue was supposed to represent history—or future intention. Probably the latter; the Xer still held a grudge against their Warlord enemies. They fully intended to retake Vardon and kill every last warrior.

He thoroughly approved.

When they reached the front of the room, the leader of the guards rounded on him. "On your knees! Now! He comes!"

He bristled at the command, but the guards were already kneeling, their armored shins ringing on the stone. Ivar shrugged and knelt.

On cue, sound roared over them—something somewhere between booming thunder and music, so deafening it made Ivar's skull ring and his breastbone vibrate. Light poured from the dais at the front of the room, a searing illumination that stabbed his eyes and blinded him. For a moment he could see nothing, hear nothing.

"This is the tool thou hast brought for Me?" The voice rolled out of the glare, silken and deep, like the echo of distant thunder. Whoever it was spoke the Xeran Priest Tongue, with its elaborate syntax and rolling syllables.

"Aye, Most Glorious," said the guard beside him.

But . . . *Tool*? He was no one's *tool*.

He lifted his head and squinted. Something huge and glowing was moving toward them. Blinking his watering, aching eyes, Ivar managed to make out what it was.

The blazing figure was nearly three meters tall and humanoid in shape, despite the light pouring from its massive body. As he struggled to make out the details, the glow dimmed a little, until it was less like staring directly into a star.

The figure was naked—and was definitely a "he." His sex hung thick and pendulous between brawny thighs as he stepped down off the dais and moved toward them. His body was powerful, so massively built it had to be genetically engineered. His face appeared human, with a broad jaw, nose a long, aquiline swoop, mouth wide but thin-lipped over a square chin. His smooth, bald head was crowned with horns—the primary set jutting from his temples, wickedly sharp, thick, curving upward like a bull's, spreading out almost the width of immense shoulders; a central spiral horn thrust from his forehead. Unlike the ones everybody else had, they didn't seem to be implants.

A big hand slammed against the back of Ivar's head, knocking him flat on his face. "Eyes down!" the guard hissed. "You are not worthy to look upon the face of the god!"

Normally he'd have hit the fucker back, but he was too stunned. *The Victor. That's supposed to be the Victor!* He'd seen intelligence reports that the Xerans' god was a living being, but he'd never really believed them.

Surprising that a supposedly advanced, sophisticated people were taken in by a little glow and surgery. He'd seen better effects in a triddie.

Naked, shining feet stopped before his eyes. Heat rolled from them in waves he could almost see. "So thou art the traitor."

Stung, Ivar started to rear up. Before he could rise, a massive hand closed over the back of his neck, lifted him effortlessly off the ground, and held him dangling like a puppy. The heat of those huge fingers seared his skin, but he refused to let the pain show on his face.

The Victor studied him. In contrast to the rest of that glowing face, his eyes were solid ovals of black, with no whites at all. Pinpoints of light swirled in them.

Ivar curled his lip. "Are those supposed to be stars?"

The Victor didn't even dignify that sneer with an answer, instead looking down at his guards, who still knelt, heads deeply bowed. "I have pinpointed the Demon's location. Police records of the time reveal he saved some female from an attacker again." He smirked, an oddly human expression. "One would think he would learn. See to setting our trap."

The chief guard bowed until his forehead touched the floor. "As Thou will, Most Glorious."

"As for you . . ." The Victor turned his attention fully on Ivar. Yeah, there were stars in those eyes. Stars, nebulae. An infinite darkness, cold and inhuman.

And insane. There was nothing at all sane in the Victor's eyes.

Suddenly all of this was a hell of a lot less funny.

"Now," the Victor said, "we shall attend to thee. Thou must have more power, if thou wouldst go against the Demon." He cocked his horned head, considering Ivar with chilling attention. "Thy computer system may be improved, I think. And the cybernetic enhancements thou art so proud of—they can be made more efficient to add to thy strength and speed."

Still holding him by the scruff of the neck, the Victor reached for him with the other hand. Ivar flinched, tried to strike out with fists and feet.

He couldn't move. The bastard had paralyzed him.

A massive finger seared the exact center of his forehead. Something pooled on his flesh like lava, seeped inside, and began to eat its way into his skull.

The pain made him want to shriek. He clenched his teeth, damned if he'd scream for this arrogant fucker.

"Pride." The Victor smiled, cold and slight. "I do enjoy breaking the pride of my toys."

The "god" took his finger away and dropped Ivar on the floor. He tried to catch himself, but his body still wouldn't obey. He collapsed in a heap, the horrific burn spreading. He fought not to writhe, but each beat of his heart sent waves of acid eating through bone and blood and muscle.

Finally, unable to hold the sound back anymore, Ivar began to scream.

He had no idea how much time went by as he roasted, howling his throat raw, in that pit of agony. Minutes, hours, days—it scarcely mattered. But finally the pain bled away, and he could see again.

He flinched like a whipped dog when he registered the glowing face looming over his.

"Now," the Victor said, crouching beside him, "let Me tell thee thy part."

· 2 ·

The Outpost

Temporal Enforcer Riane Arvid fished a piece of chiva out of its wrapper and gave it a little offhand flip, sending it arching toward her wolf partner. Frieka snapped it out of the air and swallowed happily. She dug out another nugget of the fragrant meat and popped it into her own mouth, enjoying the spicy taste of hot, rich juices.

They'd stopped by their favorite kiosk in the Outpost's concourse wing for lunch. Now they strolled along window-shopping, staring at the bright three-dimensional displays that floated in midair before the stores.

"Clothing for any era, synthesized here!" a female voice purred. "High-quality, appearing handmade! Outfit your time-travel party at affordable prices."

"Transfer your galactors into appropriate currency for your trip," said a computer-generated actor in a banker's conservative robes.

"Safe, painless, and fast—TempJump Tubes will take you to any time in complete comfort." A triddie showed a happy family of three stepping into a thick transparent tube, only to reappear a moment later in ancient Egypt.

Unlike Temporal Enforcement agents, tourists and scholars weren't permitted T-suits, which would have allowed them to Jump around the time stream at will. TE preferred to control where civilians went, and what they did when they got there.

Which was the whole point of the Outpost. A blend of police station, infirmary, and time-travel hub, the huge facility was buried deep inside a mountain in sixteenth-century North America. It was one of several installations used by temporal tourists and the Enforcers who protected them.

Riane and Frieka were among the two hundred agents stationed at the Outpost, investigating temporal crimes and rescuing tourists from accidents or attack.

It was a job Riane was well suited for. Like her father before her, she was a Vardonese warrior, stronger and faster than any normal human. A nanobot computer network wound through her brain, a match to the sensors implanted throughout her body. The comp gave her access to *riaat*, a biochemically induced berserker state that could turn her into a one-woman army. Between that and her training as a Temporal Enforcement agent, there wasn't much Riane Arvid couldn't handle.

Riane dug out another morsel of meat and let Frieka lip it from her fingers. They separated a moment to pass a bearded, long-haired man dressed in filthy buckskins. His face was gaunt, his eyes shadowed from weariness and lack of sleep. Probably an anthropologist or historian, back from a long trip experiencing life as an eighteenth-century fur trapper.

Frieka sneezed explosively. "Hey, buddy, you're home— get a bath already! You smell like a beaver."

The man looked a little startled. Probably wasn't used to cybernetically enhanced animals anymore. "Uh—sorry."

"Frieka!" Riane swatted the wolf gently on the top of the head. "Excuse him," she told the scholar. "I think his etiquette program needs an upgrade."

The cyborg wolf stuck out his long pink tongue at her, a twenty-first-century gesture he'd picked up from Riane's mother.

Genetically engineered for intelligence as well as size and strength, Frieka had a computer implant and sensors of his own. He'd been her father's partner in the Vardonese military for years. Later he'd served the family as Riane's bodyguard, tutor, and nursemaid when she was growing up.

Now, though he was a very old wolf indeed, Frieka had become her partner Enforcer. Thanks to regeneration technology and genetic engineering, Riane hoped to listen to him nag, bitch, and make bad jokes for many more years.

Abruptly the voice of Riane's computer implant filled her mind. *"Incoming message from Chief Enforcer Alerio Dyami."*

Good. A mission. *"Put him through."*

"Report to Mission Staging," Dyami said in his deep, velvet voice. *"Chief Investigator Corydon has a lead on Ivar Terje's location. You two are on the takedown team."*

"Hot damn!" Frieka bounced a little on his paws, tongue lolling in a grin. "'Bout time! I want to sink my fangs in that dickhole's butt."

"Sounds like a plan to me." Riane gave her partner a vicious smile. The last time she'd seen Ivar, he'd damn near blown her to hell during his escape from the Outpost's brig. "I'll hold him down while you dine."

Mission Staging was three floors up from the concourse. A large, brightly lit room, it lacked the usual wide window looking out over the mountains. The heavy shielding designed to control the energies of a mass Jump didn't really allow for a great view.

A long conference table in dark Temporal Enforcement blue took up one end of the room. Graceful silver chairs upholstered in the same blue surrounded it.

At the opposite end of Mission Staging, ten regeneration tubes stood on end in case something went wrong on a Jump. And it very well might, Riane thought grimly, given that they were going after Ivar. He was one nasty piece of work.

Which was probably why the rest of the takedown team looked so tense. There were ten on the team, counting Riane and Frieka, all in full armor: helmets, gloves, T-suits in the blue and silver of Temporal Enforcement, weapons belts hung with shard pistols, knives, and an array of other equipment. They were all Chief Dyami's best agents. Only Master Enforcer Galar Arvid was missing, since he was off on two weeks' leave with his beautiful new wife.

Chief Investigator Alex Corydon stood eyeing the milling Enforcers with the icy, rigid suspicion of a man who thought himself surrounded by a nest of traitors. He was firmly convinced somebody at the Outpost had been working with Ivar.

Riane curled her lip at him. He'd spent hours last week grilling her about her loyalties. The idea that anybody would think she'd stoop to working for Xerans thoroughly pissed her off. Riane had told him just how close she'd come to being raped and murdered by one of the bastards when she was barely twelve, but Corydon had only sniffed in skepticism.

Frieka had wanted to bite a butt chunk out of the human for that sniff. She'd damn near let him.

"All right, folks, attention." Chief Alerio Dyami's voice rang across the room. Instantly, the agents turned expectant gazes on him. Dyami was a big man—but then, like

Riane's father, he was a Viking Class Warlord. He was
computer enhanced and genetically engineered for battle,
and there wasn't much he couldn't do. Combat decorations
gleamed in his long, dark hair, and the gold and green tattoo of House Dyami spilled down one half of his handsome face. He turned dark eyes on Corydon and lifted a
black brow. "Senior Investigator?"

The human drew himself to his full height and puffed
out his narrow chest. "We have reason to believe that Ivar
Terje has taken refuge in nineteenth-century New York."
Corydon's teeth shone very white against the inky blue-
black sheen of his skin as his eyes narrowed into slits of
metallic gold. Hair the color of flame was bound in a se-
vere braid that emphasized the height of his perfect cheekbones. The dramatic coloring made him look intensely
alien, though in reality, he was nothing more than human.
That purebred DNA was yet another reason he hated every
genetically engineered Enforcer on the team. "There's a
great deal of temporal activity in a Brooklyn Heights neigh-
borhood which suggests a lot of people Jumping in and out
of the area. I sent a surveillance 'bot which confirmed he's
there."

He turned to the table and gestured. The Outpost computer responded, displaying a trid image obviously taken
by one of the tiny aerial couriers.

Ivar climbed the stairs of a brownstone, his big body
more than a little out of place in the careful tailoring of a
Victorian gentleman. His red hair shone like warm copper
in the light of a gas street lamp, but his eyes were as cold
and gray as an arctic sea as he turned to scan the street.

Riane frowned. The 'bot must have been heavily shielded.
The cyborg's sensors would have detected it otherwise.

"When did your 'bot shoot this?" Dyami asked.

"Ten-thirty-two p.m., May 12, 1872. We will arrive ten
minutes later." Corydon gestured, and the image pulled

out, displaying the view as the 'bot circled the building. "I want to post teams here, here, and here," he said, pointing at spots around the structure. "When I give the signal, we'll hit him. I want two teams entering through the front, and the other two through the servants' entry here."

Chief Dyami rocked back on his heels, frowning deeply. "What kind of backup does he have? You did say there were people Jumping in and out of the area."

Corydon gestured again, and data from the 'bot's sensors flashed beside the image. "There is no one else in the building during the strike period other than Ivar himself."

The Chief continued to question him, to Corydon's obvious irritation. Finally Dyami reached for his helmet and slid it on. "Let's move. We've got a spy to catch."

"We'll Jump two at a time," Corydon said. "I don't want to warn Terje with a big energy spike."

Riane saw the point—ten people Jumping at once generated a hell of a lot of energy that could be detected centuries away. On the other hand, it was equally likely Ivar would detect them as they Jumped in two at a time.

"Be ready to pursue if he initiates a Jump," Dyami said. "I don't want to lose the bastard in the time stream."

Ten helmeted heads nodded understanding as hands dropped to holstered shard pistols.

Corydon and Alerio Jumped first. Energy bloomed blue-white from the center of their suits, flaring to a blinding, eye-searing intensity that made every hair lift on Riane's body. If not for the suits' energy-damping field the backwash would have given everyone in the room a very unpleasant shock.

Then both men were simply gone, with a cracking sonic boom.

Two by two, the other Enforcers made their Jumps. Finally it was Riane and Frieka's turn. She started the procedure with the skill of long practice. "Jump coordinates?"

The wolf rattled them off. Riane checked his figures on the glowing heads-up display that had appeared on the inside of his visor. The coordinates were correct—she'd triple-checked them earlier. But you didn't play fast and loose with a time Jump.

"Initialize T-suit," Riane told her computer implant.

"T-suit initialized."

"Jump."

The moment the energy surge began, Riane knew it was all going to hell. It was way too much warp for a Jump of only three hundred years. Her suit blazed against her skin, excess energy bleeding into heat. Biting back a scream, she mentally roared, *"Abort! Abort Jump!"*

"Aborting . . ." Agony blinded her.

The comp said, *"Suit not responding."*

Shit piss fuck.

Light flooded Riane's vision, stabbing her corneas like molten ice picks. Every muscle in her body locked and jolted as if she'd grabbed a bare high-voltage line. She felt herself being ripped apart, and knew she was going to be one of the ones who went on a Jump and never came back.

The last thing she heard was Frieka's terrified howl. "Riane! Your suit . . ."

Relief pierced her fear. *At least whatever it is isn't getting Frieka . . .*

Riane materialized in the middle of a jungle, emerald green light spilling around her. She sighed. Well, she'd materialized, though the Mother Goddess only knew . . .

Oh, fuck!

Another warp was building, the heat blazing through her suit. "Abort!" she snapped, without much hope.

"Suit not responding."

"No sh—"

And she was gone again.

The Jumps came hard and fast after that, giving her no time to register anything beyond flashes of impressions: a man in a kimono, staring at her in shock; *Jump*; a burning castle in the distance; *Jump*; a herd of horses plunging away at full gallop; *Jump*; a dingy medieval street . . .

The T-suit's protection began to break down as it lost power with all those repeated warps through space and time. The burn of her body became a continuous, shrieking pain, her stomach rioting so violently every time she materialized that it was all she could do not to heave in her helmet.

This is sabotage, she realized. *Has to be. Somebody got to my suit. But how? Who? And why me?*

· 3 ·

Frieka materialized outside the Brooklyn Heights
brownstone, his heart pounding with panic. "Riane!" he
hissed, his comp sending out a simultaneous com call. "Riane, where are you?"

Desperately, he began to run around the building, his
paws thumping on the cobblestones as he scanned for his
partner. But there was no sign of her—or, for that matter,
Ivar Terje.

The last time he'd felt such fear had been when that
damned Xeran had abducted her when she was twelve.
Snatched her right off her gravboard as Frieka watched
helplessly from below. He'd run after them, howling in desperation, until the Xeran's airbike had zoomed out of sight.
I've lost her again, Baran! he thought in black despair.
And you're not around to help.

"What's going on, Frieka?" Chief Enforcer Alerio
Dyami's cool voice demanded over his comp's communication frequency.

The big Warlord seemed to appear out of thin air as he dropped his sensor shielding. Frieka sighed in relief. The Chief would know what to do. "Riane's disappeared, sir," he said, trotting to the man's side. "Something went wrong with her Jump. There was too much power in the temporal warp. Her T-suit either malfunctioned or was sabotaged."

"Given the circumstances, my money's on sabotage. Especially since Terje's nowhere to be found." The Chief turned toward Corydon, who hurried toward them, a frown on his blue-black face. "Where the hell is our spy, Corydon?"

The Senior Investigator glowered. "Someone must have warned him. It's what I've been telling you all along— you've got another mole in your organization. Probably Dona Astryr." His lip curled. "His lover."

"Dona might have been Ivar's lover once, but she's not anymore. And *my* investigation cleared her." With a growl, Dyami lifted his head and sent out a com call. *"All right, people, Ivar slipped our trap, and we're missing an Enforcer we're bloody well going to find. Let's get the hell out of here before some temporal natives show up to investigate. Start Jumping for home."* The Chief looked down at Frieka, who was trying not to dance in his anxiety. "Let's go."

With a sigh of relief, Frieka sent a command to his T-collar. A moment later, the temporal warp ripped him apart and carried him away.

Just before he vanished, he thought, *I lost her, Baran. But I'm going to get her back.*

Riane's T-suit had—just barely—enough juice to put her back together one last time, but not enough to shield her from the worst of the Jump's effects.

She crashed to her knees, blind, deaf, and sicker than

she'd ever been in all her life. She barely managed to jerk up her visor in time to avoid vomiting inside her helmet.

When she was finally done, Riane wiped her mouth, shuddering in revulsion. At least she was still alive. *"Suit status?"*

"Power levels at point-zero-zero-one percent," her comp reported.

Deader than a black dwarf. Which is no surprise. T-suits aren't rated for that many Jumps. Burned out the power pack. Which is probably exactly what that fucker Ivar intended.

Ivar had to be at the bottom of this somewhere. It just stood to reason.

"Any sign of Frieka?"

"Negative."

"Good." Riane sighed in relief. At least Ivar hadn't managed to trap the wolf, too. Though if she knew her partner, he was probably going insane with worry.

She wasn't all that happy herself.

Forcing herself to reel to her feet, Riane scanned her surroundings. She still couldn't see worth a damn. Which would make this the perfect time for an ambush . . .

"Your sight is affected by your repeated Jumps, but it is also nightfall here," her comp informed her.

"Fantastic," Riane muttered. *"Can you get me anything on when—and where—I am?"*

The comp's pause was so short, an ordinary human probably wouldn't have sensed the time lapse at all. *"I detect electromagnetic transmissions suggesting early twenty-first-century North American communications. I can decode and analyze for more information."*

"Do it. I need to know exactly where I am if I'm going to get back home." Riane's sight was beginning to clear at last, and she could make out more of the area.

She stood on a paved stretch of blacktop she recognized

from past temporal Jumps as an outdoor basketball court. Nearby were various colorful structures her comp identified as playground equipment: a swing set, slide, and other constructions designed to be clambered over by small children. There was no one to be seen, however, which suggested it was fairly late.

"The time and date are zero-zero-forty-five, May 23, 2009," the comp announced. *"I have contacted a global positioning satellite and convinced it I am a GPS unit. You are located in the southeastern United States, in Milltown, South Carolina, population five thousand. Temporal coordinates: 0302-NAC/OE-0051-0045-05-23-2009."*

"Great. Time for a hearty yell for help." Riane reached into one of the pouches on her weapons belt. Her fingers encountered the smooth, round globe of a courier 'bot and pulled it out as she mentally composed a message to the Outpost. Com messages couldn't travel through time; something had to physically carry them.

Unfortunately, the little 'bot wasn't up to the job. Normally the tiny device would feel warm in her hand, with a faint vibration of power. Now it was so cold and still, it might as well have been a rock. *"What the Seven Hells is wrong with it?"*

Her comp confirmed her suspicions. *"According to sensors, courier power levels are at zero."*

The suit had protected her, but the weapon's belt pouches had failed to save her equipment.

Riane swore ripely and started going through the contents of the pouches. As she'd feared, anything that used any kind of power source had been fried. Even her shard pistol was dead.

At least she still had her knives. She checked the combat blades, still tucked neatly in their sheaths. Unfortunately, that was the only good news. She was stranded.

Her sole hope was to find a friendly time traveler with a

functioning courier 'bot who could signal for a Jump tube pickup. *"Can you identify another time traveler in the vicinity?"*

The comp hesitated a little too long. *"That data is unavailable. I did not download updated temporal travel records for this time because we were not scheduled to stop here."*

"Yeah," she said in disgust, *"that's what I was afraid of."*

"Having trouble finding a ride home?" a too familiar male voice asked.

Riane whirled to find Ivar Terje standing three meters away in a combat crouch, a predatory gleam in the cold gray eyes revealed by his open visor. He must have been sensor-shielded to sneak up on her like that.

The big cyborg was dressed in a Xeran T-suit, its tiny scales a deep and gleaming black. Riane bared her teeth at him. "I see you're showing your true colors, you traitorous dickhole."

His lips pulled into a slow, vicious grin. "Now, is that any way to talk to an old friend?"

"You were never *anybody's* friend." Coiling into her own battle crouch, she told her computer, *"Give me riaat."* She was going to need every erg of power she could get if she intended to win a fight with the cyborg.

Riane and Ivar began to circle, watchful, waiting for an opening. Damn, she missed Frieka. She and the wolf fought like a single unit, fangs and fists and feet, overwhelming opponents with sheer vicious teamwork. Ivar wouldn't have a prayer if Frieka was with her.

But it was probably better this way. She had a feeling things were going to get really ugly. Stranded in time, no backup, no one to know if she . . .

Shut up, Riane.

She sucked in a hard breath as the biochemicals of the

berserker state flooded her bloodstream, stinging her veins like acid with a wave of white-hot strength and a sense of invulnerability. Which, unfortunately, was illusionary.

Still wearing that chilling smile, Ivar charged.

It was after midnight by the time Nick wearily walked out of a convenience store in a very bad part of town. The Stone had sent him there two hours before with a premonition of a woman in danger. Sure enough, he'd found the clerk about to be raped by an armed robber. Nick had beaten the man senseless while the girl called 911.

The two cops who'd showed up to take custody of his prisoner had questioned Nick and the clerk at length about what had happened, making both of them repeat the story several times. Probably checking to make sure their versions jibed.

Nick had not, of course, revealed that he'd intervened because the Stone warned him somebody was in trouble. He sure as hell hadn't admitted he'd blown the door open with a burst of telekinetic force. Neither point would have helped his credibility.

He sighed and scanned the darkness warily. Any dealings with cops inevitably resulted in an attack by the aliens who hunted him. He suspected they monitored police frequencies somehow. They always turned up within an hour or so of any engagement.

As if on cue, a bright emerald light lit the darkness, heat stabbing the muscles of his biceps. *The Stone* . . .

Nick stiffened as a vision swamped his mind in a kaleidoscope of images. The woman with the tattoo who'd haunted his dreams, dressed in a dully gleaming skintight costume that made the most of her long, slim curves. She slapped down the visor of a blue helmet and leaped forward with a chilling combat howl.

A man charged her. He was a good foot taller than she was, and heavier by at least a hundred pounds of hulking muscle. He wore the scaled black and red armor of the aliens. Hands the size of her head reached for her.

The vision winked out, leaving only a cold sense of anxiety—and a faint tugging sensation. Nick whirled and broke into a run, following the psychic pull.

If he didn't get to her fast, she was dead. He knew that with an ice-cold certainty that didn't permit doubt. Lengthening his stride, Nick ran hard, arms pumping, boots thudding on the pavement. He could feel her even before he heard her: desperation, rage—and a furious, icy determination.

The little girl she'd been all those years ago had definitely grown up.

He rounded a building and saw them, fighting in the illumination cast by a single streetlight. He scanned the scene as he galloped closer. One of Milltown's only parks, a tiny patch of trees and grass and a few pieces of playground equipment.

A chain-link fence surrounded it, a good nine feet high. Nick didn't let that stop him, hitting the metal webbing halfway up, hooking his fingers into the links, and swarming upward before vaulting over the top. He hit the ground with a thud and a puff of dust, then charged toward the fighters.

He'd always known he'd see her again. He just hadn't thought it would be like this.

I'm not going to be able to take him, Riane realized, *not without Frieka. Maybe not at all. The son of a bitch is stronger than ever.*

She'd pitted herself against Ivar before, during combat practice sessions back at the Outpost, and she had a good idea of his abilities. He was a cyborg, yes, but she was a Vardonese Warfem. Despite his greater size, she should be a match for him, at least with *riaat* increasing her speed, strength, and agility to superhuman levels.

She'd dodged his opening bull-like charge, only to have him tag her with a backhanded swipe of one armored paw. Despite her helmet, the impact sent fireworks exploding in her vision, and she'd gone flying like a rag doll.

Riane hit the ground in a loose-limbed roll she used to flip onto her feet. She faced him again, ignoring her ringing ears and the copper tang of blood in her mouth. *"Opponent's strength seems to have increased from prior encounters,"* her comp warned.

No kidding. She tongued away blood from her lips.

Ivar's teeth flashed white through the dark visor of his helmet. "Our Xeran friends gave me a bit of an upgrade." He flexed massive arms. Light gleamed and rippled along the slick scales of his black armor. "Enhanced the tech in my muscles, reinforced my skeleton with nanobot engineering. All in all, I'm twenty-eight percent stronger than I was before, thirty percent faster—and more than capable of kicking your Warfem ass all the way back to the twenty-third century."

She bared her teeth at him. "And one hundred percent more mouth than action."

Ivar came at her in a blur of raw, terrifying speed, catching her across the waist and slamming her into the ground with a force that drove the air from her lungs. She felt every erg of the impact, too—her drained armor had lost too much power to protect her.

A fist shot toward her head. She threw up a forearm block and banged a punch of her own at his visor. He shook it off and hit her again, rattling her skull in her helmet. She swung at him, but his massive paw engulfed hers before the punch could land. His fingers crushed around hers like an industrial vise. He jerked off her, snatched her up by her trapped hand, and flipped her over his head. She tucked her chin to keep the back of her head from slamming into the ground, but even then, the impact made her consciousness gray. The rest of her body hit the ground so hard her teeth rattled. The breath left her chest in a whoosh.

A ghostly voice sneered, *You're not the warrior your father was.* A memory, nothing more, but the words stung.

She tried to force herself to her feet, prove the Femmat bitch wrong. Her stunned, breathless body barely twitched. From the corner of one eye, she saw Ivar lift a booted foot, about to stomp down on her belly . . .

Then he was gone.

Riane blinked once at the empty sky above her. *Get up,* her mind screamed. *Get your ass up!*

. . . not the warrior your father was . . .

"Yes. I. *Am!*" Gritting her teeth, she rolled over onto her hands and knees, though the world spun in sickening circles around her.

A male voice bellowed in rage to the meaty sound of fists hitting flesh. She staggered to her feet and almost fell again as she turned, looking for the traitor, trying to determine what the hell had just happened.

Ivar was down on the ground, another man on top of him. For a moment, her heart leaped in hope—an Enforcer? Then she registered the man's twenty-first-century blue jeans and black T-shirt.

His face savage with rage, he powered a fist into Ivar's faceplate. A crackle sounded. His arm lifted and descended again, then twice more, so fast it appeared blurred even to her sensors. The tough resplas visor shattered in glittering arcs that were echoed an instant later by flying blood. She couldn't tell if it was from Ivar's face or the stranger's fist.

He's not human. No human could take Ivar down like that. "Computer, sensor scan."

The answer came back barely a heartbeat later. *"Sensors indicate subject is half-human, but his maternal DNA is Xeran."*

She cursed. What the Seven Hells was going on now?

· 4 ·

The Victor watched the fight from the darkness with His finest cohort, shielding Himself and the six priests so heavily the Enforcer would be unable to sense them. Too heavily even for the Demon's keen otherworld senses as the creature battled his spy.

"Shall we intervene, Light of the Infinite?" Warrior Priest Gyor ge Tityus asked in a hoarse whisper. He appeared perfectly calm, but the Victor could feel his vibrating eagerness to shed blood and prove himself. He was new to his post yet, having so recently advanced on Tarik ge Lothar's death.

"Not yet," the Victor said, eyes locked on the Demon with starved fascination. "I would observe."

How ordinary the Demon looked. One would have thought him the twenty-first-century primitive he believed himself to be. Yet seen in the Coswold-Barre spectrum, he blazed with energy. Exotic forces gathered around his fists and feet, giving each blow a superhuman force, protecting his bones, making him more than a match for Ivar, despite the cyborg's armor and nanobot-enhanced strength. Each time Terje tried to hit the Demon, exotic alien forces cushioned the impact. It was no wonder none of the Victor's teams had ever managed to capture the creature.

But what fascinated the Victor most was the Stone that clasped the Demon's upper arm. Staring into that gem in the Coswold-Barre spectrum was like gazing into the heart of a star. He thought He could sense some alien universe shining through its glittering green aperture.

That was true godhood, not the sham He'd constructed for His people. With such power, He could bring all human space to its knees before Him.

As it should be.

But He must acquire the Stone first, and that was not so easy. One could not simply take it, not even after killing its possessor. They'd discovered that with the Heretic's death. The priests had been unable to remove the armband, and then it had simply vanished from her body, off to find the Demon, whom it seemed to view as her heir.

No, the Demon must be persuaded to give it to Him.

Luckily, the Victor had a very good idea how to force him to do just that.

Now what? Riane watched Terje and the strange male circle, crouching, both men feral and intent. The stranger was a big man, though unlike Ivar, he was leanly powerful rather than hulking. Clasped around his upper arm he wore a glowing gem that sparked and snapped each time he and the traitor exchanged a blow. It cast a soft green illumination over the starkly handsome angles of his face. His narrowed eyes reflected the unearthly shine like a cat's in glints of green. His shoulder-length hair was thick and dark and a little shaggy, in need of a trim, giving him a wildman look that was enhanced by the snarl on his well-cut lips.

Why the hell would a half-breed Xeran intervene to help her?

As if echoing her thoughts, Ivar spat at the man in English, "This is no fight of yours. Why die for a woman you don't even know?"

The man's green eyes didn't shift their patient, predatory gaze. "I know you're trying to kill her. That's enough for me."

"Ahh—a hero." Ivar surged forward, spinning into a sweeping kick aimed at the man's legs. "I've always hated heroes."

The stranger leaped back with that inhuman agility, easily avoiding the kick. But it was a feint; Ivar drew a knife from a sheath across the small of his back.

Fuck it, Riane thought. *Whether he's half-Xeran or not, I can't just stand here and watch Ivar kill him.* She charged as the cyborg continued his whirling attack, blade slicing across the stranger's T-shirt-clad chest. Blood flew in an arcing splatter.

The stranger grunted softly, taking a staggering step backward and falling to one knee. Ivar reversed his spin, the knife now aimed at his back. Riane dove between them, sweeping her forearm up in a block.

She'd forgotten her powerless armor. The blade glanced off her arm and arced downward, slicing into her thigh. Blood flew, though thanks to *riaat*, she felt no pain.

The stranger surged upward from his knees, his body twisting as he slammed one fist into Ivar's head. The other grabbed the traitor's knife hand and twisted. Ivar howled in agony as the blade spun away. Riane drove her elbow into his face, and he fell, hitting the ground on his back.

"Opponent unconscious," her comp whispered.

For a moment, she found herself staring up into the

stranger's green gaze from centimeters away. He was a good head taller than she was, his shoulders broad under his T-shirt. The black fabric clung to the muscled lines of his body, damp with sweat and blood, smeared with dirt. He smelled of battle. Her body leaped in purely female reaction to his.

Silently, she cursed *riaat* and the need it always left after a fight. *He's Xeran, remember? I can't trust him. And where in the Seven Hells did he get those powers?*

Her visor was smooth and dark, hiding her features. But it couldn't keep Nick from sensing her reaction to him— the blend of sensual interest and acute wariness. He frowned, studying her.

Was this the girl he remembered from sixteen years ago? He wished she'd take off that damned helmet. In the vision, she'd seemed to have the same tattoo, but what if that kind of design was simply common wherever she came from?

The armor she wore was a dark blue piped with silver instead of the black and red his enemies wore, yet it was obviously the same kind of suit. She, too, must be an alien, but why had she come here? What did she want? What was her connection to his enemies?

A warning blade of pain stabbed his biceps from the Stone. He jerked his head around.

Six of the aliens appeared a bare dozen yards away, weapons flashing silver in their hands. Nick cursed and grabbed her wrist, reaching for the power deep in his mind and flinging it out around them. "Duck!"

She half turned, saw the aliens, and growled something in a language he didn't understand. He jerked her after him as enemy weapons hissed, spitting a lethal rain of silver shards. "I've cloaked us," Nick yelled, pushing her ahead of him to put himself between her and the weapons. "They can't see or hear us, but somebody could still get off a lucky shot! Run!"

She needed no further urging, breaking into a hard, fast sprint, bounding ahead of him. Nick shot a glance over his shoulder to watch the aliens scatter, trying vainly to determine which way they'd gone. He smiled in grim satisfaction.

They raced through the night together, pounding down darkened streets, veering through alleys, even jumping a pair of chain-link fences without breaking stride. She kept up with him every step of the way, her lovely body moving with a lean grace and power that made his own purr in approval.

Was she the girl he remembered?

The Victor scanned the night as His priests quartered the area. He could sense their seething frustration, but all He felt was satisfaction.

Warrior Priest Gyor ge Tityus approached Him and dropped to one knee, bowing his head in obeisance. "They have disappeared, Most Victorious."

"Good." He gave His priest a slow smile. "All goes exactly as I intend." He nodded to Terje, who had staggered to his feet, visibly dazed. "Gather that one, and prepare to Jump. Make sure the traitor goes into regeneration for his injuries when we arrive at the Cathedral Fortress. I suspect I will find a use for him again."

Riane ran beside her unidentified savior, her body still hot and buzzing from *riaat*. It felt good to run, good to burn off all that screaming energy, though she knew the metabolic crash to come would be a bitch.

The Xeran was leading the way now. She found herself watching the easy roll of his broad shoulders as his muscled arms pumped, the flex of his butt under the fabric of his jeans, the stretch and surge of his long legs. Shaggy black hair whipped in the wind of their passage. Hunger stirred in her.

You're not the warrior your father was.

Baran Arvid had spent years fighting the Xerans. They'd christened him the Death Lord because of his ability to slip through their defenses and kill any target he chose. He'd told her about some of the deceptions they'd tried on him. *Never trust Xerans,* he'd told her. *They're good at tricks, and they lie.*

So what kind of tricks was this one playing? Her eyes narrowed as she studied him with rising suspicion. Why the hell would a Xeran intervene to help her?

What made even less sense was the fact that according to her sensors, not one single molecule of his body originated in the twenty-third century. With the exception of his DNA, he seemed to be a temporal native. It was as if a Xeran female had come back in time, given birth to him, and left him here. Which was illegal as hell; you weren't supposed to pollute the human root stock with future-originating genetics, especially nothing as genetically engineered as the Xerans. True, the Xerans were a human offshoot race, which was how you could get half-breeds to begin with, but still, there were significant differences.

This whole situation stank of setup to her. The Xerans trapped her in the past and sent Ivar Terje to kick her ass. Then some half-Xeran primitive who shouldn't be here to begin with just happens to come along and save her? She didn't think so.

It had to be some kind of trap.

Obviously, somebody wanted her to think this Xeran was on her side, but why? What kind of game was he playing?

Could be they'd figured out how to hide the molecular traces of the future. Charlotte Holt had, after all. She'd been pure Xeran, yet she'd scanned as a twenty-first-century primitive to Riane's sensors.

Riane frowned. So why had they allowed her to detect the Xeran half of his genetics at all?

Should she play along, pretend she was fooled while trying to figure out his angle? Or was that simply a good way to get her throat cut?

Her gaze drifted down to his flering backside again.

Damn riaat. Those biochemicals might enhance her strength, but they also made her horny as hell afterward. She wished Frieka was here. Whenever she wasn't entirely sure of her own judgment, the wolf always knew what to do.

And just now she definitely didn't trust her own judgment.

· 5 ·

"I think we lost them." Nick let his pace slow at
last. His chest ached furiously, and he could feel the hot
trickle of blood from the knife wound where the alien had
tagged him. He thought about healing it, but decided it
wasn't a good idea to spend the power just yet. Better to
wait and get somewhere safe first.

The woman glanced at him, then slowed her plunging
pace to a walk. For a moment they simply strode along side
by side down the walkway, their boots ringing on the ce-
ment.

The moon rode high in the cloudless sky, spilling silver
illumination around them. In the distance, he could hear
the sigh of traffic on the interstate and the wail of a train
whistle. A dog barked frantically from a house nearby. He
scanned the area. Saw only a few houses, trees, and a field
of weeds, already growing tall and lush with the advent of
spring. He breathed in, finding the air cool, tinted with the
scent of distant daffodils.

"What now?" the woman asked suddenly. She was breathing deeply yet evenly, not even out of breath despite the long race.

Nick hesitated a moment, eyeing her, wishing he could see her face. *Was* she Riane? He reached out with his powers, but he still couldn't tell one way or another.

His abilities did tell him she was wounded. The alien had caught her with that knife of his. Twice, once on the arm, again on the thigh. Neither was serious, but they must hurt like a bitch. Though she wasn't even limping . . .

That decided him. Nick didn't care who or what she was, he was taking her somewhere he could heal her. "My apartment is a few blocks from here." He turned and started in that direction.

Alien or human, he'd do what he could for her.

But instead of following, the woman stopped in her tracks. Nick looked back at her, brows lifting.

"Who are you?" She tugged off her helmet and tucked it under one arm. Her hair was a dark red in the light of the street lamp, sweat-damp and hugging her small head, emphasizing sculpted cheekbones and a delicate jaw. Her mouth was lush, with a full lower lip and a deep cupid's bow. Red brows lowered over beautiful eyes, wide, long-lashed, infinitely dark and deep. Red light sparked and glittered in their depths. Enhancing the striking, alien effect, a familiar tattoo in swirling shades of red and blue spilled down one side of her face.

It's her! Elation stormed through him, and an incredulous grin spread across his face. Until a new thought chilled his joy. *But what the hell am I going to tell her?*

"I said," Riane enunciated, amusement in the curve of her lips, "who are you?"

"Nick. Nick Wyatt." Automatically, he extended a hand, before it belatedly occurred to him that an alien might not understand the gesture.

She took it and gave it a brief, decisive shake. "Riane Arvid."

Yes!

Those strange, strange eyes studied his expression, intent, acute. And suspicious. "Have we met?"

What the hell was he to say to that? *I saw you in a vision sixteen years ago. I saved your life.* She'd think he was nuts. To give himself time to think, Nick gestured for her to follow and started down the sidewalk again.

Automatically, he directed his powers in another scan of their surroundings. There was no sign of any threatening presence. On the other hand, he could clearly sense Riane's wariness. He thought there was more than a trace of sensual awareness, too, but she plainly didn't trust him as far as she could throw him.

And why the hell was she so wary? He'd risked his life to save her, dammit. What was going on in her head?

Maybe he should just tell her what had happened sixteen years ago.

No. Not yet. He had to take this slow and easy. He couldn't just blurt out the story of their psychic encounter.

Too, she probably knew something about the aliens. That suit of hers was similar to theirs, suggesting she came from the same place. Which meant that for the first time, he had a chance to learn something about the enemy who had hunted him his entire life. Questions even his mother had refused to answer. Who were they? Where were they from? What did they want? Why had they killed his mother?

He couldn't lose this chance. He had to gain her trust. After, that is, he'd figured out why she distrusted him to begin with.

Obviously he couldn't just start pelting her with questions. That might add to her evident paranoia. He considered topics, chose one that seemed safest. "Who was the man who was trying to kill you?"

Riane hesitated a long moment before she said reluctantly, "Ivar Terje. He's a traitor working for the Xerans."

"Xerans?" He managed to keep his tone casual. "Is that what the aliens are called?"

"Aliens?" Riane gave him a long, narrow-eyed look. "They're not aliens. They're a genetically engineered offshoot of humanity."

"Humans? Genetically engineered?" He frowned, thoroughly confused. "But the technology they've got—what are they, some kind of secret government program? And what government?" He remembered some of the wilder conspiracy theories he'd heard over the years. "Not the Feds? Why would the Feds be after me?"

"After *you*?" She lifted a brow. "I was the one they just tried to kill."

He snorted. "Join the club. They've been trying to kill me since I was a kid. They murdered my mother when I was fourteen."

"Why would Xerans try to kill *you*?" She frowned deeply.

"Your guess is as good as mine. I've tried asking them, but they're usually too busy trying to whack me to answer. Again, what are they? I'm not paranoid enough to think they really are Feds."

She blinked, her expression incredulous. "Feds? As in the United States government?"

Well, that answered that. "Didn't think so. So if they're not Feds, and they're not aliens, what are they?"

"They're from the future, Nick. And so am I."

The Xeran stared at her, his eyes wide with astonishment. He'd dropped his shields now that they'd outrun their pursuit, and her sensors could easily detect his emotional reactions. He wasn't faking his astonishment. He truly didn't know a damned thing about the Xerans.

Yet he was Xeran, at least in part. Did he know that? Somehow she didn't think so. And she had no idea when— or even whether—to break the news.

Normally, you didn't tell a temporal primitive a damn thing about time travel. But if he really had been hunted by the Xerans all these years, he was no ordinary primitive. Which was pretty damned obvious, considering his abilities. He deserved some kind of explanation. Besides, she wasn't convinced he really *was* a temporal primitive.

So instead she gave him the basic facts as they walked through the night: that she was a Temporal Enforcement agent sworn to prevent and solve crimes committed by time travelers. And, since he'd figure it out sooner or later, she admitted she'd been stranded in time after her T-suit had been sabotaged.

He seemed amazed by the whole concept. Not just the physics of Jumping, though he had plenty of questions about that idea. No, what really amazed him was the idea of time travel as an industry.

"Let me get this straight—you folks let people travel through time *on vacation*?" He frowned down at her as they walked along down the darkened street. "What keeps some goofball from going back and killing Hitler, or something equally major? That might save a lot of lives, but wouldn't it change history? Cause a massive time paradox?"

If this Xeran was simply acting the role of ignorant temporal primitive, he was doing a damned good job. "Nobody could kill Hitler."

"Why?"

"Because he didn't die. So obviously, if anybody went back and tried to kill him, they'd fail. You can't change history. Temporal paradoxes just aren't possible."

He tucked his hands into his back pockets, making his powerful biceps flex. "So everything's predestined?"

"Well, no. But what happened, happened. People make the decisions they make. Hitler wasn't assassinated, so trying to kill him would be pretty pointless. If you tried, you'd obviously fail. His guards would stop you or the gun would misfire, or whatever. On the other hand, if, say, he'd disappeared under mysterious circumstances and you knew it, you could go back and kill him just when you knew he vanished."

"Or you could kill him in that bunker of his and make it look like suicide."

Riane nodded. "Exactly. You'd have to go over the historical record, find out when he supposedly killed himself, and go after him then."

His eyes widened. "Police reports!"

"What?"

"I wondered why the bastards always come after me right after I save someone. I always move every few months or so, but they find me every time. They must get their hands on police reports. They go back to the time right after each incident and hit me then."

"Well, yeah. All that stuff is in historical databases. It's not perfect. Historical records are often riddled with inaccuracies, and many of them have gone missing over the years. Still, it gives you a starting point. Though they probably end up investigating a lot of dead ends."

"Dead ends?"

"Incidents that sound like you, but aren't." A thought struck her, and she stiffened. "A message. I could post some kind of ad in a newspaper or something. The Outpost would be able to track me."

He lifted a dark brow. "And so would the Xerans."

She slumped. "Good point. Unless I told them to expect a fight . . ."

"Invite everybody to a brawl? What if the wrong people lose?"

Riane rubbed both hands over her face. "Good point." Remembering his earlier remark, she lowered her hands and eyed him. "That reminds me—who have you been saving, and from what?"

"People." He shrugged, a deliciously brawny ripple of broad shoulders. "There was this convenience store clerk earlier tonight. An armed robber was trying to rape her, so I intervened."

"You just happened to be around?"

"Oh, no," he said absently. "The Stone told me." He tapped the green gem on his upper arm. "It senses when somebody nearby is about to become the victim of violence. It sends me a vision, and I go rescue whoever it is."

"You just run around saving people when that rock tells you to?"

"Something like that."

"Could you use that stone of yours to send me back home?"

He stared at her. "Three hundred years through time? I have no idea how to do something like that. I don't think it's even possible."

"It's possible. I've known people like you who could make Jumps like that."

He looked interested. "You know other people with these Stones?"

"Well, no, not with that. But they had psychic abilities. Master Enforcer Arvid's wife developed powers like yours. She Jumped back to the twenty-first century to escape Ivar after he tried to kill her."

"Arvid? Your father?" Recognition lit his gaze.

"No, Galar was just genetically engineered by the same House as my father. What do you know about my dad?"

"Oh, nothing." His gaze didn't flicker. "I just assumed from the name he was related to you."

"Sensor data indicate his heartbeat jumped. He's lying," her computer implant whispered.

No shit, she thought. He was definitely playing her. But why? *How does he know my father?*

What the hell is going on here? He seems to know nothing about the future, yet he recognizes Dad's name. What kind of elaborate scam is this anyway?

· 6 ·

Nick had fallen silent, apparently still digesting the concept of time travel, when they arrived at his apartment in a run-down brick building. Riane followed him inside to climb a set of stairs covered with worn beige carpeting, then down a dark hallway both of them navigated with ease. He opened a door at the end of the hall, flipping on the light as they entered.

Pausing in the doorway, she ran a quick scan, evaluating the results in light of what she knew of the period. It was a small apartment, as neat and starkly furnished as a monk's cell, with a kitchenette, a scarred breakfast table and three mismatched chairs, and a black leather couch positioned in front of a flat-screen television set. Her sensors told her that just down the short hallway lay one bedroom with a king-sized bed and a bureau. There was also a bathroom and a home office that held only a laptop, a desk, and a single chair.

"It's not fancy," Nick said, sounding a shade defensive.

"I've got in the habit of living a pretty stripped-down life."

She turned to find him watching her.

"There's no point in acquiring anything more when the Xerans keep finding me," he explained. "I usually end up leaving everything behind because I'm barely one jump ahead of the bastards." His smile was very slight. "I tend to shop at Goodwill a lot."

Riane nodded, though she had no idea what Goodwill was. As she watched, he reached for the hem of his T-shirt and pulled it off over his head, wincing a little.

She stiffened. Blood marked his powerful chest, trailing from a long slash that ran diagonally from left nipple to right side. Automatically, Riane started toward him. "He tagged you."

Nick shrugged. "Didn't duck quite as fast as I should have. He's a quick son of a bitch."

"Emphasis on 'son of a bitch.'" Frowning, she crouched to examine the long, raking slice. She brushed her fingers delicately over his skin. It felt warm, smooth, over the firm, well-shaped ridges of bone and muscle. Her *riaat*-stoked appetite awoke with a soft growl, but she forced it back down. "He got you a good one, there. Cut's almost ten centimeters long. You need regen . . ." Riane grimaced. "Except there isn't any here."

"I have no idea what 'regen' is, but it's not a problem." He laid a big palm across the center of the slash. Green light flared as emerald sparks whirled around his hand.

Riane's eyes widened as the light faded, the bleeding stopped, and the cut's ragged red edges sealed even more quickly than regeneration could have done the job. "How did you do that?"

"The Stone." Nick shrugged. "I've always had abilities, but the Stone makes them stronger. I've never known why, or even how they work." Eyes the same luminous green as his stone studied her with a penetrating interest. "I was hoping you could tell me."

"Got no idea."

His mobile mouth drew into a frown of concern. "Did you know you're bleeding, too?"

She rose to her feet, aware of distant aches in her thigh and arm as she moved. "My comp mentioned it, but I don't feel much pain when I'm in *riaat*."

"Comp? Ri— What?"

"*Riaat*. It's a biochemically induced berserker state. I've got an internal computer winding through my brain that can induce it on demand. The comp also gives me control of my autonomic nervous system, and information from sensors implanted throughout my body."

"Damn." His lips twitched into a grin. "Bet that makes surfing the Internet a hell of a lot more convenient."

"Inter . . . Oh, right. This time's cyber network."

"Cyber network. Riiiight." Nick's grin faded as a line of worry formed between his thick, dark brows. "Look, you've got a cut on your arm and a stab wound to one thigh, and I'd really like to tend them for you. Could you lose the suit?" He hesitated. "I can get you a T-shirt or something."

Riane considered the question. In its current powerless state, the suit was basically useless anyway. She shrugged and reached for the seal at her throat and slid her fingers down it to her pubic bone. The edges parted more stiffly than usual, and she had to peel it apart.

Looking up, she saw he was watching her with widened eyes. Belatedly it occurred to her that twenty-first-century natives had different standards of modesty. Unlike Riane, who had been taught to see nudity as something to be ignored in the crowded conditions of paramilitary life. It certainly wasn't an invitation to sex.

Except when both parties wanted it to be.

Riane hesitated, her body beginning to buzz in anticipation again. Chances were good that if she did this, they were going to end up in bed. She wasn't sure she trusted Nick—too many things didn't add up. But on the other hand, her sensors insisted he was telling the truth when he described his suffering at the Xerans' hands.

Maybe the best thing to do was to simply play it out and see what happened. That could end up telling her a great deal.

One way or another.

There was absolutely nothing coy in the way Riane stripped off the scaled suit. She was so totally unselfconscious, it was as if she was completely alone as she bent to unfasten her boots and step clear of her clothing.

Somehow that made it all even more breathtaking. And intensely arousing. Her breasts bounced as she wriggled out of the suit, pink-tipped, delicious handfuls that made him ache to touch and stroke. Her waist was narrow, with carved abdominal muscles, her hips gently curving, leading to long, luscious legs. Her skin was pale and fine-grained over lean, strong muscles. Her build reminded him of a female Olympic track-and-field athlete: sturdy, yet intensely feminine. No bony fashion-model waif here. She was a fighter, and looked it.

Especially with blood rolling from a cut across her right forearm and a deep puncture wound in her thigh. Nick frowned and forgot her nudity. He reached for her arm.

She drew back, eyes narrowing. He stopped in mid-gesture. "I need to touch you if I'm going to heal that. It's a deep cut."

Riane hesitated. "My medibots could heal it—but that would take time. And I need to be able to fight." She extended her arm, the gesture reluctant. Her eyes met his in obvious challenge.

She's ready to take my head off if I do something she doesn't like, he realized. *And she'd make sure it hurt. A lot.*

Taking a deep breath, Nick summoned the power. The Stone heated and glowed, casting a green gleam around the room. Gently, he closed his fingers around her arm, positioning them over the cut, trying not to press too hard. Carefully, precisely, he started pouring energy into the wound, envisioning it closing as the blood stopped flowing from it. Obediently, the cut began to heal with breathtaking speed, emerald sparks flashing and leaping along its length.

Riane caught her breath in a small, startled gasp. The sound was so intensely female, he glanced up. As his eyes lifted, they fell on nipples drawing into tight, rosy little points. Hurriedly, he dragged his gaze to her face.

Her eyes glowed, red-hot beneath long, lowered lashes. She licked her lips.

He sucked in a deep breath as his body leaped in response to hers. And tried not to remember just how long it had been since he'd made love.

His palm was big and intensely, surprisingly warm, his long fingers growing almost hot enough to burn as he touched her. As she watched, sparks danced around his hand. They seemed to fizz their way into her skin, making the wound heal with a strange, ticklish sensation that reminded her of champagne bubbles. The sexual hunger of *riaat* awoke again, heat flushing through her body, drawing her nipples tight, pulling into a hard, tight knot of arousal deep in her belly.

As if he sensed her reaction, Nick's eyes lifted to hers, hot and green and very male. The glow from his hand cast light across his angular, handsome face. She watched him swallow hard. "Well. I need . . . I need to do something about that leg."

Riane caught her breath as he dropped to one knee, hesitated, then covered the puncture wound with his hand. She jolted at the abrupt sting of pain.

"It's deep." His voice sounded harsh. "Am I hurting you?"

Riane cleared her throat. "No." Her eyes dropped below his belt.

He was hardening beneath his zipper, thick, delicious, and promising. Her body purred approval. Her mouth went dry.

What the hell am I doing? He's half-Xeran!

. . . not the warrior your father was . . .

But he also seemed oddly innocent of Xeran fanaticism, as if his mother truly had abandoned him in the past with no knowledge of his history. And these strange abilities of his were definitely not Xeran.

Actually, they were more like those of the alien Sela than anything else. Riane frowned at the thought. Charlotte Holt had been Xeran, and she'd had psychic abilities that she'd somehow gotten from those telekinetic aliens . . .

So what was *he*?

Before she could pursue that question any further, power poured into Riane's wounded thigh, a sweet, searing flood that stole her breath and distracted her from every other thought. She swayed, growing dizzy as light flashed before her eyes and the wound closed in a rush. She could feel herself going wet, ready. Her gaze dropped to his cock again.

I want him. I don't care what he is. I want him.

So why not take him? Heat rolled through her in dark, creamy waves. *If he's what he seems, what can it hurt? And if he's not, he'll think he's got me fooled. And I'll have the advantage.*

As her father always said, you had to outthink the bastards if you wanted to win. *Find their weaknesses, and exploit them.*

And looking into his hungry green eyes, Riane suspected she'd just found Nick's.

Her thigh felt warm and firm and deliciously smooth under Nick's hand, the injury healing in a rush as it responded to his power. His heart beat hard, the thick pulse in his cock echoing its demanding thump. His mouth was dry as sand with need.

And he could smell her arousal, every bit as potent as his own. In this position, her softly curled red bush was at his eye level, temptingly close. He wanted to bury his face between those luscious thighs, taste and lick.

With any other woman, he'd have quickly produced sweatpants and a shirt, then hustled her out the door as soon as he had her healed. No civilian, after all, had any business in the crosshairs with him.

But Riane Arvid was not a civilian. She was a warrior with powers every bit as exotic as his own, just as willing—and able—to fight.

Still, he didn't want either of them mindlessly swept up in a passion they later regretted. Nick rose to his feet and met her gaze. "Do you want to get dressed?" His voice sounded embarrassingly hoarse.

Her hot eyes met his. "No. No, in fact, I want *you* naked."

The cool, steady admission stole his breath. Without another word, he reached for his zipper.

Riane watched, breath held, as Nick unzipped his jeans, toed off his boots, and peeled his pants down brawny thighs. As he kicked them aside, he rose to his full height and met her gaze.

For a long moment, they stared silently at each other, enjoying the mutual rise of heat. Riane was no stranger to beautiful bodies—Enforcers were genetically engineered for physical perfection.

Yet there was a tough, lean elegance about Nick that appealed to her. He was broad-shouldered, long of arm and leg, with big, calloused hands and brawny feet. Dark hair dusted his wide chest and trailed its way down his muscled belly, fluffing around the thick organ that angled up from his groin. She eyed it, thoroughly approving its plump, rosy head and long, veined shaft. His balls were round and heavy, drawn tight with his arousal.

Unable to resist, Riane reached out and wrapped her fingers around his cock. It bucked in her hand, a jolt of delight, the skin like hot velvet. The thought flashed through her mind again: *He's Xeran* . . .

And she found she no longer cared. There was absolutely no calculation in those deep green eyes, no sense of hidden plots or secret agendas. He was a man, and she was a woman, and that was all that mattered to either of them.

Riane purred in approval and tugged gently, drawing him closer.

Nick chuckled, a pleasant male rumble of sound. "Demanding wench, aren't you?" His hands came to rest on her hips, warm and a little rough.

"Life is short in my line of work," she told him, smiling up into his eyes. "I don't believe in wasting time."

"Really?" Long fingers traced their way up her ribs to cup her breasts. "Personally, I like to *take* my time."

Lowering his head, he found her mouth with his.

· 7 ·

It was a slow, lazy kiss, a thorough exploration of
tongue, lips, and teeth that made Riane moan with pleasure deep in her throat. He tasted minty and hot and very
male. As Nick pulled her in close, she reached up to wrap
her arms around his neck, enjoying the hard, muscular
heat of his body. It had been a very long time for her, so
long she had trouble remembering when last she'd sought a
man's arms.

His hands made a leisurely exploration of her ass, cupping her curves, tracing up her back along the sensitive ge-
ography of muscle and bone. And still he kissed her, deep
and hungry.

When he finally drew away, they were both out of breath
as they hadn't been from the battle with Ivar. Her heart was
pounding in eager thumps, and she smiled up at him, loving
the sensation. He reached up to cradle her face in his hands,
a sweet and tender gesture. His thumb traced the lower
edges of her tattoo. "This is beautiful. *You're* beautiful."

Riane gave him another smile, though she knew his twenty-first-century standards were low. "So are you." She meant every word; he might not be genetically engineered, but there was a rough beauty to his chiseled features and gleaming hair.

Nick trailed one hand down to take hers, drew her after him down the short hallway. Toward the bedroom. The band around his upper arm cast a bright, dancing light as they went. Tiny sparks bounced around them both like fireflies. Under other circumstances, she'd have wondered what energies the Stone was producing, maybe done a scan. At the moment, she was far more interested in the long, beautiful wedge of his back and the way his glutes shifted as he moved. His legs were powerful, dusted in dark hair, arousing and very male.

As they walked into his room, an array of candles burst into flame on top of the small oak bureau. A floor-to-ceiling bookcase stood on the opposite side of the room, where a wisp of smoke curled up from a golden ball studded with tiny square holes. It smelled of some faintly woody, exotic spice she couldn't identify.

"I meditate," Nick said, as if by way of explanation. "The incense and candles help."

"I like it," Riane decided, looking around the room. His bed dominated the space, a sprawling structure in blond oak covered in a thick forest green spread embroidered with a curling pattern of leaves.

Nick pulled her toward the bed, the eager jut of his cock angled upward in lusty promise. Riane eyed it. "That's really tempting." She trailed her fingers along the sensitive shaft, which bounced a little under her hand. He stiffened, lips parting, eyes darkening.

Unable to resist, Riane dropped to one knee and bent in for a sampling taste. Against her tongue the skin felt like velvet over a core of heated steel, and he smelled deliciously like sex and clean male effort. A drop of pre-cum flavored the tip of the shaft, tangy and a little bitter. She licked it away, then wrapped her fingers around his width and engulfed him for a slow, teasing suckle.

Nick threw back his head at the amazing sensation of her wet, soft mouth closing around his cock. Her graceful hands stroked him, cupping his balls in long fingers, spinning delicious curls of heat through his belly. Her tongue flicked over the head, swirled, teased the tiny opening until his every nerve quivered in delight.

"God," Nick rasped, "that feels so damned good. But I want to touch *you*." He caught her shoulders.

She gave him a wicked grin and allowed him to draw her to her feet. "If you insist."

Nick bent, caught Riane behind the thighs and across the back and swept her into his arms, then strode to the bed with her. Riane gave him a slow smile as he lowered her to the mattress. She stretched seductively, a long feline extension of her lean body. His mouth went dry at the sight of those lovely, pink-tipped breasts, the beautiful legs, so endless and strong, with that neat little russet nest between them.

He slid a knee onto the bed and braced himself on his arms as he bent for her lush, curving mouth. Her lips felt exquisitely soft as they opened under his. Her tongue slipped into his mouth, stroked, teased. Nick moaned in pleasure and drew her hard against him. She arched, wrapped her legs around his waist, and his head spun at the sensation of lush, smooth skin, the erotic scent of a woman in need.

With a hungry growl, he sought out her breasts.

Pleasure swirled in liquid delight through Riane's body, in time to every flick of his tongue. Her hands caught his head, threaded through his thick, dark hair, long and silken under her palms. Teeth raked, and she shivered.

Slowly, he started working his way down her body, spinning spells of pleasure with clever, calloused hands and wicked mouth. She sat up on her elbows to watch his progress, letting herself enjoy his luscious attentions. Her eyes widened.

Sparks jumped and swirled around his armband, then rained down on her skin like fireworks. A quiver of unease stole down her spine.

What were those sparks *doing*?

Nick nuzzled his way between Riane's thighs and began to lick. Heated to a roiling boil by a combination of *riaat* and his sizzling attentions, Riane's body overrode her wariness. She threw back her head and arched at the searing pleasure.

Hunger roared high, too fierce and demanding for even a pretense at passivity. She reared under him, grabbed him by his brawny shoulders. He was kneeling by the bed, but his weight was nothing to her genetically engineered strength. Riane flipped him onto the bed and pounced. Grabbing his cock, she angled up the strong, thick shaft and slung a leg over his hips.

"Wait!" he gasped. "Let me put on a condom . . ."

"Don't need it," she growled. "I won't get pregnant, and my nanobots kill any bug I'm exposed to. We're both safe." Without waiting for further argument, she impaled herself in a sweet, delicious rush.

Riane caught her breath at the sensation of his shaft, so broad, so long. Almost too much after so many months between lovers, filling her more full than she could ever remember being filled. But he'd made her slick and eager, and she didn't wait long before she was moving, almost gently at first, a slow and teasing jog.

"God," he breathed. "You're tiny!"

She grinned, eyes shuttered. "You're not."

"So I've heard." He gave her a deliberately cheeky grin in return, but it faded into a touch of anxiety. "Not too much?"

Riane planted her palms on his belly and rotated her hips. "I think I can rise to the occasion. I'm tough."

His hands clamped around her hips, holding her still as his gaze searched hers. "I'm serious. If it's too much, there are other things we can do."

Riane blinked down at him in surprise. "You sound like a Warlord."

His head rocked back, and he looked rather offended. "A what?"

"The men of my people. Warlords. They are . . ." She searched for the English word. "Chivalrous like that." Rising to her knees, she slid downward, sighing in pleasure at the way he filled her. "But I don't need your chivalry." Riane smiled down at him like a cat. "I just need this big, delicious cock."

God, Nick loved the way her mouth looked, shaping that word. He'd never met a woman like her, so bold, so incredibly strong. A match for him in every sense.

She gripped him like a slick, tender vise, her breasts bouncing as she rose and fell. Long thighs worked, all smooth skin and rippling muscle as she braced her hands on his belly. No centerfold could ever look so beautiful in his eyes, so strong, yet quintessentially female. His heart hammered as he watched his cock slide in and out of her pink, fragile lips.

Nick shuddered, loving the dizzying rise of pleasure that spiked higher with every stroke, loving the sight of her riding him like a Valkyrie, red hair whipping around her shoulders as she rose and fell. Heat surged in him, a ferocious need, and suddenly it was no longer enough to be ridden. His hands caught her waist, rolled her over. She laughed in delight as her back hit the mattress.

He rose over her with a growl. "My turn!"

"Fine, you do the work." Laughing, she wrapped her long legs around his waist as he positioned himself.

His initial stroke drove so deep they both gasped. Hungry for more, he braced his arms beside her head and began to drive.

The first molten wave of orgasm made Nick grit his teeth and fight to keep from coming too soon. He looked down into her face.

Riane gasped, eyes wide and blazing that bright, glowing red. The glow should have looked alien, a little threatening, yet on her it was simply exotic, another mark of her delightful differences, like the tattoo that adorned her face. Her legs tightened around his waist, and she began to lift herself into his hips, grinding hard. His other senses told him she quivered on the edge of climax. So he let go, plunging hard, giving her what she needed. What they both craved so ferociously.

Fire exploded from his balls, a blazing fountain of delight that seared its way up his spine. He bellowed, the raw male sound mixing with Riane's scream of climax.

Panting, sweating hard, Nick collapsed beside her. "God, that was amazing."

"Mmm," Riane agreed, then blinked at the sated purr in her own voice. Xeran or not, the man knew his way around a woman's body. And he didn't mind giving her what she needed.

She frowned. None of that sounded like what she'd come to know about those bastards. He should have been selfish, taking his pleasure and letting her find hers only if she could. Figuring she didn't deserve it if she couldn't.

Nick reached over to draw her gently into his arms. Also out of character. Still, he felt damned good, though her *riaat*-induced hunger had passed off. She lay her head down on his broad chest and listened to his heartbeat slow. In minutes, he was asleep.

Awfully trusting for a Xeran killer.

It was impossible to feel properly paranoid lying in sated bliss beside a handsome, thorough lover. Especially one who slept as bonelessly as a boy.

Riane sighed and put aside her distrust as she stared into the darkness. Her thoughts drifted to Frieka.

Poor wolf. He was probably going out of his mind with worry. She stirred, wishing there was some way she could let him know she was all right. Frieka had always had a fatherly streak, carefully hidden beneath bad jokes and bluster.

She had to get the hell back to the Outpost. Unfortunately, there wasn't a damned thing she could do about it right now.

Putting aside her various worries, Riane let herself drift off to sleep.

· 8 ·

"Riane!" Frieka called, his voice spiraling peril-
ously near a howl. He felt sick, a little woozy, and he
cursed his T-collar. It didn't offer as much protection during a Temporal Jump as his full T-suit, but he hated wearing the suit. It was uncomfortable, and it looked stupid.

But he'd be willing to endure that to find Riane.

"She's not here, Frieka," Dyami said gently, one big
hand falling on the wolf's head. "We've lost her."

"One more Jump, Boss." He knew he was begging, but
he didn't give a damn. "We can go back to her last location, and I can recalculate. I know I can triangulate where
she went if I try one more time . . ."

They'd successfully followed her through three Jumps,
calculating her next destination based on the residual
power left behind. Thing was, that only gave them a rough
radius in time and space. She could be at any point along
that vast temporal circle. Landing at just the right spot to
find her would be a matter of dumb luck.

They'd guessed wrong every time since.

Dyami sighed and dropped to one knee beside him, the better to look into his eyes. "Your collar doesn't have enough charge to keep Jumping like this. It's time to go home. Maybe one of the other teams will find her." The Chief had sent out every spare agent he had on the search.

Frieka turned to look out across the darkened medieval street—to meet the wide, terrified eyes of a man in the ragged garb of a peasant. The man made a forking gesture the wolf recognized as a sign against evil, then sprinted off, yelling about demons.

Frieka felt too discouraged to care. "She's trapped in time, Boss. That's what all those Jumps were designed to do—burn all the power out of her suit. She's stuck somewhere. Alone."

"Yeah." Dyami rose to his feet. "Probably. But at least she's alive. If they'd really meant to kill her, they'd have programmed the suit to self-destruct. Or materialize her in the caldera of a volcano."

"Hey, thanks," Frieka muttered. "A whole new nightmare for me to enjoy."

"Cut that out," Dyami said sternly. "Riane's young, but she's tough, intelligent, and gutsy. She can handle whatever they throw at her. And she's smart enough to figure out how to leave a clue in the historical record for us to find. All we have to do is look."

"Assuming that record survives." And there was no guarantee it would. Hundreds of years was a very long time for a temporal SOS to travel.

"So she'll leave more than one. Quit being a furry pessimist."

The sound of shouts rose in the distance. "Witches! Get the witches!"

"Oh, shit." Dyami sighed. "Not again. Come on, Frieka. Let's Jump before they try to burn us at the stake."

The thunderous boom of their joint temporal leap made the mob scatter with screams of terror.

It was a *beautiful sunlit day on Vardon as Riane Arvid rode her gravboard through the park. Frieka followed patiently just below, zigzagging down the pedwalk after her as she jinked around the tall, ferny trees of her home world.*

Safety boots clamped her to the board, holding her in place as the cool breeze of her passage blew in her face. The sun felt pleasantly warm on her shoulders, and she grinned in pure enjoyment.

"Hey, you're getting a little high there," Frieka called up at her. "Come down a meter."

"Oh, don't be such an old Femmat," Riane said, leaning left a little and bending her knees. Her board obediently arced right and climbed another meter higher.

"Riane, dammit!" Frieka growled over the approaching whine of an airbike. "Get down here before I bite you!"

She laughed down at him. "Gotta catch me first!"

The Xeran came out of nowhere, hitting her like a swooping hawk. One brutal kick of his boot smashed her gravboard into two pieces and snapped it loose from her feet. Stunned, Riane watched the broken halves tumble out of the sky as a hard arm clamped around her waist. Whipping her head around, she realized her captor was riding an airbike.

Frieka dodged the pieces of her gravboard, his horrified gaze on hers. "Riane!"

She twisted to look at the man who'd grabbed her, about to demand he put her down. Her eyes fell on the glint of silver at his temples.

Horns. Oh, sweet Mother Goddess! He was a Xeran!

He grinned into her face, his pupils red, reptilian slits.

"Yes, you little bitch. You're dead!" He laughed, the sound nasty, suggestive. The most evil sound she'd ever heard. "Scream for me. Scream for your furry friend down there!"

Fury stormed through her, almost hotter than the icy spear of terror piercing her heart. She balled a fist and slammed it at his face. He only laughed harder.

Kicking, struggling, swearing uselessly at her captor, she barely heard Frieka's terrified howls as he raced after the airbike climbing into the cloudless violet sky.

Riane jolted awake, sweating, her heart thumping a violent beat. She lay against a hard male body, the scent of him flooding her head. Jerking away, she scanned him wildly.

Xeran!

She rolled out of bed so fast, her back hit the wall.

Green eyes flared open, and light burst from the Stone clasped around his upper arm. He bounced out of bed and into a combat crouch, his gaze sweeping the room as though looking for whatever alarmed her. "What?"

Seeing nothing, he turned his attention on her. She was shaking, her skin ice-cold with remembered shock and terror. Nick's voice went low and soothing. "Hey, it's okay. Nobody's going to hurt you."

The bedside lamp flicked on, flooding the room with a soft light. He hadn't touched it; apparently he'd activated it with psychic ability alone.

It's Nick, Riane told herself, bringing her mind back to the here and now. She forced her body to straighten and relax.

"Nightmare?" he asked, his eyes warm, sympathetic.

"Yeah." She raked a hand through her hair, pushing it out of her eyes.

"Want to talk about it?"

"Not particularly." There was more than a trace of snap in her voice. She was damned if she was going to hand a weakness like that to a potential enemy.

He didn't appear to take the rejection personally. "Want anything?"

"Just the bathroom." She already knew where it was, of course, but it gave her something to say—and an excuse to get the hell away from him for a few minutes.

"Across the hall." He jerked a thumb in the direction of the doorway.

Riane escaped across the narrow corridor and closed the bathroom door behind her, then let her back fall against the cool painted wood.

Xeran. He was Xeran. How had she allowed herself to forget that?

Thing was, he didn't look Xeran, didn't act Xeran. Was that because he was exactly what he seemed—somebody who'd been abandoned in time—or was he trying to run some kind of elaborate scam on her?

Dona Astryr had been the victim of just such a scam. She'd thought Ivar Terje was a loyal Enforcer, right up until he'd tried to kill both her and Galar's lover, Jessica Kelly. As a result of his betrayal, Dona had fallen under suspicion of being a traitor, too.

Of course, there had been indicators that Ivar was lying. He'd used his computer's sensor shields to hide the brain activity that went along with lying. Dona would have caught it if she'd been looking for it.

"Have you seen any indication that Nick has lied to me?" Riane asked her computer implant.

"Affirmative."

She tensed. *"When?"*

"When he said he knew nothing about your father."

"Anything else?"

"Negative."

"Has he been shielding brain activity?"

"Negative. Sensor data suggest he has been honest in all statements, except when talking about your father."

"Now, what the hell does that mean?" she muttered under her breath. "How would a twenty-first-century primitive have encountered my father? Especially one who claims to know nothing about time travel."

None of this made sense. Somebody, presumably Ivar, had sabotaged her suit to trap her in the twenty-first century. Ivar then attacked her and was about to kick her ass until Nick showed up just in time to save her.

And yet they had to know *she'd* know he was half-Xeran. They hadn't even made an effort to hide it. So what was the point? What were they trying to accomplish?

Or was she overthinking all this? Nick could be exactly what he seemed: a decent man with remarkable abilities who just happened to be half-Xeran.

Should she just confront him? Demand to know what he knew about her father? Even if he lied, the lie itself would tell her something. Or should she go on pretending to believe him, while watching every move he made?

Watch him, Riane decided. *Watch him very, very closely.*

Nick lay with one arm bent to pillow his head as he stared at the ceiling. Wary suspicion radiated from the bathroom in waves he could almost see.

Riane didn't trust him, even after everything he'd done. Yet she'd given herself to him with hot abandon just three or four hours before.

The dream. He wished to hell he knew what it was about, because it had obviously triggered her doubts again.

That hurt.

He supposed it was a little ridiculous to feel wounded at

her distrust. Yes, sixteen years ago he'd saved her life. And yes, he'd always sensed that somehow they'd meet again. Though if he'd known she was from the future, he probably wouldn't have been quite so optimistic about the odds on that.

But she didn't know any of that.

He could tell her, of course. Nick frowned, troubled. Would she believe him? Or would it just make her more wary, more convinced, as she obviously was, that he was lying to her for some reason?

No, better wait. Let her get to know him a little better, realize that he had no intention of hurting her. He'd win her over.

Eventually.

The door swung open, and he lifted his head to watch as she walked naked into the room. His mouth instantly went dry. That long, gently curving body, lean and lithe as a cat's, red hair tumbling around her shoulders in tousled waves. The tattoo added a flourish to her exotic beauty. He cleared his throat. "You all right?"

"Fine." Without looking at him, she slid into the bed and curled up on her side facing away from him, her lean back stiff.

Fine. Yeah, right.

Sighing, he reached over to the bedside table and turned off the light.

· 9 ·

Frieka padded into the Outpost mess aching as if someone had beaten him with a board. His eyes felt sandy with exhaustion, and his stomach growled in demand. Too many hours of fruitless searching lay behind him. Dyami had finally thrown him out of Central Computing and ordered him to go eat.

Scanning the room, he saw Dona Astryr sitting at one of the tables that stood around the vast space. She was staring out the enormous window that dominated the Outpost mess with a breathtaking view of the rolling Blue Ridge Mountains. Since Frieka was desperate for company—hell, for *any* diversion at all from his dark thoughts—he trotted over. "Hey."

She startled and looked down at him. "Oh. Hi."

"Mind if I join you?"

Dona waved a hand. "Go ahead."

Frieka jumped up into a chair and told the table, "A

double order of chiva." He turned his attention to Dona, glad for the distraction from gnawing worry.

He supposed a human male would consider her beautiful, with those high, dramatic cheekbones and big violet eyes. Her navy blue Enforcer's uniform, piped in silver, hugged a lush, athletic body. Like her former partner, Ivar Terje, she was a cyborg. Unlike Ivar, she was also one of Riane's closest friends.

"Any luck?" she asked.

He sighed. "Not so far. We've been combing the historical record for any sign of her. Nada."

Dona frowned, a line of worry forming between arching dark brows. "How the hell did Ivar get to Riane's suit? I thought the Chief and his tech team had made sure he couldn't get through the Outpost's defenses."

"They did." A small door slid aside in the center of the table, and a plate rose into view. Dona reached out and pushed it over in front of Frieka. "Thank you." The chiva smelled delicious, and he buried his muzzle in it. The vocalizer around his neck allowed him to continue talking even as he devoured the rich meat. "The Chief suspects the Xerans have someone else on the inside."

"Yeah," Dona said bitterly. "Me."

Chewing, Frieka shot her a look. "If he really believed that, you'd be in the brig right now. His investigation cleared you, remember?"

"Corydon thinks otherwise. And I'm afraid he's almost got the Chief convinced. Dyami certainly seems to be keeping an eye on me."

"Dyami always keeps an eye on you." Frieka snorted and took another huge bite. "And it's got nothing to do with suspicion. He just likes your ass. And your tits. And probably your—"

"Well, Corydon doesn't," Dona said, her high cheekbones

coloring. "He keeps dragging me into the Chief's office and grilling me."

"Alex Corydon is a dick," Frieka growled. "He was a dick when I met him twenty-six years ago, and his dickishness has only ripened with time. Kind of like one of those really stinky cheeses."

"You've known him that long?" She lifted a dark brow and swept a lock of curly hair back from her face. "How did you get that bit of misfortune?"

"He transported Baran and me to the twenty-first century to save Jane from Jack the Ripper. Who was actually a Xeran named Kalig Druas. Turns out there was no Victorian killer, just a bastard leaping through time committing the Ripper's crimes."

She cocked her head in interest. "Jane, as in Riane's mother?"

"Right. She's from the twenty-first century."

"Riane never mentioned that."

Frieka grimaced. "She doesn't talk about her parents much. People tend to make too many assumptions."

"About her mother?"

"About her father." Instead of going into details he'd just as soon avoid, Frieka continued, "Corydon thought the Ripper was supposed to kill her because she disappeared from the historical record. 'Cause, you know, she moved *here*. But when we succeeded in saving Jane anyway, Corydon tried to kill her himself to prevent a temporal paradox."

Dona frowned. "But paradoxes are impossible."

"Yeah, we know that *now*. *Then*, everybody thought the universe would end if you changed history. So Corydon was all for murdering her until Baran forced him to transport all of us back to the twenty-third century." He chewed the chiva thoughtfully. "None of which did much for Corydon's career. I think he's still carrying a grudge."

Frieka suddenly noticed Dona had gone still as she gazed across the room, an expression of mixed longing and deep misery in her violet eyes. He followed her gaze.

Chief Alerio Dyami crossed the room in long, powerful strides. He dropped into a chair at another table and glanced in their direction. Dona quickly looked away.

For just a moment, the Chief gazed at her, his expression dark with a kind of haunted need.

"Humans," Frieka growled in disgust. "Always have to make everything so damned complicated."

"What?" Dona asked, looking confused.

"Nothing."

Corydon had just walked in, looking like he had a metal rod up his butt. Catching sight of Dona, he strode across the room toward them.

"Watch it," Frieka growled. "Dickhole on the approach."

The Senior Investigator stopped beside their table. After sweeping a contemptuous glance over Frieka, he looked down his nose at Dona. "Report to my office, Enforcer. I have some questions."

She ground her teeth. "The same questions I've answered a dozen times already?"

Metallic golden eyes narrowed, and his thin lip curled. "You may have your chief fooled, but I know exactly what you are. And I'm going to prove it. *Report to my office.* That's an order." He turned on his heel and stalked away.

Frieka looked at Dona. She was sheet-pale except for two flags of angry color riding her knife-blade cheekbones. "Want me to bite him?"

"No," she gritted. "You might catch something."

The bedroom was quiet except for the soft sigh of slow, deep breathing and the occasional stir of sleeping bodies.

Riane's T-suit lay tumbled and forgotten on the floor of

the living room. Its scales gleamed dully in a thin shaft of moonlight flooding in through the room's sole window.

One of the scales stirred, moonlight sliding across its surface like oil over water. Five thin pseudopods extended from its slick blue body, then slowly straightened, pulling it free from its fellows.

Free, it scuttled across the suit and onto the floor. It altered the moment it touched the new surface, taking on a nubby brown that perfectly matched the carpeting. Quick as a cockroach, it made for the window. The climb to the expanse of glass took little effort, its pseudopods clinging to the smooth paint. Anyone looking for it would have been unable to see it at all, so perfectly did it match the wall.

The closed sash cost it a few minutes. It had to flatten itself thinner than a sheet of paper before it could wiggle through the tiny gap between the window and its frame.

Out on the brick lip of the window, the thing went still, taking on the appearance of the surrounding brick.

Beneath the window, in the shadow of a stinking green Dumpster, a small fist-sized globe stirred, then floated quietly upward. A camouflage field surrounded the metal globe, shielding it so perfectly that it went undetected by Riane's computer implant.

The globe stopped before the window. The scale spat a burst of data in a tight, quick beam. The courier 'bot replied with a quick burst of its own, then zoomed upward as if shot from a catapult. It Jumped the minute it was far enough from Nick's apartment to avoid detection.

The planet Xer, the future

He existed in the heart of a howl. Data raged around Him, a storm of bits and bytes that thundered against His consciousness like hail. Every computer and cyborg and sensor on the planet contributed to the storm, information coming so fast even His inhuman consciousness couldn't process it all. Voices spoke to Him in a senseless babble, human and machine blending into one feral roar.

Goiva said she . . .

Sensors indicate atmospheric . . .

. . . honor to the Victor . . .

I would make a better priest than that fool.

Chemical reaction between sodium and . . .

. . . myself a perfect tool for His hand . . .

. . . never good enough . . .

. . . why won't he listen when I . . .

I must prove myself to . . .

Soil temperature of 28°C results in . . .

Engines at full power . . .

She lies, lies! It's all lies, the bastards need to die . . .

What if they find out?

On and on it went, shards of knowledge pelting Him, acid fragments of emotion making no sense, forming no connections.

Sudden pain sliced through His awareness, and He seized it gratefully. Pain stabilized His thoughts, gave Him something to focus on.

Somewhere on Xer, a penitent was making sacrifice to Him, wrapping a piece of spiked wire in an intricate braid around the worshiper's own erect penis. He dragged the sufferer's pain into His mind, savored its razor sharpness. Felt Himself integrate around the act of worship.

He was the Victor. He was the god of Xer, the Most Glorious, the Conqueror, He Who Walks in Victory.

And He was *not* mad.

Most Glorious?

He ignored the courier's hail, busy drinking in the penitent's sacrifice. Through His worshiper's ears, He heard blood droplets strike bare stone in a swift, sweet patter as the man prayed, praising the Victor's wisdom and power.

This concerns the Demon, Most Glorious.

The Demon? He jerked to full awareness, Himself again, sharp and coherent. He remembered He'd placed a nanobot colony on the Warfem's T-suit and sent a courier to follow it. "What news?"

The courier spat out its load of data in one rapid squirt. The Victor absorbed the recording, watching and listening as His targets circled each other, wary as a pair of cats.

Damn that Warfem. Her distrust of the Demon was a barrier the Victor had not anticipated. He needed to force her to turn to the half-breed. To trust, or His plans would never reach fruition.

Fortunately, the answer to that problem was obvious. There was a risk, of course—there always was in such cases. Still, the Demon had been more than a match for everyone the Victor had ever sent after him. There was no reason to believe he wouldn't meet this challenge as well.

And if he did not—perhaps his Stone would fall into the hands of someone who would be easier prey.

Return to the girl, the Victor told the courier. *Log their location, and wait for My team's signal.*

Milltown, the Present

The nanobot colony writhed its way under the window sash, then froze, sensors scanning the room. Its targets still slept. No surprise, as it was surrounded by a field that rendered it invisible even to Riane's computer.

Reassured, it crept down the wall and scuttled toward the bed, moving in a blur of psuedopods. It scaled one leg of the bed's headboard, then skittered across the pillow toward Riane's head. Delicate as a whisper, it found her braid, crawled up among her combat decorations, and wrapped itself around one shining bead. Then it settled down to wait.

And record.

· 10 ·

꧁꧂

Riane woke to the smell of frying bacon. Yawning, she stretched lazily, enjoying the sense of well-being that radiated through her sated body.

A completely inexplicable well-being. She frowned. The sex had been delicious, true, but the fact was, she was still trapped in the twenty-first century with a dead T-suit and no way home. And the man who had given her this delicious sensual buzz was half-Xeran.

She rolled out of bed and looked around for something to wear. The T-suit was stiff and uncomfortable without power, so she scooped up the first item of clothing she saw and slipped into it. It turned out to be a black T-shirt of Nick's. He was considerably taller and broader than she was, and the shirt hung to the top of her thighs.

It also smelled like him. Without really intending to, she took an appreciative sniff, enjoying the sensual scent of clean male. There was no trace of that faintly reptilian tang the Xerans so often carried.

No wonder he kept sneaking past her defenses. The man even smelled good.

And he was cooking bacon.

Her mouth watering, Riane padded barefoot down the hallway into the little kitchen.

Nick stood at the stove in nothing but a pair of blue jeans. Riane eyed his bare back, admiring its strong muscled contours. *Half-Xeran, remember? A half-Xeran who showed up a little too conveniently. As Mom would say, I can't trust him as far as I can drop-kick him.* She cleared her throat. "That smells good."

He turned to give her a smile, though she thought there was a hint of wariness in his eyes. "I wasn't sure if you'd like bacon and eggs, but I really didn't have anything else."

"Well, normally I eat gaksnake pancakes for breakfast, but I'll make do." He blinked, and she grinned. "I'm kidding."

"Oh."

"I'd never put gaksnake on pancakes. It's pretty good on crackers, though." His expression of revulsion made her laugh. "You are so easy. Seriously, my mother is from the twenty-first century. She makes bacon and eggs all the time." She inhaled deeply. "Reminds me of home." And it did, as much as she hated to admit it.

He started plating the bacon with deft flips of his spatula. "How did you end up with a mother from the past?"

"Dad rescued her from a Xeran killer."

"Wish he'd been around to rescue mine from hers." He put the plate aside and started cracking eggs into a bowl. "You like your eggs scrambled?"

"Definitely." Riane filched a piece of bacon from the plate and crunched into it. It was perfectly done, smoky but not overcooked. She frowned. "You mentioned that before—that the Xerans killed your mother."

"Yeah. It was . . ." He paused, as if thinking back. "Sixteen years ago now. I was fourteen. We'd been running from the ali— the Xerans for years, but apparently there were too many of them that time."

She winced, imagining the scene. "And you witnessed it?"

"I wouldn't be here if I had. I was home playing a video game at the time." Nick tapped an egg a little too hard on the lip of the bowl and cursed as half of the smashed shell fell into the yolks. Retrieving his fork, he started fishing out the fragments.

"Why were they after her?"

Nick shrugged broad shoulders, his expression brooding. "Don't know, but I think it had something to do with this." He tapped his armband with one finger, then started beating the eggs.

Riane hesitated, watching his face. *"Does he believe what he's saying?"* she asked the comp.

"Affirmative."

She took a deep breath. Should she do this? Did she have the right? Maybe not, if he was the innocent he appeared to be. But if he wasn't . . . if he was indeed a Xer spy, he'd probably put on a very revealing act. Either way, his reaction just might tell her what she wanted to know. Riane took the plunge. "Nick, did you know your mother was Xeran?"

He froze, his eyes widening. As she watched, the blood drained from his face, leaving it white as the broken shells of those eggs.

Well, she thought, *there's a reaction impossible to fake.*

"Bullshit." A muscle flexed in his jaw, and anger blazed in his eyes. His armband began to crackle and flash like distant lightning before a storm. "Who told you that?"

Fuck, he really hadn't known. Well, it was too late to stop now. "My sensors. Your maternal DNA is Xeran."

Nick turned back to the eggs, the movement jerky, agitated. The fork clattered furiously against the bowl's ceramic walls as he beat the mixture. A muscle worked in his cheek. Without turning around, he said, "You're wrong."

"No. I'm not. Your father was human, possibly from this time. You're definitely from this century—there's no other sign of twenty-third-century molecular structures in your body other than half your DNA. If you'd ever been in the future, there'd be some traces of it in your body."

He slammed the fork down on the countertop and spun with a snarl. *"My mother was not a fucking alien!"*

She winced. "I told you, Xerans aren't aliens. They're an offshoot of humanity. Otherwise, humans wouldn't be able to crossbreed with them."

"Let me get this straight." Nick took a step closer, looming. "You're saying my mother lied to me my entire life."

Riane refused to back down from his angry glare. "Did she ever tell you that you *weren't* Xeran?"

"No." Doubt stirred in his eyes before he turned back to the stove again. "But that's not the kind of thing you forget to mention."

"It's also the kind of thing you might hesitate to tell a child. Particularly if your own people are trying to kill you. That pan is starting to smoke."

"Shit." He poured the eggs into the skillet with automatic skill, then shot her a look. "You're sure about this?" He wasn't asking about the skillet.

Riane shrugged. "Sensors don't lie."

"And I wouldn't have been able to sense that she was Xeran until I got the Stone." A muscle flexed and rippled in his tight jaw. "And I never saw her body after I got it."

For a long moment there was no sound except the soft sizzle of frying eggs. Riane watched him cook and wondered if she should have kept her mouth shut.

No. She'd had to know whether she could trust him.

After a moment, Nick plated the eggs with the same deft skill he'd displayed before, then carried them and the plate of bacon to the table. It was already set, including a pitcher of orange juice.

He put the plates on the table and turned to her. "Please serve yourself. I've got something to take care of."

Riane watched, frowning, as he headed back down the hall. *Well,* she thought, *that didn't go the way I expected. "Computer, did you detect any sign he was lying?"*

"Negative. He was not aware that his mother was Xeran."

But what did that mean?

Nick felt as if an earthquake had struck, knocking everything he thought he knew into a shambles. He couldn't believe it was true. Didn't want to believe it was true.

How could his mother have hidden something like that from him? And if she'd lied about that, what else had she lied about?

And why the hell did he believe Riane over his own mother?

He walked into the bedroom and knelt on the worn carpet. The room still smelled faintly of the sandalwood he'd burned the day before.

And Riane. Her scent lingered in the air, intoxicating and exotic. He breathed in deeply without really intending to, trying to identify the delicious underlay. Aroused woman and something else, some exotic smell he'd never sampled before, rich and strange.

She'd turned his world upside down, made him doubt everything he'd thought he knew. Resentment stirred. Irrational, of course, and he knew it. It was better to know the truth than fumble in darkness.

So he closed his eyes and reached for the Power.

He found it as he always did, hot and sure, as much beneath his skin as inside the Stone. But instead of directing it outward as he usually did, he turned it within himself. It poured through him, touching each cell, testing for the truth.

And finding it.

Riane stood in the bedroom doorway, her breath caught.

Nick floated six inches over the floor, emerald light swirling around his body, bright sparks shooting into his chest and out again.

The hair rose on the back of her neck, and she knew. Regardless of his DNA, this man was no ally of Xer. If the Xerans had access to abilities like his, they would have already conquered the Galactic Union. Which explained why they had been after him all these years.

They want his power.

Which in turn meant he was no enemy. Something deep inside her uncoiled and relaxed.

Of course, that left the question of where these abilities of his came from, if not from the Xerans. Still another issue was the question of what kind of game the Xerans were playing. Somebody had definitely sabotaged her suit to bring her to this particular location at this particular time. All of which suggested her meeting Nick was no accident.

Which in turn suggested an entirely new and very troubling question.

"Your eggs are getting cold."

Riane startled.

He knelt, watching her, his body now firmly on the floor. "You were right, by the way. I am half-Xeran." His gaze was steady, but there was pain in his eyes.

Riane shifted uncomfortably as guilt stabbed her. "I'm sorry."

He rolled his broad shoulders in a shrug, then rose to his feet with easy strength. "Xeran or not, my mother was a good woman. I can't even count the times she risked her life for me. I don't know why she didn't tell me the truth about herself. I'll probably never know now." His lips twisted bitterly. "Since she's dead." He drew his shoulders back, straightening to his full, impressive height. "But I know the most important things about her. I know she died protecting me. I know she believed she should only use the power she had to protect the innocent. I know she believed those who hunt us are immoral bastards who want only power, and aren't picky about how they get it." His eyes narrowed thoughtfully. "Maybe that's all I need to know."

"Any sign he's lying?" Riane asked her comp, a question born of sheer reflex.

"Negative."

She took a deep breath. "There is another question. One that just occurred to me."

"And that would be?"

"The Xerans sabotaged my suit to bring me here. I thought it was a little too convenient that you happened to show up where I got dumped, just in time to save me from Ivar."

Nick's green eyes narrowed thoughtfully. "Especially since you knew I was half-Xeran." He swore ripely. "No wonder you were suspicious. It was logical to assume I was part of some kind of Xeran trap."

Riane nodded. "The trouble with that is—why? I'm just an Enforcer. Why go to all that effort to mind-fuck me? It doesn't get them anything. But what if *I'm* not the one the trap is aimed at? What if it's you? You're the one with the powers. You're the one with the"—she gestured at the armband—"magic rock."

He considered it, then nodded. "Makes sense."

"But if that's the case, where's the trap?"

He lifted a dark brow. "Your large, homicidal friend?"

"Ivar? Nah. You blew through him a little too easily. There's got to be something else. And since *I'm* certainly not working for the Xerans . . ." She went still. "My suit."

Whirling, she pounced on it. "Dammit, I should have thought of this earlier. We already know they sabotaged it to dump me here, so . . ."

Shaking it out, Riane held it at arm's length. *"Comp, give me a full spectrum scan of this. Every last centimeter. Look for any sign of tampering."*

But the comp's scan turned up nothing. Neither did Nick's paranormal examination, complete with dancing sparks and glowing eyes.

"So what does that mean?" he asked her finally.

Riane sighed. "Not a hell of a lot. The suit's dead. The Xerans must have hacked the onboard computer system in order to redirect my Jumps, but without being able to power it up, there's no way to tell."

That still didn't answer the main question, though. If Nick was the target of this scam, where was the trap?

And when did the Xerans intend to spring it?

·11·

꧁꧂

"So," Nick said after they returned to the kitchen and reheated breakfast. "What is it that you want to do now?"

Riane took a thoughtful bite of bacon. "Well, obviously I need to get back to the Outpost—our headquarters. Frieka's probably going out of his furry little mind by now." She took another bite, then explained. "Frieka's my wolf partner. Genetically engineered and cybernetically enhanced." Grinning, she added, "He also takes pride in being a pain in the ass."

Nick grinned back. "Everybody needs a hobby."

"Oh, yeah. But he also loves me, and I hate the thought of him being worried."

"But how are you going to get back to the future? Because I don't happen to have a DeLorean handy."

Riane blinked at him, mystified. "A what?"

"Never mind. Movie reference." Nick waved a hand. "I mean, how are you going to get home if your suit is dead?"

"Good question." She scooped up her braid and twirled it between two fingers. "Either I need to find another time traveler who can send a courier 'bot back to the Outpost, or . . ."

"Or?"

Riane hesitated a moment. "You could use your powers to send me home."

Nick shook his head. "I told you, Riane, I don't know how to do that. What if I screwed up? Those kind of energies could fry you like bacon." He picked up a slice of bacon off the plate and snapped it in two before eating the pieces in decisive bites.

"But I can't stay here, Nick. And the problem is, I don't know where to find another traveler from my time. It's not like I can Gaggle them."

Handsome lips twitched on the verge of a smile. "I think you mean 'Google.'"

"Google, Gaggle." She glowered at him. "You know what I mean."

Nick sighed. "Yeah, I know. What I don't know is how to create some kind of space-time warp that will transport you three hundred years into the future without shredding you like toilet paper."

"Okay." She raked both hands through her hair. "Okay, I see your point."

"And I see yours. Let me think about this. Maybe I can come up with some way to do it safely."

Riane took a deep breath. "Thank you."

"In the meantime," he said, eyeing her, "you're going to need something more to wear than one of my T-shirts. Which means we need to go shopping."

"With what? I wasn't expecting to come to this time. I don't have currency for the twenty-first century."

"Luckily, I do. Money's not a problem." He stood and began to clear off the table.

Riane, picked up her own plate and walked to the trash can to dump the remains. "Why not? What *do* you do for money?"

Nick laughed. "You know, that's not considered a polite question in this time."

"I've never been considered all that polite even in my own. So?"

He smiled slightly. "The Stone provides very good stock tips. My mother made a lot of money playing the market, and I've made even more."

"Are you saying you're rich?"

"Does it matter when I have to live like this?" Nick grimaced, gesturing around at the Spartan apartment. "All the money means is that I can afford to run when I have to. Or buy you a new pair of jeans."

She inclined her head. "Thank you."

"Not," he added with a roguish twinkle at her bare legs, "that I object to the view now."

Riane eyed his broad, bare chest and smiled back. "Neither do I."

His gaze heated, but then he cleared his throat and got to his feet. "I'd better find you something you can wear in public."

Nick dug through a drawer, looking for the pair of sweats he'd accidently washed with a bunch of towels. They'd drawn up in the hot water until they hit him at mid-calf. They should fit Riane . . . not that they'd do that luscious body justice.

Bending, he pulled open another drawer and absently pushed a pile of underwear aside.

He could almost hate her for the way she'd turned his life upside down. There'd been something almost . . . testing in her eyes, like she was waiting to see how he'd react to having his whole fucking life blown up around him.

Nick took a deep breath and closed his eyes. The center of his chest ached with a dull pain. All these years, his mother had lied to him. She'd known exactly what the Xerans were—hell, she was one—and yet she'd never told him. And he'd asked.

Why? Why hadn't she told him? It was like being abandoned all over again.

He slammed the drawer closed. *She didn't abandon you, you dumb shit. She was murdered.*

He opened another drawer, burrowed.

And Riane had known it. And she'd just slid the knife right between his ribs.

It was ridiculous to feel so betrayed. He knew that. She'd suspected him of being some kind of Xeran plant. She had no way of knowing he'd been waiting for her for sixteen years.

Which, now that he thought about it, made him sound like some kind of stalker. Better not share that little data point with her. She'd probably go all paranoid on him again.

Lifting a stack of underwear, Nick finally spotted the pants and pulled them out. He stood to find her standing in the doorway in his T-shirt, looking leggy and entirely too delicious. He stalked toward her and handed her the pants. "Here." Suddenly he had no desire to watch her slide into them. "Excuse me."

She stepped back, frowning up at his face. "Something wrong?"

"Not a damn thing." He escaped into the bathroom without looking back.

* * *

Aliens, **Ivar thought,** his big hands tightening on the van's steering wheel. *Bastards have teamed me up with aliens. I* hate *aliens.*

The van rocked on its wheels. Probably the Tevan moving around in the back. The reptilian warrior was more than two meters tall, with orange scales, spined red armor, and a temper as ugly as his four-eyed face.

Ivar didn't actually mind the Tevan that much. It was the freaking Her-Gla that gave him the chills. She was coiled in the passenger seat next to him, watching him with the unblinking attention of a snake. Her claws clicked restlessly as her long, pointed tongue flicked in and out of her triangular muzzle, tasting the air. To Ivar's eyes, she looked like a genengineer's nightmare, not even vaguely human. Her skin was a gleaming blue-black, and she had a trio of snaking arms tipped with multiple tentacles rather than hands. Three claws tipped the end of each tentacle. Her three legs were powerfully muscled, giving her the ability to leap long distances.

But it was her eyes that really disturbed him. There were six of them, faceted like an insect's, three arrayed on each side of her long head. Her mouthful of triangular razored teeth reminded him unpleasantly of a shark.

Ivar himself had been upgraded again, a process that had been no more pleasant the second time around. His body had jolted painfully every few minutes all day afterward, as if in the grip of a series of vicious electric shocks. He'd been told his strength and speed had more than doubled, but he couldn't help but wonder about side effects from all that Xeran tech.

His lips peeled off his teeth. Fuck it. As long as it let him get revenge on the gods-cursed Enforcers, he didn't care.

Starting with that bitch Riane Arvid.

He straightened in interest, watching intently as the

primitive and the Warfem came out of the apartment building. They got in a long, low black car and pulled out into
traffic. Ivar waited a few minutes, sensors locked on the
BMW's distinctive pattern of emissions, before he, too,
pulled out and followed.

The Outpost

Punching the Senior Investigator in the mouth would
be a very bad idea. Dona Astryr pasted an expression of
polite attention on her face and straightened the fingers
that wanted to curl into fists. *I'm not going to hit him. I'm
not going to hit him.*

"You're telling me you had no idea your lover was a
spy?" Corydon lifted his upper lip in contemptuous disbe-
lief. "You worked with Senior Enforcer Ivar Terje for more
than a year—even slept with him—yet your sensors never
once told you he was lying to you?"

How many times had she already explained this? Ten?
Fifteen? She'd lost count. Fighting to control her irritation,
Dona looked out the wall-length window at the rolling,
tree-covered flanks of the Blue Ridge Mountains as they
dozed in the sunlight, painted with indigo shadows. It was
a beautiful view, one that normally never failed to soothe.

Today it barely kept her from breaking Corydon's exquisite nose. *I know how this works, dammit,* Dona thought.
*I've interrogated more than my share of subjects. Pissing
them off is all part of the game. An angry criminal makes
mistakes.*

But she was no criminal. She was a Temporal Enforcer.
She'd spent eight years chasing killers and thieves through
time, and she didn't deserve Corydon's suspicion.

Taking a deep breath, Dona returned her attention to
the Senior Investigator, who sat behind Chief Dyami's

massive black desk as if he owned it. Her commanding officer had loaned the human his office for these relentless interviews of the Outpost staff.

"Ivar apparently used his internal computer to hide his reactions whenever he lied," she explained, wrestling her temper into submission. "There were no physiological changes for my sensors to detect."

"You told Chief Dyami your lover's computer was active even in casual conversation. You never even entertained the thought that he might be a traitor?"

"Do you ever wonder if *your* friends are traitors?"

"Actually, yes, I do." Corydon's tone was icy. "I'm always alert for signs of treason."

I'm not surprised.

"Your commanding officer told me he considers you an intelligent and capable agent." His chin set at a contemptuous angle. "Your record doesn't seem to indicate any real incompetence. You've been an agent of Temporal Enforcement for eight years now. Decent case solved rate. Adequate string of commendations—even a Silver Dragon for bravery under fire." He sniffed. "But then, you *are* a cyborg. I'd imagine it's easier being courageous when you're so hard to kill."

Her mouth tightened. "I was awarded that for chasing a berserk Tevan cyborg through twentieth-century Chicago after he murdered my previous partner. I managed to keep him from killing any temporal natives, but I damned near died doing it. The medtechs had to resuscitate me twice after they got us back."

"A Tevan?" Corydon's aristocratic nostrils flared. "Tevans have no business time traveling to Earth. They can't pass for human."

"Since they're two and a half meters tall, scaled, and orange, no. And this one was completely insane. That's why we were chasing him."

"An impressive arrest, I suppose." He glanced down at his comp slate. "Of course, it would have been more impressive if you were human."

I'm not *going to hit him.*

· 12 ·

The bra was a confection of lace and netting that didn't look as if it could support a baby hamster, much less Riane's round, lovely breasts.

Unfortunately, Nick's mind persisted in picturing her wearing the thing, those rosy nipples peeking through the sheer black fabric . . .

He swallowed hastily and hung the bra back on the rack. Its hanger rattled loudly against its fellows, and he cast a furtive glance around for other customers. Like the ones who might think he was some kind of pervert.

What the hell had possessed him to take her to Victoria's Secret?

Though, it *had* seemed the logical thing to do at the time. Apparently twenty-third-century people didn't wear twenty-first-century-style undergarments. And Riane needed them, a fact that became obvious when he watched her walk around in his clothes. Her pretty breasts swayed under the black tee in a way that had riveted his hapless attention.

Her nipples jutted under the soft fabric like pencil erasers. Or pieces of candy.

Pink, delicious pieces of candy, all rosy and . . .

Bra, he'd thought desperately, as various anatomy south of his belt buckle woke up and took notice of his fantasy life. *The woman needs a bra.*

"Now I know why my mother hated these things."

He wheeled in relief as Riane emerged from some mysterious back room of the store. Her expression was disgruntled in the extreme.

"Just look at this thing!" She whipped the hem of the T-shirt up, displaying her bra-clad breasts. Lace veiled the pretty cream mounds, just barely, the rosy shadows of her nipples peeking through.

He lunged forward, grabbed the hem, and jerked it back down. "Don't *do* that!"

She frowned at him. "What?

"You don't show your breasts in public!" Nick hissed, glancing around to make sure no one was running for mall security.

The frown deepened. "But there are pictures of breasts on the wall." She gestured at one of the huge posters.

"They don't show *nipples.* Have you paid for that yet?"

"Yes, of course." Elaborate patience rang in her voice, as if she was speaking to someone of very limited intelligence. Which wasn't far off, considering that his entire blood supply was headed south for the winter. She displayed the shocking pink bag that held the rest of her purchases. "Just as you instructed, I told them the airline lost my luggage. The clerk let me wear a bra and panties out of the store." She frowned, her mind apparently returning to the Great Tit Debate. "We passed a picture of a bare-chested man in the corridor. His nipples were showing."

"It's different when it's a woman." He caught her elbow and steered her hastily out of the store.

"Why? A nipple is a nipple."

"Children." Nick could hear the growing desperation in his own voice. He lowered his voice to a hiss. "We don't like children to see women's nipples. Or ... ah ... the genital ... parts of either sex."

"That's stupid." She eyed him in disapproval. "If you teach children that the human body should be hidden like something dirty, you risk instilling a sense of shame that can lead to sexual pathology later in life. It's no wonder you have so many sexual predators in this century."

"Would you *please* stop talking about time travel?" Judging from the heat in his cheekbones, he was blushing like a thirteen-year-old caught with a skin mag. By a nun. "Look, let's just concentrate on finding you some clothes, okay?"

She leaned closer suddenly, and her eyes crinkled with amusement. "You're blushing!"

"Cut it out."

"It's cute."

"Please. Shut. Up."

Riane discovered leather.

She spotted the leather pants in the display window of a store whose usual clientele ran to people with exotic body piercings. Before Nick could protest, she sauntered inside to investigate.

"It's not armor," she announced, running one hand down the butter-soft hide, "but it would be better than those jeans you're so fond of."

"Better for what?"

"Battle."

Nick blinked, mouthing, "Battle?"

He watched, bemused, as she worked her way through the rack without checking sizes before whipping out a pair. "These."

They did look long enough to accommodate her impressive leg length. "You sure they'll fit?"

She shrugged. "Comp says they will."

And her computer would know. "Get three pairs."

They took the pants to the cashier and bought them on the spot, Nick wincing just a little at the price. Riane, who evidently had no idea of the relative cost of things, didn't even blink.

She went off to the dressing room with one pair and donned it. Apparently she was tired of hitching up his too big sweatpants. When she emerged a moment later, Nick barely kept himself from swallowing his tongue.

The pants were long enough, but they fit her muscular legs like a layer of black vinyl spray paint. She bounced a little on her toes, frowning, then suddenly pivoted on one foot and snapped the other leg up in a kick that stopped just shy of Nick's jaw.

"Umm," he said, one hand wrapped around her ankle. He'd blocked the kick before he realized it wasn't actually going to land.

"They're a little stiff," she told him. "I'm going to have to break them in."

"You do that." He released her ankle as she smoothly pivoted away. "Just don't break *me* while you're at it."

As Riane moved off to investigate a rack of leather jackets, Nick met the startled gaze of the store clerk. "She does Women's Ultimate Fighting." He'd learned how to lie like a psychopath before he could shave.

"They've got that?" The clerk's eyes, ringed like a raccoon's with eyeliner, widened in interest. Both her tongue and her nose were pierced.

"It's new."

"I like these," Riane announced, returning with a leather jacket, three tops in various colors, and a length of thick chain that appeared to be some kind of belt.

"What's with the chain?" he asked, interested.

"Weapon." Having dumped her selections on the counter, she started examining a pair of gloves. Metal studs ran the length of each leather finger. They looked like something Billy Idol would have worn in a video twenty years ago, but Nick imagined that a punch with them would hurt. A lot.

"Want 'em?"

"Yes, please." She watched as he added them to her purchases. When the pierced clerk gave him the total, Riane frowned.

As they walked out of the store, she caught his forearm. "That was a lot of money, wasn't it?"

Nick shrugged. "If it keeps you from losing skin the next time Ivar comes after us, it's worth it."

"I'm not sure how I'm going to repay you." Riane paused as if thinking it through. "Though I suppose I can come back after I get my suit repaired."

"Don't worry about it," he told her gruffly. "Money isn't an issue with me. I've got more than I can spend as it is."

She looked relieved. "That's good. But I'll still come back."

Damn, he thought, *I hope so.*

Next she found a pair of black Timberlands to replace her blue uniform boots. She bounced around on her toes for a while before she pronounced herself satisfied. "I'll be able to kick with these."

Nick contemplated the boots' heavy soles. "And your target won't be likely to get up afterward."

Hungry after their shopping safari, they stopped at a pizza kiosk in the food court. Nick was looking forward to introducing her to a new food, but it turned out pizza had been a favorite specialty of her mother's. The taste, she told him, chewing happily, reminded her of her childhood. "Frieka hates pizza, though."

"Yeah?"

"Too much dough, not enough meat."

After dinner, they hit a movie. Since it was Wednesday night and the film in question had been out several weeks, they had the theater to themselves. That turned out to be a good thing, because Riane critiqued the cop hero's intelligence and technique, as well as the general believability of the action.

Nick found himself agreeing with her, and soon both of them were tossing popcorn at the screen every time the cop did something particularly stupid.

They threw a lot of popcorn.

A growl rumbled from the back of the van, a wordless sound of savage impatience and frustrated bloodlust.

"Keep your armor on, Tiny," Ivar growled back. "They'll come out of there eventually. And when they do, you'll get to play."

"*Che-cler effa.*" The Her-Gla clicked her claws twice.

"*Erita kator che!*" The van rocked violently as the Tevan lunged forward in offended rage.

"Back off!" Ivar roared, jerking around in the driver's seat. "Don't make me come back there, Tiny. You won't like it."

"*Ai cleta, Ivar.*"

Ivar knew enough about Tevans to interpret that hissing tone as the equivalent of sneering laughter. "You want to get paid, asshole? Keep it up."

Kavar's Bleeding Balls, he hoped their targets came out of that theater soon, or his so-called "allies" were going to turn their collective psychopathy on each other—and him.

·13·

꒰꒱

Dona Astryr stalked into the Enforcers' training gym. She needed to hit something. Hard.

Even as the doors closed behind her, she almost turned and ran out again.

Chief Enforcer Alerio Dyami stood in a corner of the gym holding a gravbar, pumping out repetitions with a Warlord's effortless strength. He wore only a pair of black snugs that left most of his big body deliciously bare. His black hair fell in a thick mane to his broad, sweating shoulders, one lock braided with a string of gemstones that were actually combat decorations on his home planet. An intricate tattoo in vivid shades of gold and green covered the right side of his face, stretching from above one arching brow halfway down his elegant cheek.

Each part of the swirling pattern meant something; she'd looked it up once. The gold and green color of the tat represented House Dyami, the company which had genetically engineered and trained him. The triangular design running down his cheek meant he was a Viking Class Warlord, the most physically powerful subclass of his warrior people.

And the empty circle that lay directly underneath that meant he was unmated. Which intrigued Dona entirely too damned much, considering that male Vardonese warriors were renowned for their sex drive and erotic skill.

He's your commanding officer, you moron, she told herself impatiently. *Eyes off.*

Dona jerked her head away and stuffed her fascination for her chief back into its mental box. She'd been infatuated with Dyami since joining the American Outpost two years ago. Which was why she'd gotten involved with that treasonous asshole Ivar Terje. When the big redhead had been assigned as her partner last year, she'd thought he was the perfect antidote to Dyami. He was even taller and more massively built than the Chief, with a handsome angular face, cool gray eyes, and a talent for making her feel she was the center of the universe. Instead, Ivar had turned out to be a murderous spy for the Xeran Empire.

Oh, yeah. She definitely needed to hit something.

Sweet Mother Goddess, Dona had just walked in. With an effort, Alerio managed to keep his eyes from drifting in the cyborg's direction as she strode across the gym on those long legs of hers.

Even in a time when genetic engineering had made beauty commonplace, Dona was nothing short of heartstopping. Tall and lean, she had the long, strong build of a fighter, yet there was more than enough curve to her breasts and ass to draw his hot-blooded attention. As usual, she wore her long, dark hair in intricate braids that called attention to her striking violet eyes. Her features were precisely sculpted, cheekbones high and rounded, with a firm chin and a soft, sensual mouth.

That mouth had been the focus of far too many of his most erotic dreams.

It was an entirely inappropriate attraction, and he knew it. She was his subordinate. Though it wasn't against Temporal Enforcement regulations to take a lover from among one's staff, doing so was a very bad idea. How was he supposed to maintain objectivity about a woman who'd obsessed him for the past two years?

To make matters worse, Dona returned his interest. She'd never said so directly, of course—she was as aware of the inherent problems as he was. But her powerful female response to him was entirely too clear to a man with sensor implants.

Unfortunately, Alerio wasn't the only one who'd sensed her interest.

At first, he'd been relieved when Dona had gotten involved with Ivar Terje. Terje, however, had proven to be a jealous son of a bitch who'd made Dona's life hell even before he'd revealed himself to be a spy. He'd treated Dona so badly, Alerio had itched to call him out for a Warlord-style duel.

Meaning no weapons, no rules, and no mercy.

As the couple's commanding officer, however, Alerio hadn't been able to do that. Now, though, he could finally give Terje the beating he'd been begging for. If he ever actually caught the bastard anyway.

Brooding, Alerio rotated the gravbar, ignoring the ache of his straining arms. The bar basically functioned the same as an antigrav unit, but in reverse. Its actual weight was only a kilo or so, but he'd adjusted its field generators until its mass was closer to four hundred. Controlling that mass deserved every bit of his attention and strength, but it was all he could do to keep his gaze from drifting to Dona.

She opened one of the lockers set in the wall and activated the combot it contained. The towering gray android stepped out of the locker and trailed her over to the circular combat mat in the center of the gym.

Dona and the combot bowed to each other, signaling the beginning of the session. An imagizer field flared around the android, abruptly transforming it into the likeness of Ivar Terje.

He winced. *Why had she programmed it to . . . ?*

Her elegant features twisted into a chilling mask of rage at the sight of her ex-lover's face. Dona flung herself at the practice android in a flurry of punches and kicks, driving the combot into retreat.

Never mind.

Alerio deactivated his gravbar and turned to watch. Three weeks before, Ivar had sabotaged a combot and programmed it to kill Jessica Kelly. The machine had damned near choked Jess to death, and would have had she not blown it apart with telekinetic abilities she'd acquired from the alien Sela.

Alerio and Galar, Jess's lover, had supposedly plugged the security holes Ivar had used to program the combot to kill. But considering what had happened to Riane Arvid's T-suit, he wasn't in the mood to take chances.

Not that keeping an eye on Dona was a hardship. She wore black snugs and a matching breast band, and her long, elegant feet were bare. It was the sort of costume that showed off her lean, lush build in a way that made his dick do a happy little dance.

But it wasn't just the barely clothed contours of her body that enthralled him. It was the way she moved.

Each attack flowed into the next until it was impossible to tell where punch ended and block began, where roundhouse

kick became spinning retreat. The combot had been programmed to mimic the raw, physical power of Ivar's fighting
style, his vicious intensity and mercilessness. Dona was every bit as ferocious, but she met his power with blurring
speed and agility. It was like watching a mongoose fight a
cobra.

Long minutes went by in a hypnotic rain of blows as
Dona took out her rage on the combot. Until at last she
landed a kick to the android's head that was so clean, so
powerful, that the machine simply stopped and announced,
"Killing blow."

Dona turned to Alerio, sweat streaming down her lean
body, her breath coming in rasping pants. Her face was
white with rage, and her violet eyes blazed. "Do you really
think I'm part of that bastard Ivar's treason?"

Alerio shook his head. "What I think is irrelevant.
Headquarters sent Corydon to investigate, and I can't—"

"Fuck Corydon and his investigation," Dona snapped,
stepping right up to him and meeting his eyes in bold demand. "I want to know what you believe. *Do you really
think I'm capable of treason?*"

He found he couldn't lie to those eyes. "No. I don't think
you had anything to do with any of it."

Tense muscles relaxed in her strong, feminine shoulders. "That's all I needed to know."

And as he watched, she turned and left the room.

Alerio turned to the combot. "New session."

"Affirmative."

He bared his teeth. "And keep the Ivar Terje image."

Then he launched himself at the combot like a missile
of pure, blazing rage.

Nick and Riane strolled out into the parking lot after the
movie, as if they were an ordinary couple on an ordinary

date. He had to admit, he thoroughly enjoyed the illusion.

"What an idiot," Riane groaned, the combat beads of her braid clinking as she shook her head. "Why did Grayson charge in alone like that? Any cop with the brains of a chio would have waited for backup."

Nick looped an arm around her neck as they walked along together. "My mother had a very wise saying whenever I asked a question like that as a boy."

"Yeah?" Riane lifted a red brow. "What?"

" 'It was in the script.' "

"Being stupid was in the script?"

"It was a very stupid script."

As she laughed, he automatically scanned the parking lot. And felt the hair rise on the back of his neck. It was almost midnight, and the lot was virtually empty. "Let's get to the car," Nick said, tensing. "This is a really good place for an ambush."

"You know," Ivar Terje said from behind them, "that's just what I was thinking."

· 14 ·

Something out of a horror movie was stalking
Nick. The thing had three . . . arms? . . . that ended in a
trio of tentacles tipped in claws. It moved on three muscled
legs, its six faceted eyes focused on him with unnerving
intensity. Its open mouth looked like something off a boxed
set of *Jaws*—way too many triangular teeth and truly ugly
intentions. Its skin gleamed dully black, iridescence rippling along its flesh like oil on inky water.

Nick retreated warily, moving into an easy, fluid
stance. His mother had enrolled him in martial arts
classes the minute he could walk; he'd long since stopped
keeping track of which degree black belt he was. But he
wasn't at all confident he was up to taking on the thing
with all the teeth. Not even with the Stone reinforcing his
strength.

He shot a glance over at Riane. She had problems of her
own—seven feet of brawny orange warrior who was moving stealthily toward her like a cat creeping up on a canary.

Nick badly wanted to help her, but he didn't dare divert his attention from Jabber Jaws.

To make matters worse, Ivar was hanging back, watching both of them with an expression of profound enjoyment. He'd be on them like a shark on sushi the minute one of them tried to help the other.

An indescribable hissing, clacking sound snapped Nick's head around. Jabber Jaws leaped toward him like a misshapen flea, tentacles whipping.

"Fuck!" He ducked, spun, feeding the Stone's power into his fists, his feet. His booted heel caught the thing in its . . . head? The end with the teeth anyway. Jabby hit the ground hard, flinging out its legs to stop its roll.

A tentacle whipped around his ankle with the speed of a striking rattlesnake. It snatched him off his bracing foot, yanked him through the air like a rag doll, and slammed him against the blacktop. The Stone's power absorbed most of the fall's force, but it still rattled his teeth. He rammed his free foot into the thing's head, amping the kick with the Stone. Moving with blurring speed, he kicked it again. And again. The grip of the tentacle loosened, and he flipped onto his feet. Jabby lunged at him like a gator, teeth snapping.

Nick leaped back, slamming a fist down on the top of the thing's head. A clawed tentacle raked his arm. Scarlet flew.

First blood to Jabby.

At the sight of that welling crimson slash, something dark stirred in Nick. A black and familiar rage, a craving for the release of violence and revenge. A craving that could only be sated by the death of his enemies.

He gritted his teeth and forced the darkness down. He didn't want to lose it in front of Riane.

* * *

Riaat **sang its** deadly song in Riane's blood, bringing a
dark euphoria and insane strength that might not last long
enough. Not against a Tevan warrior.

He was well over two meters tall, scaled and orange in
bright red armor, claws tipping his big, seven-fingered
hands. According to her sensors, his skeleton was reinforced with titanium laminate, while nanocybernetic muscle implants boosted his already considerable strength.

Mother Goddess, Riane thought grimly. *Dad would
have trouble with this fucker.*

And if the Tevan was a match for a Viking Class Warlord, she wouldn't have a prayer.

*Shut up, Riane. I've got to take him, so I'll by the Mother
take him.*

She threw herself toward the mercenary, clearing six
feet in one leap. In the endless instant of her flight, her
knives glittered in either hand as she watched his four yellow eyes narrow. He held blades as long as her forearms in
those big, unhuman hands. If he caught her with one, he'd
cut her in two.

She hit him like a missile. He parried one of her knives
as she passed, blade clashing on blade before she could
slice his throat. Riane saw his other knife swinging in a
long, deadly arc, and twisted like an acrobat to avoid the
attack. Felt the chill breeze of the swipe, saw the flash of
the moonlight on metal. He spun and charged as she hit the
ground behind him.

Riane ducked, whirling, slashing. One knife met his
steel, but the other grated on armor and was deflected
away. She saw the flash of his blade, jerked around to bring
her own up. Too late. Cold stung its way across her belly,
followed by a hot runnel of blood.

She leaped back—*too late, too late, too . . .* Saw an
opening, bounced forward, slashing. *Caught him!* Violet
blood splashed from the wound across his bearlike muzzle,

and he roared in pain. Yellow eyes flared with battle madness as he struck out. She jolted away, avoided the knife
by a whisker, slid in again, and leaped, slashing at those
four eyes. He cursed her, ducked away from her attack,
then stabbed straight in. Riane had grown too used to
fighting in armor; she almost let him drive the blade into
her belly. At the last instant she threw herself to safety,
twisting, off-balance.

He kicked out, caught her in the side of the thigh, barely
missing the knee he'd been aiming for. Her leg buckled
under her. She went down hard.

The Tevan pounced, two hundred kilos of scales and
armor plummeting toward her, both knives seeking targets
in her torso. She flipped clear in a back-twisting convul-
sion of muscle and desperation. When he hit the ground,
the boom of armor and reptile warrior striking pavement
sounded like a shuttle wreck. One of his knives rammed
into the blacktop. And lodged there, wedged deep by his
alien strength.

He jerked it free, swearing, and turned on her. Riane
surged desperately to her feet. Sucked in a gasp as her
thigh almost collapsed under her. It didn't hurt—it wouldn't
in *riaat*—but it definitely wasn't working right.

"What's wrong with my left leg?"

*"Fractured femur. If not for your reinforced skeleton,
the bone would have been crushed when he kicked you."*

Great. Just great. A leg injury in combat was the kind of
thing that would get you killed.

The Tevan's yellow eyes glittered, and she knew his
sensors had detected the weakness. "Now," he growled in a
rumbling basso, baring an impressive array of teeth, "Now
we finish it."

Oh, fuck.

* * *

Nick and Jabber Jaws circled. The alien moved in an insectoid skitter, claws clicking and snapping eagerly, as if it couldn't wait to sink them into his flesh.

Nick watched it warily, keeping his distance. How the hell did you fight something like this anyway? All those arms, all those claws.

All those teeth.

He wanted to kill it. He wanted to watch its blood fly . . .

Stop it, Nick. Just get it done and get out.

From the corner of one eye, he caught a blur of motion. Sensed a flare of grim fatalism as loud as a scream. Nick knew better than to take his eyes off an opponent, but he couldn't help himself. He looked.

Riane backed away from the big orange lizard thing, which was chasing her, swinging his knife like a reptilian Iron Chef. She was bleeding from long gashes across her chest, her belly, her arms, thighs. Her teeth were set in her bloody face as she struggled to parry his flashing attacks. As she took another step backward, her left leg juddered under her, almost giving way before she caught herself.

Nick got no sense of pain from her, despite all the blood. Only fatalism and a grim determination to go down fighting. *Oh, hell. That leg . . .*

Pain slashed across his chest, a vicious ripping sensation tearing through skin and muscle. He jerked his head around again. Jabber Jaws! The damn thing was right on top of him, tentacles whipping, slicing at him with five-inch claws, teeth snapping.

Dammit, he didn't have time for this. Riane was going down if he didn't do something *now.*

So he let go. Let the bloodlust surge through him, filling him with the hot, vicious euphoria he'd been fighting to contain. He swung one fist in an explosion of force, connected with a deliciously meaty thump.

Jabby just snapped at him, damn near taking a chunk out of his arm. He jolted clear barely in time. Snarled. The bastard was just laughing off his punches.

Well, Jabby wouldn't be laughing for long.

Nick sent his will whipping into the Stone, drew power in a furious stream. Struck out in a whirling roundhouse kick, all speed and brutal power, catching Jabby cleanly across the chest. The alien went flying like a football off a tee.

Nick whirled toward Riane, who was down on one knee now, cutting grimly at the reptile's legs as he danced around her. Her knives glanced off the alien's armor, rattling, raking, doing nothing. "Hang on, Riane! I'm coming."

"I don't think so, hero." A redheaded mass of muscle and bone stepped into his path. There was a big-ass knife in Ivar's hand, more sword than anything else. The cyborg grinned like a psychopath. "We've got other plans for your little friend."

I definitely don't have time for this. "Forget it, motherfucker," Nick snarled. "You're not taking another woman away from me."

A roiling stew of fury and frustration blasted into the Stone and out again in a white-hot surge. He struck out, a fist swinging in a brutal arc even as the other hand slashed forward. He hit the cyborg in the side of the head and grabbed Ivar's knife hand. Crunched, twisted, wrenched. Ivar screamed, and Nick grinned in pure, feral pleasure. The cyborg dropped, leaving his knife in Nick's hand.

As Riane parried blow after savage downward blow.

Nick forgot the cyborg. With a roar, he charged, his new knife a cool and satisfying weight.

The lizard wheeled, startled, knives whipping around. Not fast enough, not against Nick when the darkness was on him. He slid right past the reptile's guard to drive his blade right in the middle of that armored chest. Metal grated, shrieked, and the armor cracked like an egg. Four yellow eyes widened, startled. Glazed as the big warrior dropped where he stood.

Nick felt the grin stretch across his face just as he met Riane's astonished gaze. He wiped the grin away and caught her upper arm to haul her to her feet.

She fell against him. Concern instantly banished the last of his battle lust. "Can you walk?"

"My leg's broken. Bastard kept hitting it when he saw I was injured. Shattered the damn thing."

No time to heal her. He snatched her off her feet, slung her into a fireman's carry, and ran toward the car.

Behind them, Ivar bellowed a curse. Claws skittered on pavement, coming closer. Dammit, it sounded like Jabby was right behind him. Nick ran faster.

"Thanks," she gasped, bracing herself against his back as she hung upside down. "He had me. I was done. How did you drive that knife through his chest plate? My comp says the blade should have shattered before the armor did."

When Nick was in the grip of his darkness, he could do all kinds of shit he shouldn't be able to do. "I have no freaking idea." He sent a wave of telekinetic force ahead of them, flinging the car's doors open. "Watch your head."

Nick ducked, slid her into the passenger side, then scrambled right over the hood, his boots thudding on the metal.

Jabby lunged up at him, snapping ferociously as he started to drop off the hood. He kicked out, catching the alien hard under the jaw, sending it flipping backward through the air.

"You fucking coward!" Ivar roared. He was on his feet again, though blood slicked the side of his face. He didn't look steady on his feet as he ran after them.

"Yeah, yeah, kiss my ass, Benedict Arnold." No time to fumble with the keys. Nick dove into the driver's seat and slapped his palm over the ignition. A snap of power started the engine. He stomped his foot on the gas and sent the Beamer fishtailing toward the mall's exit.

"Kavar's Bleeding Balls!" Ivar snarled, wheeling back toward the van. "Grab the Tevan and get in the van."

The Her-Gla loped back and scooped the massive corpse into her muscular tentacled arms, claws clicking an irritated tattoo. He threw open the doors and jumped into the passenger seat as she tossed the body into the back, then scrambled in after it.

The van roared in pursuit of the primitive's car even before she'd slammed the door.

"Hirglir ak cok vira ba, I'Var!" the Her-Gla snarled.

"Vira ba back at you, bitch." Ivar floored it. "Who'd have guessed the primitive little bastard was strong enough to slab a Tevan?"

· 15 ·

"Can you use a gun?" Nick demanded, muscling the wheel as the black Beamer shot into traffic.

Riane stared at him. "You've got a gun? Why in the hell didn't you use it before now?"

He shot her a fulminating look. "It's in the glove compartment. It's not legal to carry concealed into the damned mall."

"Since when do you *care*?"

"Since the last time I got busted, the freaking aliens came right into the jail after me. Damn near killed three cops and some poor bastard in the drunk tank."

She fumbled a moment until she figured out how to get the compartment open, then pulled the big Glock out. Nick hit a button to roll the window down. "Are you sure you know how to use that?"

Riane snorted. "I can load and fire a flintlock in under thirty seconds. I can damn well shoot the wings off a fly with an automatic." She twisted around in the seat and rose on her good knee, leaning out the window.

"A flintlock? Why would you need to . . . ?" He shook his head. "Time cop. Never mind."

Riane grunted, watching the van draw closer through the rear window. Blood ran, wet and sticky, into her eyes. Her head spun from a combination of blood loss and exhaustion. She'd burned through her *riaat* reserves fighting the Tevan, and her hands were shaking. She steadied herself on the frame of the window and exhaled, readying herself for the shot.

The van roared closer, obviously intent on ramming the car. Riane took aim through the tinted windshield at a spot right in the center of Ivar's forehead. The cyborg's eyes widened, and he jerked the wheel in the instant she fired. The roar of the gun was deafening, and the car filled with the smell of cordite. Ivar yelped as he ducked.

"Get him?" Nick demanded, taking the corner with brakes squealing.

"He swerved. Bullet grazed his ear." Coolly, she took aim again, this time on the van's tires. Her next two shots did not miss. Both front tires blew, and the van swerved and spun out of control. She watched with grim satisfaction as the big vehicle hit the curb, ran onto the sidewalk, and slammed into a light pole.

"Good shooting!" Nick said, sounding vaguely surprised.

"I'm a Warfem. I hit what I aim at." She twisted around and dropped back into the seat, grunting in pain.

"How badly are you hurt?" Nick asked as the car shot through the night.

She shrugged. "Leg's pretty bad. Blood loss isn't good, but most of the knife wounds are minor. I can dance my way through a fight pretty good when I have to, even half-crippled." Raking a hand through her blood-sticky hair, Riane shot him a look. "So what's our next move?"

"We run like hell. We don't dare go back to the apartment; they've obviously figured out where it is, since they followed us here."

Riane shook her head. "No, we've got to go back. My T-suit's there."

"And there's a real good chance a hit team is, too. We can't risk it."

"Nick, we've got no choice. You don't leave twenty-third-century tech where the natives can find it. That's the kind of shit that gets Enforcers court-martialed. Even Ivar went back for the Tevan, and he's not even *in* the agency anymore. I'll bet he didn't even think about it; it was sheer reflex."

"Fuck." Nick glared out the windshield, then threw up a hand in disgust. "Fine, we'll go get the damned suit. I just hope we don't get killed in the process."

Despite his considerable misgivings, Nick left Riane in the car with the gun when they reached the apartment. She wasn't up to climbing the stairs to the second floor with that leg, and he didn't dare take time to heal it now.

He bounded up the steps three at a time, his nape crawling as his every instinct howled that the aliens—no, Xerans—would attack any minute.

His stomach heaved. He always felt a little sick when he cut loose. It was one thing to kill, particularly since the bastards would have gutted both him and Riane given the chance. But there was something about the unholy joy he felt when he cut loose that bothered him.

What if the next time he started killing, he wasn't able to stop?

Shut up, Nick. You stopped. You're fine.

He found the suit draped over a chair and stuffed it into a gym bag. What the hell, as long as he was here, he might as well grab a few things. Being no stranger to speed packing, it took him no time at all to bundle a few pairs of T-shirts, jeans, socks, and jocks into the sack.

Five minutes later, he threw the bag in the back of the car. Riane, gun in her lap, pale as milk, barely looked up as he slid into the driver's seat. Having left the engine running, Nick hit the gas and took off at a speed just barely legal. He really didn't want to get pulled over.

"I don't get it," he growled the fifth time he checked the rearview mirror only to find it empty. "Where the fuck are they?"

"Maybe they were killed in the crash."

"We're not that lucky."

Hidden behind a sensor shield to keep Riane from spotting it, the courier 'bot followed the car . . . and the shielded nanobot spy hidden in her combat decorations.

The trip to Xer was a bitch. No surprise, considering they had to cross three centuries and four hundred light-years to get there, all while lugging the Tevan's corpse.

The three first materialized in twenty-third-century Atlanta. A ten-year-old boy on a gravboard gaped at them in wonder. Either the kid had never seen anybody make a Jump before, or a dead Tevan, Ivar, and a Her-gla made a particularly striking combination.

Ignoring the boy, Ivar and the surviving alien made the next Jump in the trip, this one designed to take them one hundred light-years through space.

They materialized on Kardiv next, then went on to Uty, then made two more Jumps, each time materializing on worlds farther and farther toward the edge of the Galactic Union.

Five more Jumps carried them into the heart of the Xeran Empire, to Xer itself.

They materialized at the coordinates they'd been given, an outer courtyard of the Cathedral Fortress. The first thing Ivar saw when the sickening dazzle of the Jump faded was an armored guard with a quantum sword, standing less than a meter away. The glowing blade made a musical chime as the guard lifted it. "Prepare to be searched," the man snarled.

The Her-gla growled something guttural at him. Ivar told her to shut the fuck up, and she subsided sullenly. He wasn't real thrilled either, but considering how thoroughly they'd screwed the mission, they were in no position to get pissy. Particularly since there was a good chance they could end up as dead as the Tevan; the Victor was not exactly known for his forgiving nature.

So they endured the searches. A body tube arrived, and the Tevan was loaded into it with no ceremony at all. Finally a team of armed priests arrived to escort Ivar and the Her-Gla off to the Cathedral Fortress's great audience chamber.

Then it was a matter of cooling their heels until the Victor decided to grace them with his glow-in-the-dark presence.

The wait apparently got on the Her-Gla's nerves as badly as it did Ivar's, because she spent the entire time clicking her claws until he was seriously tempted to slap her upside her toothy head. Only the realization that she'd probably eat his face made him keep his hand to himself.

Finally the familiar music swelled into thunder, signaling the Victor's arrival. Ivar felt sweat break out between his shoulder blades.

The sweat became a cold trickle down his spine as he

recounted the day's disaster to the god's pitiless black eyes. He badly wanted to lie, but he knew the Victor would sense it. And he had heard enough to know the Xeran's idea of atonement was even worse than his idea of upgrading.

"The little bastard was dancing around the Her-Gla as if he was scared of her," Ivar said, forgetting his fear as he got into the frustrating details of his story. "Then he realized that little bitch Riane was about to get whacked. And all of a sudden . . ." He shook his head. "That fucking arm thing of his started glowing. He hit the Her-Gla, and she just sailed off like—"

The Her-Gla interrupted with a rapid-fire stream of guttural protest.

"Silence!" the Victor snapped at her, without turning those black eyes away from Ivar. "I have no interest in thy excuses. Continue, traitor."

Ivar wanted to grind his teeth at that "traitor," but he knew better. "Then he went after the Tevan, and I tried to stop him. Sparks just came pouring out of that arm gem, and he started glowing like a damned laser torch. And when he hit me . . . I've fought Tevans, Warlords in *riaat*, Rivarian combat 'bots—you name it—and I have *never* been hit like that. He shouldn't have been that strong. He just shouldn't. And then damned if he didn't drive my knife right through the Tevan's chest plate. That blade wasn't rated to penetrate combat armor. I have no fucking idea how he did it."

The Victor smiled, a tight curve of his glowing lips. "I do." He leaned down to look into Ivar's eyes. Ivar fought the urge to back away. "So he called more power because the girl was in danger?"

Ivar nodded cautiously. "That's the way it looked to me. Which would make her his Achilles' heel."

"Yesssss. It does seem that way." Those black eyes narrowed. "However, I am not particularly happy with your performance on this mission. I think you need a bit more . . . power."

Oh, shit.

Riane rested her forehead against the car's cool window. She felt as if she swam in a stew of exhaustion, weakness, and the kind of dull lack of sensation she associated with her comp's blocking a great deal of pain.

Worse still was the sense of defeat. The Tevan had beaten her. If not for Nick, she'd be dead.

You're not the warrior your father was.

No. No, she wasn't. True, Baran Arvid would have had trouble with the Tevan, but in the end her father would have defeated the big mercenary. She, on the other hand, had let him break her freaking leg.

Moron. Clumsy. Stupid. Moron.

If Nick hadn't appeared like an avenging angel from one of her mother's stories—*glowing*, for the Mother's sweet sake . . . "Where'd you learn to fight like that?"

He shot her a worried look, then managed a smile. "Well, I've been taking martial arts classes ever since I can remember. Trouble is, we kept having to move, which made it really hard to learn. I got so desperate I started using my powers to absorb the knowledge I needed."

She lifted her head off the cool glass and stared at him. "Absorb? How?"

Nick shrugged. "I'd find someone with the abilities I needed, and I'd tell them what I needed to know and why."

"You'd just tell them. That you were being stalked by aliens. And they *believed* you?" Many people in this time didn't think life on other planets was even possible.

He snorted. "If I want to be believed, I'm believed. Then I ask them whether they'll let me draw the experience I need from their minds."

"Do they ever say no?" *Can* they say no?

"Sometimes."

"What does this . . . process do to them?"

"Nothing. I don't drain the memories. I just use the Stone to implant those techniques in my own brain. Of course, then I have to practice like hell so I can incorporate them, which usually takes a couple of months. But that's still faster than spending years studying. And it works. I've learned everything from the operation of financial markets to aikido that way."

Riane contemplated the idea, decided it wasn't so alien after all. "So it's kind of like an EDI."

"A what?"

"Educational data implant. It's a medical technique that implants information directly into the brain. Allows people to learn a skill in minutes instead of years."

"Yeah, basically."

"So if they say no, what do you do?"

He shrugged. "Same thing I do if they say yes, except for absorbing the abilities. I make them forget about me. As far as they're concerned, none of it ever happened."

Riane shook her head. "That's a scary set of abilities."

Nick shot her a pointed look. "Would be if I misused them."

Question was, where the hell had those powers come from? She kept circling back to the Sela—and Charlotte Holt. Charlotte was a Xeran, but her abilities had been different. She'd been able to transport herself through time, yet she hadn't seemed to have the pure, raw power Nick had.

Could *she* have been his mother?

Of course, the Charlotte Riane had encountered had appeared to be barely thirty in the year 2008. Nick appeared to be around that now, and it was what, 2009 . . . ?

Time travel. What if she traveled back in time to give

birth to him? "Oh, Mother Goddess, I really am a moron!"

"Okay, that's it." Nick took the nearest exit ramp, then veered off down a dark country road.

She gave him a wary look. What did he have in mind now?

· 16 ·

❧❀❧

Nick pulled onto the shoulder of the road and turned off the engine. A meadow stretched away to the left, ringed by trees. The moon rose fat and full, edging every weed and leaf in silver.

Riane tensed, feeling disoriented. Blood loss was getting to her. The entire car smelled like copper, and her clothes were sticky, glued to her wounds. "What? What are you going to do?"

"What the hell do you think?" He got out. She watched as he walked around the BMW, pulled open her door, and crouched on the ground beside the car. "You," he told her, "have a broken leg and way too much blood loss. I don't know what all your little nanothings are doing, but you're about to get a dose of Nicky's special magic."

She sighed, feeling weary and discouraged. "I won't argue with you."

"Good, 'cause I would ignore your ass if you did." He touched her leg with gentle hands and frowned. "That's not a good break, Riane. There's a lot of damage and swelling. Oh, hell, I should have pulled over a lot earlier." He cupped his fingers over bloody leather. "It doesn't hurt?"

Riane shrugged. "My comp does a really good job with pain."

"Again, good. Healing something like this isn't going to be any fun." He frowned deeply as green sparks poured out of his palms and began to dance over her leg like fireflies. A sensation that reminded her of ants crawling began to swarm up her thigh. Muscles jerked and shivered, with no command at all from her. Something *shifted*, and she gasped.

"That hurt?"

"No." She ground her teeth. It didn't, but deep inside the leg she could feel something weird happening.

Green light swirled in his eyes, hypnotic and alien. She had the feeling he was looking inside her, as if her skin had gone transparent. The flesh on the nape of her neck chilled.

"You did well in that fight," he told her absently. "I was impressed."

"You must be joking."

Nick lifted his head to stare at her. "You had a broken leg, and you were fighting a guy more than eight feet tall— from your knees. *And* holding him off. That's pretty damned impressive. . . . Fuck. Hold on. I need to align this bone."

He wrapped both hands around her thigh and yanked, hard. Riane managed to swallow a startled yelp. Sweat broke out on her forehead. "I'd still be dead if you hadn't intervened."

"That doesn't make it any less impressive."

"I shouldn't have let him break the damned leg. Clumsy." Her head was swimming, and she closed her eyes, swallowing hard. Her stomach rolled in an alarming way. "I'm just not the warrior my father is." Another ferocious jerk, and she ground her teeth. "Being half-human"—she stopped to gasp—"doesn't exactly help. Plus, I'm not a real Warfem."

"A what?" He seemed to be concentrating on the leg, his tone distracted.

"A Warfem. Female warrior. Genetically engineered, with computer implants. I've got the implants, but I'm not genetically engineered. My dad *is* genetically engineered . . . but he and Mother . . . had me the old-fashioned way." She was babbling, but she didn't care. There were some seriously unpleasant things going on in her body. "I was one of a handful of kids on Vardon who weren't genengineered."

"Really? What was that like?"

Riane suspected he wasn't really listening, so she was more honest than she normally would have been. "Kind of sucked, because you know"—she drew in a hard breath as something seemed to wrench and tear—"I'm ugly."

He jerked his head up and stared at her incredulously. "*What* did you say?"

Panting, she looked at him. "Ugly. I'm ugly."

His jaw dropped. "Are you fishing for compliments? That's the most ridiculous thing I've ever heard. You're gorgeous."

Riane shook her head. "You don't know. You're not from Vardon. Mother refused to put me in the Warrior's Creche because she and Dad wouldn't be allowed to see me. So I went to school with the children of the Femmats and Hommes."

He shook his head and went back to work. Once again, sparks began to flow from his palms. "Which are what?"

"Vardon's aristocracy. Genetically engineered for beauty and intelligence. Those kids were . . . exquisite." She stopped to pant. "Every one of them was like . . . a work of art in flesh and bone. And me . . ." Bone grated sickeningly, and she swallowed hard. "My nose is too long, my jaw is too square, and I'm not even going to talk about my mouth. They really made fun of my mouth."

He snorted. "And then there's that whole delusional thing."

"You're not Vardonese, Nick. I'm telling you what those kids always told me. And I was always too big. Those children were built like little fairies. Delicate, tiny. I was always the tallest kid in the class. My dad is a Viking Class Warlord, and he's built like a human tank. I have his bone structure, so I was this . . . gawky giant."

Nick shot her a look under his brows. "There's *nothing* tanklike about you, Riane. These kids sound like assholes."

She shrugged. "Aristocrats."

Closing both hands around her ankle, Nick gave it another hard tug. He stopped and stared down at her thigh, a deep groove between his dark brows. "I'm having trouble getting this bone straight. This is a lot more complicated that just closing cuts."

Her stomach rolled. *"Do not dare let me throw up,"* Riane told her computer.

"Understood."

Swallowing hard, she went on a little desperately, "Then I got into the Vardonese interstellar service. My dad is a legend in the service, which became kind of a problem. My first commander was a Femmat aristocrat. She hated the fact that I wasn't genengineered. Insisted I wasn't built right, wasn't as strong, wasn't as smart as I should have been. Just inferior all the way around."

"I hope you didn't buy that bullshit." He stroked his big hands up and down her leg, heat and light spilling after his palms in swirling patterns.

Riane closed her eyes, leaning back in the seat. "Finally my mother told me it was time to quit beating my head against Vardon bigotry. Get off-world, go somewhere I wouldn't run into all this crap. So I decided to go into Temporal Enforcement. My dad had never served in the agency, so there was no baggage. I never looked back."

"Sounds like that was the only thing you could do." Nick rocked back on his heels and studied her. "Okay, I think I've got the leg solid again. Swelling's down, blood supply is back up. Still got to heal those knife wounds, though."

"Yeah, sure." *Just finish.*

But the rest was far less unpleasant. She lifted her shirt for him, peeling it away from sticky wounds. Nick ran his big hands over the injuries, and they closed in a swirl of light.

Finally he rose to brace a forearm against the roof of the car. He looked weary.

Riane blew out a breath in relief. "Thank you." She reached for the door frame. Nick stepped back to let her lever herself to her feet. Straightening her shoulders, she took a step. When her leg didn't give under her, she carefully began to walk along the shoulder.

The smile Riane turned on Nick was dazzling. "Comp says everything is solid. Thank you!"

"My pleasure." He watched as she tried bouncing on her feet, then pivoted on the formerly broken leg to snap a lightning kick into empty air. *Figures that the first thing she'd do is make sure she can fight.*

Nick sighed and rolled his shoulders. His head was pounding, and his body felt stiff and aching. "I'm wiped. We need to find a hotel or motel. Hell, I'm not picky—I'll take a wide spot in the road."

Riane stopped kicking and stared into space, her gaze abstracted. He was about to ask her what the problem was when she suddenly snapped back into focus and turned a smile on him. "My comp says there's a motel about ninety miles up the road. I can reserve a room for us if you've got a credit card."

He blinked. "Your comp can access the Internet?"

She shrugged. "Of course."

"Of course." He reached into his back pocket and pulled out one of several credit cards, then handed it over.

Riane looked down at it, read the name. "Joseph Baker?"

"I've had to create a lot of identities with a lot of different bank accounts to keep the aliens off my ass."

They got back in the car and pulled off the shoulder while she performed her Internet magic.

"Done," she announced, and handed the card back. Nick slid it back into a pocket.

They drove on in silence for a time. He glanced at Riane, who was staring out the window. She looked tired, which was to be expected given the fight. But there was also discouragement in her eyes, and that bothered him.

"What you said about . . ." He broke off, unable to come up with a delicate way to put it. Being ugly? Not being strong enough, fast enough, good enough?

Riane made a dismissive gesture. "I was just babbling to distract myself. All of that stuff is ancient history anyway."

"Didn't sound like it to me."

"I'm an Enforcer now." Her elegant profile was set like stone. "I've put my life on Vardon behind me. My fellow agents know my capabilities."

But do you? Nick thought the words, but decided not to voice them. He knew the answer anyway. It was painfully obvious she had lingering doubts about her own worth and abilities. Which was really no surprise. If you spent years telling a kid she wasn't good enough, she'd start believing it after a while. The fact that she was so dazzlingly competent anyway was probably a testament to her own stubborn determination, as well as her parents' love. Baran, after all, had been coolly willing to kill for his daughter.

Yet whatever her doubts, she didn't let them stop her when it came to a fight. Even though the Tevan was damn near two feet taller and probably three hundred pounds heavier, Riane had refused to give up, even with a broken leg. She just kept slugging. He'd never sensed fear from her, even when she'd obviously thought she was going to die.

Nick liked what that said about her. Liked it a hell of a lot.

He even liked the fact that she'd refused to call for help, but hadn't hesitated to thank him when he'd saved her. She was proud, but she wasn't arrogant.

And no matter what she thought, she was one of the most beautiful women he'd ever seen.

Ugly, my ass.

· 17 ·

※☙☙※

Riane's pain and exhaustion seemed to have van-
ished like mist. Whatever Nick had done when he'd healed
her leg seemed to have eliminated her usual post-*riaat*
funk.

But with that rising energy, she also felt the bloom of
desire, hot and expanding down low in her belly, making
her shift restlessly in her seat.

She was acutely aware of his body, of the way his hands
moved as he turned the wheel, of the flex and play of muscle as he drove.

Need built, hot and dark. She remembered that luscious
moment when he'd slid that big cock into her, when he'd
kissed her and run his strong hands over her body.

And she wanted that again.

But I shouldn't. Riane shifted in her seat again, this
time with unease. This . . . thing between them got more
intense every time they touched. And his power only added
to that intensity. Giving in to it was simply not a good idea.

Eventually, she'd be going home, and he'd have to stay here in the twenty-first century, where he evidently belonged.

Giving in to the passion between them would only make the coming separation more difficult.

Riane curled her hands into fists and tried to ignore the slow, honeyed rise of desire. The silence grew weighty between them.

Oh, hell. He feels it, too.

His eyes slid toward her, and his nostrils flared. Sparks began to flit around his armband like amorous fireflies.

Yeah, he felt it.

Her eyes drifted to his lap. A massive ridge grew behind his zipper. She felt her mouth go dry, imagining the rolling pump of his hips, driving his width relentlessly deep, sating that carnivorous ache between her thighs . . .

Cut it out, Riane. This isn't a good idea.

But the desire grew anyway, defying all the good reasons against it, a prowling need that had her heart pounding, her sex going wet. Images flashed through her mind—the brawny line of his torso, his strong hand moving between her thighs, his tongue dancing over one pebbled nipple.

And that cock. Thick, flushed, a long, elegant shape jutting from its curling nest of dark hair.

His fingers drummed on the steering wheel. His jaw flexed.

She found herself fascinated by his mouth. It was so . . . sensuous. The full lower lip, a bit tight now, as if he was fighting for control. The upper lip, with its curve and deep cupid's bow.

Riane wanted to feel those warm, surprisingly soft lips on hers. She loved the way he kissed. Sometimes slow, gentle, coaxing; sometimes so hungry and devouring, he could make her wet with a kiss.

"If you don't quit looking at me like that," he growled, "we're not going to make it to the motel."

She knew better. Really, she did. But she found herself sitting back in her seat and giving him a feral smile. "This is a problem?"

"It is if you don't want to find yourself ass down in the weeds."

"Who says I'd be the one on my ass?"

He barked a laugh. "You're a bad, bad girl, Riane."

"So I'm told." Also more than a little stupid, but that had never stopped her before.

She told him which exit to take. He took it a little fast. The growl of the engine seemed to echo her hungry body.

At last he wheeled the car into a parking spot. Both of them got out and headed for the office, walking a little too fast.

Nick fell in behind Riane. She glanced back at him, lifting a brow.

His smile was dry. "I'd just as soon not walk up to the motel desk with a hard-on that could choke a horse."

Riane pointedly looked down. "And yet, it seems you are."

"Why do you think I'm walking behind you?"

She whooped a laugh.

"Shut up. This is all your fault." But his lips twitched.

They checked in, then had to find their room. By the time they finally got inside, neither was in the mood to laugh.

Even as the door swung closed behind them, Nick jerked Riane into his arms, swooped in for a kiss, and spun her against the wall. She kissed him back, openmouthed and fierce. His tongue swirled a wanton circle, thrust and retreated. Purring, she draped her arms around his strong neck, rolled her hips against his. Felt his cock, hard and urgent, behind the rough fabric of his jeans. She reached down, found snap and zipper. He wore cotton boxers beneath, and the soft, thin fabric strained to contain his eager cock. The head peeked above his waistband, and she explored it with her fingers. Velvet soft, beaded with precum. She smeared the drop with her fingers, traced a teasing circle over sensitive flesh until he shivered, going rigid with his fight for control.

"Living dangerously, Riane."

"Nothing new about that."

Nick bent, caught her under the thighs, lifted. Riane wrapped her legs around his hips as he turned with her, carried her toward the king-sized bed. She concentrated on his mouth, tugging his lower lip with her teeth, licking and nibbling as they walked.

He tumbled her onto the bed, reared off her only long enough to strip away the leather jacket and black top. Paused to study the bra, his gaze heating.

Riane looked down to see her own nipples pushing against the delicate white lace. "Hmm," she murmured. "Okay, I begin to understand the bra concept."

"You sure?" He tugged one cup down, just far enough to liberate a nipple, then swooped in for a teasing tongue flick, and gave her a wicked grin. "I can provide an illustration . . ."

Nick licked the peak until it blushed a bright rose. Raked it with his teeth. She squirmed, gasping. Finally his mouth closed over the hot little tip, suckling fiercely, deliciously. Riane let her head fall back and moaned at the burning pleasure of his mouth, the way that tongue danced, circled, the skillful bite and rake of his teeth.

The man definitely knew his way around a woman's body.

Nick shaped and stroked her other breast, his thumb flicking back and forth over its lace-covered nipple, teasing delightfully.

"You're really good," she managed, between pants.

"Thank you." Green eyes flashed up at her. He gave her

a slow, considering lick, then smiled lazily. "I could say the same of you."

"Oooh." She bit her lip as his hand wandered down to her waistband to unbutton and unzip. Long fingers dipped behind the waistband of silk panties, paused to explore her stomach in tickling circles. She squirmed and gasped, "Thank you."

"Believe me, it's my pleasure."

Riane slanted him a look. "I'm not exactly finding it a hardship myself." She contemplated his black T-shirt. "Though you *are* wearing too many clothes."

Catching him by one shoulder, she flipped him onto his back. He blinked up at her as she flung a leg over his hips and straddled him. "Damn, Riane, you're strong."

"Why are you so surprised? You've seen me fight." She dragged his T-shirt off over his head.

"I thought that was *riaat.*"

"Not all of it." She rose off him just long enough to drag his pants off. Tossed them aside before attacking his boxers. His cock sprang free. Bobbed, long and thick and promising. She started to grab for it, but he promptly flipped her onto her back and grabbed her wrists. "No, no, no." He grinned down at her. "You interrupted me in mid-nibble. I have plans."

"But so do I." She gave him a toothy grin and jerked her hands free so she could grab for him.

A brisk wrestling match ensued amid much laughter and yelps of protest. She quickly discovered that he was stronger than she was. Instead of killing the mood, it somehow intensified her need. The surge of muscle against muscle, the strain and arch of body against body. Laughter died in the rich, rolling rise of creamy heat.

Somehow she ended up on her knees, her face pressed into the bedspread with him on top of her, both her wrists held behind her back, his cock teasing her butt. He gave her a suggestive roll of his hips. "Now, this is more like it."

She rolled her eyes back and grinned up at him. "It certainly is."

"Mmm." He crouched behind her, still holding her hands pinned. She jerked as his face nuzzled against her ass. His tongue pushed between the lips of her sex, made a long, wet swipe. Riane squirmed at the sweet jolt of pleasure, gasping. Using his free hand, he parted her sexual lips and started licking, nibbling, teasing.

"Sweet Mother Goddess!" she gasped.

He only rumbled at her and kept using that incredible tongue, drawing luscious circles around her clit.

Orgasm gathered deep in her sex, a pulsing heat that tightened and tightened, maddening her. She tossed her head, her hair whipping her shoulders. "Niiick!"

"Yes?" He paused in his wicked licking to give her behind a nip.

"I want you!" She craved the hard thrust of his big cock, the pumping force she knew would kick her over the edge.

"Do you?" A slow circle around her clit, not quite touching, only jerking her need into a tight, aching knot.

"Yes! Fuck me!"

"Not yet." And he gave her another slow lick.

Riane bucked against his hold, her gorgeous ass rolling. Nick tightened his grip on her wrists, barely holding on as she fought him.

God, this was hot. He didn't think he'd ever known such clawing lust. The scent of her, the taste of her, ripe and utterly erotic. She was incredibly hot, her inner flesh ripe and wet as a peach. He could feel his balls drawing tight and firm as a pair of apples. His cock was so hard, he swore he could drive nails with it.

He was dying to thrust into her, to lose himself in her tight, creamy depths. Instead, he tightened his grip on both his self-control and her narrow wrists, then reached his free hand under her body and began teasing her nipples. She gasped and arched into his hand, pushing her hips back toward his face.

He licked her slowly, intent on driving her lust higher and higher. She squirmed deliciously, moaning in a way that made his cock jerk.

Suddenly she convulsed, shouting in raw delight. Unable to resist, Nick released his grip on her breast and reared behind her. Still holding her wrists, he grabbed his cock with his free hand. And began to push inside.

The sensation was incredible. Wet, swollen so incredibly tight he had to force his cock home inch after delicious inch. Riane yowled, throwing back her head so hard, her hair whipped the small of her back.

At last he was all the way inside and began to pull out. The going got easier, and he started pumping, keeping it slow, letting the pleasure build. And build. And build.

He shuddered at the way she felt, so creamy. Her firm, satin-skinned ass met his every thrust with her own, rolling against him. Utterly perfect.

She humped harder, demanding more. "Nick! Nick, I want you. Please! Harder, oh, Goddess!"

Silken walls clamped down on him. He jerked. And control skidded right out of his grip.

Unable to resist any longer, Nick began to drive, hunching harder, deeper. Faster. And she met his every thrust, panting, shivering, her moans spurring him on.

Until she yowled and writhed and reached yet another climax.

The hot ripple of her interior walls maddened him, driving him into short, hammering thrusts. Pleasure curled around his balls, yanked tight.

He came with a shout in a storm of blazing sensation.

They sank down together, panting, sweat streaming off their bodies. Nick crawled up and curled around her back, wrapping both arms around her, craving contact with that long, lusciously feminine body.

Riane sighed and twisted her head around. He reared up and kissed her hungrily, savoring the taste of her mouth. She smiled up at him. "Thank you."

"Oh, baby." He smiled back, even as he strongly suspected the smile looked a little sappy. "Thank *you*."

Riane settled down, deliciously exhausted, as Nick curled around her, warm and strong. Closing her eyes in lazy contentment, she tried to remember the last time she'd had sex this good.

And couldn't.

She frowned uneasily as all her earlier doubts came rushing back.

Nick was a twenty-first-century man. His home was here. Eventually she'd go back to the Outpost, and he'd have to remain, fighting his battles with his Xeran enemies. By Galactic Union law, the only way he could go to the future was if there was evidence those of this time believed him dead. Otherwise, even if she tried to take him, he'd be sent back, and she would face charges.

Paradoxes might be impossible, but that didn't mean

Enforcers were allowed to change things on a whim. If he belonged in the past, that's where he'd eventually end up, no matter what either of them wanted.

All of which meant that no matter how delicious their relationship was, it couldn't last.

· 18 ·

The Her-Gla was on a tear. She had come to Ivar's quarters, snapping her teeth, clicking her claws, and swearing viciously in Linga Galactic. Her tentacles lashed as she complained about the treatment they'd received at the hands of the Xerans. She was a mercenary, she said, and she refused to sit still for being held prisoner on this wretched planet. She would certainly have never acceded to having alien comp tech forcibly implanted in her system. It was an outrage. In all her years as a merc, she had never been treated with such cavalier disrespect.

Worst of all, the Xerans had not paid her yet, may the Great Black God curse their eggs to rot.

She wanted her galactors, she wanted the Xeran tech removed, and she wanted off this egg-rotting planet.

Ivar agreed with every word of her rant. Especially the part about wanting off Xer. Actually, at this point he'd be willing to forgo payment, if he could only get the fuck away from these lunatics.

Why, oh, why, had he agreed to work for the Xerans to begin with? True, he'd been royally bored. His career in Temporal Enforcement had begun to seem a little too easy. The thought of turning traitor had sounded exciting, the kind of pure adrenaline rush he craved. God knew, the money had been very tempting.

And for the first few years, it had been everything Ivar had dreamed of. His life had become one long, delicious grav-sled ride over an imploder minefield. He'd loved fooling his commanders and fellow Enforcers, thoroughly savored his corruption.

Until they'd ordered him to kill Jessica Kelly, and the little bitch had developed psychic powers no one could have predicted. His life had gone straight to shit from there.

"*Ke-cha ki'tor, Ivaritu,*" the Her-Gla said cajolingly. "*Ei til revoth kelar Galactors.*"

"I don't think it's going to be that easy," Ivar warned her. "We don't want to piss them off. Because believe me, pissing them off is a bad idea."

She sneered that the hatching of his eggs was highly doubtful, a deadly insult among her kind.

He told her he preferred his eggs over easy, with a side order of roasted kela.

She called him a perverted sucker-of-eggs. Before the conversation could disintegrate any further—say, to drawn blades and teeth—Ivar agreed to back her up in her petition to their priestly liaison.

What the fuck. He'd always enjoyed living dangerously.

They found the priest in his new quarters—distinctly better decorated than their own barren monks' cells.

Ivar's first clue that things were about to get seriously fucked was the fact that Warrior Priest Gyor ge Tityus knelt naked on the black stone floor, wreathed in that smoke the bastards loved to inhale, the kind that intensified sensation and arousal. Personally, Ivar would have used it as a sex aid, but the Xerans were less enlightened.

Gyor had wrapped his erect penis in a cage of silver wire studded with barbs. He was apparently doing penance, which probably meant he was in a very bad mood. Ivar would have dragged the Her-Gla out on the spot, but cultural differences threw a sonic torch in the stew. She set her tentacles and refused to go, instead spewing a torrent of Her-Gla-style abuse on the priest.

Ivar would have abandoned the idiot to her fate, except the priest looked up at him. The man's slit-pupiled eyes burned, and he discovered he couldn't move.

Oblivious, the Her-Gla ranted on, insulting the priest roundly. She went on to demand her money and her release, and hissed that nobody had asked her permission to implant alien tech in her comp system.

Gyor ignored her, merely gazing coolly at him and lifting one brow.

Ivar found himself looking around the room. He spotted an antique steel sword next to a display of—were those skulls? Looked like it.

Compelled, though he had no idea why, he walked over and picked up the blade. In the back of his mind, some panicked part of him babbled, *What the fuck am I doing?*

That quickly became obvious. Ivar walked up behind the Her-Gla, still in mid-rant, lifted the sword in both hands, and brought it down with all his strength. The alien's blood flew across the room in a rain of azure drops, and the creature fell into two halves. She'd never known what hit her.

She should have. Her sensors should have warned her. But they hadn't. Obviously, they hadn't because the Xerans hadn't wanted them to warn her.

Ivar looked up at the priest, feeling stunned, disoriented. God knew he'd killed plenty of people, some of whom had deserved it far less than the Her-Gla. "I have no idea why I did that."

"Because the Victor wanted you to." Gyor gestured at the bisected body, his expression dismissive. "Clean that up."

"Why?" Ivar asked numbly. "I mean, why did the Victor want her dead? She was damned good in a fight."

"She was too alien," the priest said indifferently. "He did not care to hear her thoughts."

Ivar looked at the priest. A thought flashed through his own mind—*I'm not a cleaning, 'bot!* He firmly suppressed it. The Victor might be listening in. "Where are the cleaning supplies?"

Master Enforcer Galar Arvid sprawled in a chair in the Chief's office, a lazy smile on his face, his eyes positively sated. Drumming his fingers restlessly on his desk, Alerio studied his friend and second-in-command with naked envy. "You look downright smug. I gather your leave on Vardon went well."

"Jess told me about this twenty-first-century tradition called the 'honeymoon.'" The big blond's lids drooped to half-mast. "Three weeks of sex on the white sand beaches of Vardon." He sighed happily.

Alerio's mind flashed to Dona with a spurt of longing. He firmly dragged it away. "No wonder you look like a soji dragon gorged on a herd of beefer."

His friend studied him with perceptive green eyes. "You, on the other hand, look like hell."

The Chief shrugged. "I lost one Enforcer, and the agency's chief investigator is convinced another is a traitor. And a third Enforcer definitely *is* a traitor. Since all of that happened on my watch . . . well, I don't exactly have job security."

Galar winced. "Alerio . . ."

He waved a hand in dismissal. "It was my responsibility, Galar, and I didn't catch Terje until people damned near ended up dead. I'm not sure I deserve to keep my job."

"That's beefershit, and you know it. You're a damned good investigator, not to mention the best commander I've ever had the pleasure of serving. That moron Corydon—"

The door chimed, and the Outpost computer intoned, "Chief Investigator Alex Corydon wishes to see you."

"Speak of the devil." Alerio sighed. "Probably wants to try to convince me to arrest Dona again—on the strength of no damned evidence whatsoever. I don't know why he's got such a bug up his ass about that woman." He lifted his voice. "Let him in, computer."

The door slid open and Corydon bulled through, a smile on his face that was nothing short of smug, his eyes dancing with triumph.

Alerio's heart sank.

Riane opened her eyes to see a truly mediocre painting on the motel room wall. Nick cuddled around her from behind, brawny arms circling her waist. He felt good. His warm breath gusted against her nape, slow and deep. Still asleep.

He stirred, made a deep purring sound in his throat, and kissed her nape. She smiled sleepily.

"Want a shower?" he asked, stroking a hand up her torso and cupping her breast in his palm.

"Mmm. Yeah. Feeling a little . . . sticky."

"Me, too. Sex is one thing, but stale combat sweat is something else." He rolled off the other side of the bed and strode naked toward the bathroom off the bedroom. She admired the working muscle in his glutes a moment before scrambling up to follow him.

The bathroom was a stark, white-tiled affair with primitive plumbing and thin towels. Riane watched as he turned the shower on, adjusted the water, and swept the plastic curtain aside. She stepped under the hot, pattering stream and sighed in pleasure.

Nick joined her a moment later, a small tube of shampoo in one big hand. He squeezed the thick green liquid into his palm, then started working it through her hair. It smelled of some Earth plant she didn't know the name of. "You want to do something about that braid?" Nick asked. "You've got blood in it."

Eyes shuttered in pleasure, Riane went to work on the braided lock, pulling out the combat decorations and putting them in the soap dish.

He glanced into the dish curiously. "Pretty beads."

"They're not beads. They're military service medals from my home world. Not a very impressive collection, but then neither was my Vardonese career." She grimaced and lifted one shoulder in a shrug. "I should probably stop wearing them, since I'm an Enforcer now. But most warrior Enforcers still bead their braids, so I do, too."

He stroked a forefinger down her facial tattoo. "What about this?"

"Now, that I'll keep. The color signifies House Arvid, which genengineered my father." She tapped the intricate design over her eye. "This part is my father's genetic creator, while this," Riane touched the triangular shape over her cheekbone, "means he's a Viking Class Warlord. The empty circle here means I'm unmarried. It will be filled in when I'm mated."

"So all of this is about your father, not you?" He traced the intricate inked coils, fascinated.

"Yes, since I'm not really genengineered myself." She shrugged. "Mom and Dad had it done when I was five years old, at the same time my nanobot enhancements were implanted. My parents wanted to acknowledge my heritage. Besides, they figured I'd want a military career, and my not having a tat would cause unpleasant talk."

Nick studied her as he absently worked a small cake of soap in his hand to create a froth of bubbles. "*Not* having the tattoo would cause talk? Why?"

"People would say I was trying to pass myself off as a Femmat—one of the female aristocrats. And that would simply not be acceptable." She tried to keep the bitterness out of her voice.

He fell silent, concentrating very hard on slicking the soap over her skin. She sighed and relaxed into the pleasure he spun with those clever fingers. "Damn, I wish I could take you back to my time."

Nick went still. "Why can't you?"

"Because you belong here. The only way I could legally take you to the twenty-third was if I had evidence you'd disappeared without a trace from this century. Otherwise I'd end up facing charges, and they'd just return you."

And damn, didn't that just suck?

The silence grew a little thicker, broken only by the musical patter of the shower. After they got out, dried off, and walked back into the bedroom, Riane decided to play a hunch.

"Computer, generate trid of Charlotte Holt."

It took the comp a little over fifteen seconds to render a three-dimensional image based on Riane's memories of the Xeran woman. Nick started when the trid appeared—a petite woman with a lush build and a froth of red curls. Her eyes were the same deep leaf green as his.

Nick drew in a sharp breath, staring at it in stunned amazement. "Where did you get a picture of my mother?"

· 19 ·

Frieka sat curled up next to Dona on the green velvet settee. Jessica Kelly Arvid stood at a towering wooden easel, carefully stroking oil paint over the canvas with a long, fine brush.

"So how was your . . . What was the word?" Dona asked.

Jess smiled slightly. "Honeymoon. And . . . incredible."

Frieka sniffed and pretended to cough. "Why does the air suddenly smell like sex?"

Dona lightly popped him on top of the head. "Cut it out, wolfie."

The exchange made him miss Riane all over again. He dropped his head to Dona's knee with a sigh. She looked down at him and scratched him between the ears. "Riane'll be home soon," she whispered. "We'll find her."

Jess shot him a sympathetic glance around her easel.

"Could *you* find her?" Frieka asked the artist, lifting his head. "You've got those powers . . ."

She turned to her art table to swirl her brush in a jar of

turpentine. The expression on her delicate face turned
brooding. "Yeah, I do. And I could transport her back to this
time—if I knew where she was. Trouble is, I have no idea.
And I have looked." She sighed. "But I'll keep looking."

He knew she meant every word of that. "Thank you,
Jess."

A chirp sounded, and the studio door slid open. Galar
and Alerio walked in. Corydon followed, smirking, entirely too damned pleased with himself.

The Chief Enforcer's handsome face could have been
carved in ice. "Enforcer Dona Astryr, you are under arrest
for acts of treason against the Galactic Union."

Startled, Frieka stared up into Dona's face. She looked
as if Alerio had just buried his fist in her belly—pale,
stunned, eyes wide and shocked.

Corydon tried to conceal an obvious grin of delight.
Not very convincingly.

"Oh, come on!" Royally irritated, Frieka sprang down
from the settee. "I can't believe you're listening to this
dickhole, Chief. He's a moron."

Corydon lost the grin in a snarl. "Oh, really? Take a
look at this, dog. Outpost computer, display security video
from 10.2.34.9820, Armory."

A three-dimensional recording of the armory appeared
in the air over their heads. A figure who was unmistakably
Dona Astryr strode into view, heading toward the bank of
lockers where the Enforcers stored their T-suits.

Instead of keying open her own locker, the recorded
Dona stopped in front of the unit shared by Riane and
Frieka. Reaching into a uniform pocket, she withdrew a
small device and pressed it against the door, which obediently opened. She removed Riane's T-suit and keyed the
unit closed again. Her movements brisk, unhurried, she
stepped to her own locker, took out her suit, and started
putting it on.

"That didn't happen." The real Dona's voice sounded unnaturally high with panicked desperation. "Alerio, I didn't do that! You know how easy it is to fake security recordings!"

"Oh, I know," Dyami said with icy contempt. "Which is why I checked out the whole damned cam system, as well as the image itself. None of it shows any sign of tampering."

As Frieka watched in frozen shock, the recorded Dona Jumped, disappearing in an explosion of light.

"She did not file a Jump plan with the Outpost computer, yet it alerted no one," Corydon said. "She'd obviously hacked the comp."

"We believe she must have taken Riane's suit to Xer to have it reprogrammed." Rage blazing in his eyes, Alerio turned on Dona, his lip curling with contempt. "Did you have a nice visit with your lover while you were there, Enforcer?"

"I didn't! Alerio, you've got to believe me!" Dona unconsciously rested a hand on Frieka's head.

Rage washed over the wolf in a red-hot flood. An image flashed through his mind: Riane at twelve, her eyes pleading in her white face, staring down at him over her Xeran kidnapper's shoulder as he carried her away.

Frieka spun and threw himself at Dona's throat.

She reacted with a cyborg's speed, jamming her wrist between his teeth, blocking his lunge even as she went down beneath his weight. He tasted blood. "Frieka, it wasn't me!"

He ignored her protest, ripping his head back to free his jaws for another lunge. More blood flew. Alerio's massive arm snapped around his neck and jerked him up short. "Get off her, Frieka!"

"Let me go!" the wolf roared. "I'm gonna rip out her fuckin'—"

"You're not judge and jury!" the Chief snapped in his ear. "Get it together, Frieka, or you're going in the brig right next to her!"

"Fuck you, Chief!" He tore free and made another lunge for the traitor. Galar grabbed him around the hips, and the two men lifted Frieka bodily into the air.

"Calm down, Frieka!" Suddenly Jess was in the way, shielding the female cyborg with her own body. "This isn't helping Riane." Her gaze bored into his with sudden fierce power. "And she wouldn't want you to hurt her friend."

The blind rage drained away. He stopped fighting the Warlords' hold and let them drag him back. "Get him the fuck out of here," the Chief ordered Galar. "Go!"

Galar fisted one hand in Frieka's neck ruff and started pulling him toward the door. "Come on, you dumb furball. What the hell were you thinking?"

As the Warlord hauled him out, he heard Dona's broken voice say, softly, hopelessly, "Frieka—*it wasn't me . . .*"

Nick stared at the three-dimensional image in stunned shock. His mother stood there, a faint smile on her face. She looked years younger than his memory of her, and she wore her red hair in a loose, curling style. She was dressed in a tight black skirt and a snug shirt like some young woman with club-hopping on her mind.

He licked his lips. "Where did you get that image?"

Riane sighed as she moved to sit down on the edge of the bed. "Actually, I recorded it just a couple of weeks ago, my time."

Nick flicked her a look before he went back to studying his mother's image. Except that was impossible. "Then it isn't her. She's been dead for years. So who is it? A twin, a clone, what?"

"I doubt that. It probably is her. She could easily have gone back in time after I made this recording. What year were you born?"

"1979."

She shrugged. "There you go."

He turned to stare at her. "But I don't understand how you'd just happen to have a recording of my mother. This is just too damned weird. Too many coincidences."

Riane shook her head and crossed her long legs. "I doubt seriously there are any coincidences to this situation. We just don't know what's going on yet."

Nick moved to sit down next to her. His thick dark brows were drawn into a troubled frown. "But how did you meet my mother?"

"That's where it gets complicated."

He snorted. "You mean it's not already?"

"Just wait. She was posing as a twenty-first-century woman named Charlotte Holt—"

"Her name was Carolyn Wyatt."

Riane shook her head. "Hate to tell you this, Nick, but that was probably just one of a number of aliases." She leaned back on her elbows. "At the time, Charlotte was rooming with an artist named Jessica Kelly. My team and I suspected a time-traveling art thief was going to attempt to kill Jess."

"Why?" He propped his head on his fist and studied her, his green gaze brooding.

"According to historical records, twenty-first-century officials believed Jess was murdered, but her body was never found. Because her paintings are worth millions of galactors in our time, we suspected a thief had Jumped back to the twenty-first century, meaning to kill her and steal her work to sell for a tidy profit back home. We wanted to prevent that."

Nick frowned, trying to work through the sequence of events. "But wouldn't that cause a paradox?"

"No. All officials ever found was a whole lot of blood, which implied we might be able to step in and save her. If we could prevent her murder, we could take her back to our own time to live out the rest of her life. Which as Temporal Enforcement agents, we're legally obligated to do, since it was a temporal crime."

Nick nodded slowly. "Okay, I think I've got that."

"Except we'd completely misread the situation. The thief was actually a Xeran assassin, and his real target was your mother. He attacked Jess in an attempt to force her to tell him where Charlotte was."

Nick blinked. "Why was he after my mother?"

"Because she knew where alien refugees called the Sela were hiding."

"Wait—*aliens*? Sela? What the hell is a Sela?"

"Fuzzy little six-legged creatures. I've got an image on file." Another three-dimensional picture appeared, this one of a big-eyed, vaguely feline creature with too many legs and glossy dark fur.

Nick stared at it, dark brows lifting. "And my mother was involved with those things? Why?"

"That's a really good question. Apparently, the Xerans invaded the Sela's home planet about a year ago, our time. The Xer being religious lunatics, they decided the Sela were abominations and attempted to exterminate them. For reasons we still don't understand, some of the Sela escaped back into Earth's history, where they passed themselves off as human."

"How the hell did they do that?"

"Apparently the Sela have pretty impressive psychic abilities. Among other things, they can create very convincing illusions."

"Okay, but what was my mother's connection with them?" His eyes narrowed in calculation. "And why do I get the distinct feeling they're the missing piece in all this that I've never been able to figure out?"

Riane hesitated. "Well, according to Jess—who had a vision about all this—Charlotte was a member of a Xeran team that went back in time hunting the Selan ship. They found it, but when your mother encountered one of the Sela, she decided she didn't want to kill them. Her fellow Xerans had other ideas, so a firefight ensued. Charlotte ended up wiping out her whole team."

"Why would she kill her own people?"

Riane lifted one shoulder in a half-shrug. "Apparently, Charlotte liked the Sela a lot more than her fellow Xerans."

Nick snorted. "I can believe that."

"Charlotte went on the run with the Sela, so the Xerans declared her a heretic and sent an assassin after her. To evade him, she started Jumping through time, trying to keep the killer from finding her furry friends."

"So what was she doing with this artist?"

"That's another really good question. Apparently the Sela had instructed her to implant Jessica with a blend of Xeran and Selan DNA, which gave Jess psychic powers similar to the Sela's."

Nick stared. "But why?"

"Jess says it was all part of some kind of test the Sela were administrating."

"Who were they testing?"

"Us."

"Again, why?"

"Who the hell knows? They're *aliens*. They don't think like we do, and they're not inclined to explain themselves."

Nick grimaced in frustration. "None of this makes any freaking sense."

"Oh, I'm sure it does—to the Sela." Riane stretched out beside him and crossed her ankles. "Trouble is, we're not Sela."

"Wonder why the Xerans are so hot to kill them?"

"The Xerans don't like anybody they consider a threat, and the Sela have some pretty interesting abilities. *And* they have something the Xerans want. It's a Selan artifact called the T'Lir. I saw it when we intervened in the last big confrontation between the Xerans and the Sela. It looked like a cheap little snow globe, complete with a really kitschy Santa inside. Yet it can amplify psychic abilities to godlike levels."

He stared at her. "Why would an advanced alien species create a psychic amplifier that looks like a Santa snow globe?"

"Apparently, they can make it look like anything they damn well want to. It was on display in a coffee shop the Sela were running, in the middle of a collection of other snow globes."

His eyes widened. "Camouflage."

"Exactly. Worked, too. The Xerans looked right at it and had no idea what it was. After we kicked the Xerans' collective ass, your mother and the surviving Sela Jumped who knows where, taking the snow globe with them. They've probably turned it into something else by now."

Nick's gaze shot to his armband, eyes widening. "My Stone!"

"Yep."

"Damn," he said slowly, "if you're right, all of this finally makes sense. Sort of. They've been trying to kill me all this time over the . . . What did you call it?"

"The T'Lir."

"So what do you suggest I do about all this?"

She gave him a long, steady look. "It's your rock."

"That's a big help."

"Hey, I'm not the one with"—Riane waggled her fingers in a spell-casting gesture—"powers."

"But you do know more about the Sela than I do." His eyes narrowed. "And that gives me an idea."

· 20 ·

Frieka lay on the bed in Riane's quarters. The bunk smelled like her, that clean, distinctively Warfem scent he associated with home and happiness.

Sitting beside Baran and Jane, watching a little girl with a cloud of red curls race in merry circles. The sweet waterfall of her giggles.

"Giddyup, Frieka!" *The thump of tiny heels against his ribs as she tried to ride him like a pony. He could barely feel her weight.*

The wolf heard a soft moaning sound of pain, and knew it came from his own throat.

Dona had betrayed his baby. How could she sit there, scratching him between the ears, knowing she'd left his child trapped in the past? How could she curse Ivar Terje as a traitor while committing treason herself?

How could she look him in the eye and say in that crushed voice, *"It wasn't me"*?

She'd sounded so damned truthful. Her heartbeat hadn't

jumped. His sensors swore she was telling the truth. Or what she believed to be the truth.

Could she be telling the truth? Or had she just invented a way to fool sensors so well, you couldn't tell she'd done it?

"Outpost," Frieka said aloud. "Run the recording of Dona taking Riane's suit."

He lay his head on his paws and watched the recording through once, then again. Then yet again.

Something wasn't right. It nagged at him like a flea-bite, an itch of *wrongness*. Frieka watched the recording through again. His head jerked off his paws. "Outpost, pause recording!"

The image stopped. Frieka hopped off the bed and moved closer. "Zoom in on the device in Dona's hand."

The image instantly popped into a close-up of the thin controller. The wolf reared onto his hind legs and balanced there, studying it. "Yeah, that's a personal code breaker, all right."

He'd found his nagging flea.

Frieka had watched Dona hack high-security computer systems as easily as a child getting cookies from a vendser. "Why the hell would Dona Astryr need a code breaker?"

Answer: she wouldn't. Which meant she was right. The recording couldn't be genuine.

Why hadn't the Chief realized that?

The answer to that was equally obvious: the Chief didn't trust his own judgment. He was so obsessed with Dona, he assumed any doubts were the product of hormones instead of rationality.

Unfortunately, the only way to get evidence of Dona's innocence was to hack into the Outpost comp and discover how it had been diddled. Frieka normally would ask for help from one of the other Enforcers, but Corydon was right: there was at least one mole on the Outpost. And if

Frieka accidently enlisted that traitor's help, it would be the last thing he ever did.

Which would be no help at all to either Dona or Riane.

So he could afford to tell no one what he intended. Yet hacking a computer without backup was a good way to end up dead if you triggered a lethal virus, Trojan, or data bomb.

Still, if he could find out where Riane had been sent, the risk would be worth it.

Riane stared at Nick in horror. "You're nuts."

"Riane, I've already told you about this." He rose restlessly from the bed and began to pace. "I've done telepathic links any number of times to learn all kinds of techniques. And it never hurt anybody. It's not going to hurt you either."

"Nick, all those people knew how to do what you needed to learn." She sat up on the edge of the bed, frowning at him. "But what you need to learn now is how to use your powers to find the Sela. And I have no frigging idea."

"But you've met the Sela." He turned and spread his hands. "I could use your memories to track them down."

"You want a memory? I can give you that now." She ordered her comp to generate another trid image of a Sela, which obligingly popped into midair. "There. No brain scan necessary."

Nick cocked his head and considered the image. "You know, those things remind me of Japanese cartoons. All fuzz and outsized eyes." Then he shook his head. "But no, a picture's not going to do it. I need concrete sense details like scent, sound, touch. What being in the presence of a Sela is really like. Then I'll be able to lock on and find them."

"But, Nick, what if something goes wrong? I don't particularly want my brain hacked." She hesitated before finally voicing her deepest fear. "Of course, you could *make* me cooperate . . ."

He gave her a long, cold stare. "Oh, that was just insulting."

"Yeah." She scrubbed her hands over her face, feeling a little ashamed of herself. "My mother would have called it a cheap shot."

"Yes, but I guess it's understandable." He rubbed the back of his neck as if trying to release a knot of tension gathered there. "Look, I need to find these people, or aliens, or whatever the hell they are. I need to find out if they're really the source of my abilities, and if they are, how I can use my powers more effectively. I might even be able to send you back home with that knowledge. Maybe I could finally stop the damned Xerans."

Who needed telepathy when he knew exactly which buttons to push? She shot him a resentful glare. "I'm just not comfortable having anyone poke around in my brain."

"I have no intention of 'poking' around. I'm not interested in anything but finding out about the Sela and the T'lir."

Despite the simmering paranoia he'd managed to kick up, Riane knew he was telling the truth. "Give me time, Nick."

He looked at her a long, steady moment, then rose to his feet. "You've got it." Stalking to the door, he pulled it open. "If you need me, I'll be in the parking lot."

As the door closed behind him, Riane threw herself back on the bed and stared at the ceiling. The thought of allowing anyone—even Nick—into her mind made her stomach twist into an aching knot. Especially given that even he didn't fully understand his own powers.

What if something went wrong? She'd be completely vulnerable, with no way of defending herself.

Every Enforcer knew what could happen if you hacked

the wrong computer. Twenty-third-century viruses were designed specifically with cyborgs in mind, and they could cause a lot more damage than software crashes. They could stop your heart, send your own nanobots to attack your organs, trigger massive seizures, paralyze breathing . . . The list was endless and ugly.

No, she didn't want to give Nick access to her brain. Even though she knew he had no interest in killing her, something could still go wrong. She could fight a virus, but she couldn't fight his kind of power.

Shoulder propped against one of the pillars support-ing the overhang, Nick stared out across the parking lot. The sun was coming up across the trees, spilling golden light through the low, pink-tinged clouds. The air smelled of spring, and birds were singing.

Nick felt as if Riane had kicked him square in the stom-ach. Which just illustrated how stupid he'd been. She'd become his obsession when he was a boy, and he'd never outgrown it. Then she'd actually shown up and become his lover, with the kind of uncomplicated passion every man dreamed of.

In retrospect, it was obvious he'd unconsciously hoped she'd return his feelings.

Idiot.

The fact was, she'd never trusted him. With her body, yes, but not with her heart.

Nick took a deep breath and blew it out, letting his shoulders slump. It was time to face the fact that she was going to leave. She'd made it clear he didn't belong in her world, and she couldn't stay in his.

And even if she decided to allow him to link with her, that wasn't going to change.

The motel room door swung open. Riane stared out

at him, her expression grim, her face dead pale. "Let's do it."

Nick's brows flew up. "I thought you needed to think about it."

"I did." She grimaced. "Until I heard my own thoughts and realized how cowardly they sounded. Frieka would have given me holy hell and a nip on the ass."

So it wasn't that she'd suddenly discovered she trusted him—her pride just wouldn't let her back down from a situation she considered dangerous. "We wouldn't want you to be cowardly."

Riane frowned at him. "What's your problem? You look like you've bitten into a sourfruit."

"Nothing." He strode toward her and caught the door over her head. "Let's do it."

She glowered into his eyes and backed into the room. "I repeat: What in the Seven Hells is your problem?"

Nick stepped inside and slammed the door behind him. "You wouldn't even be alive right now if I hadn't used these powers you're so worried about to save your ass. So come off it!"

"Look, I know you saved me during that fight. But—"

"I'm not talking about that damned fight. I'm talking about sixteen fucking years ago!"

She stared at him as though he'd lost his mind. "Sixteen . . . ?"

"When you were twelve years old and the Xeran kidnapped you." He bared his teeth in something not even vaguely close to a smile. "Who do you think told Frieka where you were? You think he followed your fucking scent through the air?"

"You . . . traveled through time?" Riane blinked at him, obviously taken aback.

"No, I had a damned vision! I was fourteen, and Mom had died two days before, and I was sitting there trying to work up the guts to kill myself. So the Stone sent me a vision. Of *you*."

Her dark eyes went wide. "Me?"

"You. It told me you were going to die unless I saved you. It showed me the whole thing. You, tied down in front of that obscene damned sculpture, and that sick fuck Xeran telling you he was going to *rape* you. A twelve-year-old girl!" It made him sick to think about it, even all these years later.

All the blood drained from her face. "You saw that?"

"Oh, I sure as hell did. I didn't have the power to save you myself, so the Stone told me to reach out to your daddy. Only I couldn't get through to him, so I touched your wolf instead. I told him where you were, and he led Baran to you."

"That's how you knew my father's name." Riane's voice sounded uncharacteristically faint. "You saw us all."

"Exactly. And you want to hear something funny? All this time, I knew I'd see you again. I could feel it, and I never doubted. I had no idea you were three hundred years in the future, but if I had, it wouldn't have mattered. Because I knew the Stone would bring us together. What I didn't realize was that you'd see me as some Xeran halfbreed you don't trust."

She winced. "It's not about you being Xeran, Nick. I know you're not running some kind of scam on me for the Victor."

"Oh, yeah, you know that. But don't fool yourself—it's still about me being Xeran."

A flush of pure anger spilled across her high cheekbones. Her eyes narrowed, glittering at him like a pair of dark gems. A dangerous flicker of red sparked in their pupils, revealing her growing fury. "So what are you saying— I'm some kind of racist?"

"Oh, not consciously. But you grew up hearing about

how they tortured your father until he had to hunt them down for what they'd done to him. And then one of them damn near killed you, solely because you were Baran Arvid's child. When you grew up, Xerans were always the enemy. Bouncing through time, killing innocent women." His anger began to wind down into weary resignation. "I guess it's no wonder you don't trust anybody with Xeran DNA."

"I'm not a bigot." She lowered her head and glared at him. Her face flushed, and the red in her eyes grew into a bright blaze. "You want this mind link of yours? Fine. Do it. Get it fucking over with and *send me home*!"

· 21 ·

Alerio walked into the Outpost infirmary, his steps heavy, his mind a stew of pain, anger, and confusion. Not to mention dread. He wasn't looking forward to what he had to do, but he'd never ducked an unpleasant duty in his life, and he wasn't about to start now. Which was why he was escorting Dona himself, rather than delegating the job.

The infirmary was dimly lit this time of day. A circular room ringed by medical offices, it took up one entire level of the Outpost. For once, there were only a couple of glowing patient domes arranged around the room. Each dome held a bed inside a sterile field designed to both protect the patient from infection and maintain privacy. Sensor data flickered across the fields—body temp, blood pressure, heart rate.

Dr. Sakari Chogan stepped out of one of the domes, the expression on her pretty face dispirited. Her iridescent green hair was gathered up into an untidy knot on top of her head, and her blue medical robes flared around her booted ankles.

"How is she?" Alerio said.

Chogan tucked a stylus into her hair in an absent gesture. "Considering Frieka tried to rip her throat out, pretty damn good. The damage to her wrist has regenerated nicely." She shook her head. "But emotionally . . . Well, some things not even regen can cure."

"Given that she's a traitor, I don't particularly care," Alerio lied.

The doctor gave him a long, steady look that succeeded in making him feel even more like an idiot. "Anyway," she said, "Enforcer Astryr is all yours. You can take her to the brig with a clear conscience."

He set his teeth. "Thank you, Doctor." Without another word, he stepped into the globe.

Dona looked up from sealing her bright yellow prisoner's uniform. Her face was white and utterly expressionless, but her eyes . . . The devastation and silent accusation in that violet gaze felt like a blow to the center of his aching chest.

His hands curled into fists of angry frustration. Damn her for putting him in this position anyway. "Let's go."

Dona squared her shoulders and started past him, then paused and looked up into his eyes. Hers were steady, without any flicker of deception. "I didn't do it, Chief. And considering how easy it would be to fake a recording like that, I can't believe you bought it."

"As I told you, I checked the image out thoroughly," he gritted, goaded into a reply. "It tested as genuine."

Dona curled a lip. "If you checked it with the Outpost computer, I'm not surprised. Corydon has been gunning for me since he arrived. Looks like he finally figured out how to get me."

He snorted. "Alex Corydon doesn't have the skills to

fake a recording like that, much less make it appear genuine. I checked his personnel file. That man couldn't hack a vendser into producing a cheese sandwich."

"Then with all due respect, *sir*, how did he resurrect a recording he claims I erased? Do you really think I'm that incompetent?"

That was a damned good question. One that had been nagging at him like a sore tooth. "I don't want to hear it, Astryr. Let's go." He reached for her elbow.

Ignoring his hand, she stalked out of the globe, her carriage erect as a queen's. Grinding his teeth, Alerio followed.

Maybe he should have assigned a couple of Enforcers to escort duty after all.

Nick's green eyes went narrow, and he started to turn away. "I have no intention of attempting a mind link at the moment."

Fury stormed through Riane. She grabbed him by the shoulder and dragged him around to face her again with the easy strength of a Warfem. "Wait just a damned minute. You demand I submit to some alien psychic procedure, then accuse me of being a bigot when I express doubts? Then get into a snit and stalk off when I do agree? I don't think so!"

"I didn't say we weren't linking, period," he said through gritted teeth, jerking free of her grip. "I said we're not doing it *now*. I don't want to try something that delicate involving your mind when I'm this pissed off." He took a deep breath and blew it out, seeking control. "I need to calm down."

"Yeah? I know just the thing." Riane grabbed the back of his head, dragged it down, and took his mouth with all the fury storming through her. His mouth opened under the hard pressure of hers, with astonishment as much as anything else.

Then he started kissing her back.

It was a punishing kiss, just shy of savage on both sides, as much teeth as lip. Riane thrust her tongue into Nick's mouth as he jerked her full against him. Even in her temper, she was aware of his sheer muscular strength, warm and firm.

Hooking a leg over his hip, Riane ground against him. To her angry pleasure, she could feel him hardening against her belly.

Nick groaned, then pulled away to meet her glare with a snarl. "I know what you're doing. You're going to get me hard and leave me aching."

Riane stiffened. "I don't play games like that."

He glared down into her face in hot accusation. Then his gaze softened. "No, you don't play games." A ghost of despair flickered in those forest green eyes. "But you will leave me aching."

This time he went for the kiss. The anger was gone, but she could still taste the pain. Pain that leached her own guilty anger away.

He cupped her head between his broad, strong hands. His lips brushed hers, clung, tasted. Seduced. His tongue slid along the seam of her lips. She opened for him, let him thrust deep, slow. Sighed at the rise of desire through her dying anger, like a flower blooming in the barren expanse of a cooling lava field.

Nick reached for the hem of her T-shirt and stripped it over her head. Her hands dragged at the soft fabric of his shirt, tugged it upward, and tossed it aside. Her fingers found warm, smooth skin. He unfastened the front clasp of her bra, and she let it slide down her arms. His palms cupped her breasts in tender warmth. Her head fell back with a moan as his mouth found her nipples, hot and greedy.

And incredible.

Nick licked. First back and forth over the reddening point, then in slow circles. Finally he started to suck, deep and hard, until pleasure swirled through her in hot, creamy waves. With a soft growl, he went to work on her pants, unsnapping, unzipping, tugging them down her legs.

Riane threaded her hands into his long, dark hair, enjoying the silken texture against her fingers, pulling him even closer.

She rose up on her toes with a startled gasp when one long finger found its way into her sex. He pumped slowly, raking his thumb across her clit. The combined pleasure of his mouth and clever fingers made her writhe in delight.

Riane looked down to enjoy the lush sight of Nick making love to her breasts. He brought a kind of total attention to every flick of his tongue, as if he loved what he was doing for its own sake rather than as a necessary step to orgasm.

As Riane and Nick strained together, sparks poured from the Stone to swirl around them both. One flew into her side, and she gasped at the sudden hot delight. "Did you do that?"

He lifted his gaze to hers and managed a "Nope." And immediately returned his mouth to her nipple, suckling with urgent hunger.

With every tug of his mouth, more sparks danced around them, zipped in and out, leaving hot, buzzing little points on her skin.

Nick dropped onto his heels, parted her sex with his fingers, and leaned in to lick. Riane moaned as his tongue danced, teasing her clit, thrusting between her lips. The whole time, he used the other hand to continue the long, spearing strokes of his fingers.

She closed her eyes, rolling her hips against his face, allowing herself to simply enjoy the sensation of his tongue, his hands, his mouth. The sparks circled them faster, zipping in and out.

Finally Nick drew away from her, his mouth wet from her juices, his eyes a glowing green. "Do you want me?"

"Mother Goddess, yes!" She bent over him as he knelt, diving for a deep, drawing kiss.

When he pulled away at last, he pushed her back to sit on the edge of the bed so he could untie her boots and pull off her leather pants. She watched him, her body buzzing with hunger. When he finally stood, she sat up fast, eager to free the thick ridge of his erection.

Nick was so hard, it was difficult to unfasten his jeans, but she was determined. Finally he spilled out into her hands, rosy, eager, and deliciously promising. She stroked him slowly, almost purring with anticipation, until he caught her wrists.

"Maybe . . . you might want to hold off on that." He was breathing hard, his eyes glowing bright and green.

"Okay." Grinning, Riane sprang off the bed and into his arms.

Nick caught her easily, laughing. "You don't believe in playing hard to get, do you?"

"I don't believe in playing, period." She wrapped her long, bare legs around his waist as he positioned her over his cock. His hands felt big and warm on her backside.

They both sucked in a hard breath as he impaled her. "God, that feels good." His head fell back, emerald eyes closing.

Riane growled in approval and leaned in to bite the strong cords of his throat in small, goading nibbles.

He chuckled. "Carnivore."

She tightened the grip of her thighs and twined her

arms around his neck, then used her strength to pump up and down on his cock.

Nick's eyes widened. He tightened his grip on her butt and began to hunch back at her, matching her stroke for long, strong stroke.

Moaning in chorus, they worked his big erection in and out. Each thrust tugged and twisted her slick inner flesh, filling her, feeding the orgasm she could feel hovering just out of reach.

Riane breathed in hard, savoring the musk of male sweat and female arousal, enjoying the galloping erotic music of flesh slapping flesh, the mingled gasps and grunts and soft moans, the softly stinging whip of hair on bare skin. Hands that gripped her ass just shy of bruising, his hard, muscular shoulders going sweat-damp under her arms.

And the light of the Stone, glowing brighter and brighter, verdant sparks flying around them as if caught in a furious updraft, stinging, urging them on. Spiking the surging pleasure, building relentlessly.

His gaze met hers. The reflection of emerald sparks swirled in his eyes, catching her attention. Circling faster and faster, hypnotic. Her head grew light even as her orgasm gathered tighter and tighter.

Then, at last, it exploded.

His bellow echoed hers as they came together. Suddenly it seemed she could see herself out of his eyes, feel her own body gripping his cock, feel the hot spill of his climax.

And the spinning green light in his eyes dragged her in. Dimly, she felt him stagger, hit the edge of the bed with his thighs. His hands gripped, convulsively bracing her as they tumbled to the mattress.

The green blaze swirled their shared consciousness away.

* * *

Nick's eyes were wide open, a solid sheet of green light, matching the emerald blaze of the Stone. Riane's shone with the same pure blaze. Time ticked by with no movement except the synchronized rise and fall of their chests.

Finally, the nanobot unwrapped itself from the bead in Riane's hair. Cautiously, it crept onto her face on its pseudopods, scanning them both with its microscopic sensors.

Neither so much as twitched.

Reassured, the nanobot turned and scuttled for the motel room window, moving with all the speed it could manage. The Xeran courier 'bot floated just outside, waiting to carry its message to the Victor.

· 22 ·

Dona Astryr lay on the narrow bunk, staring sight-lessly at the ceiling of her cell. It was a stark little chamber, so tiny its white walls seeming to crowd in on her. It held nothing more than the bunk, a sanitary unit, and the vendser that would produce food and water on a specific schedule.

There were no apparent bars across the empty doorway, but Dona knew better. An invisible repeller field would blow her across the room with a painful shock if she got too close to the opening.

As if that wasn't enough, two Enforcers stood guard outside. One might think that was overkill, except some-body had broken Ivar out of the brig two weeks before. Agents had been injured in the raid, and the enemy's self-destructing combots had blown craters in the floor. The damage had only just been repaired. So she supposed it was understandable that Chief Dyami would take precautions.

At the thought of the Chief, Dona's chest ached with a deep, relentless throb. The really pitiful thing, she thought,

was that the pain was not because she faced the likelihood
of a long sentence in a penal colony if she was convicted
of treason. It wasn't even that her friends and coworkers
thought she had betrayed them, risked their lives, and
stranded her best friend in time.

No, she was hurt because Alerio Dyami thought she was
a traitor. Alerio, who had been her obsession for entirely
too damn long. She never would have gotten involved with
Ivar to begin with if it hadn't been for her commander.

There was no real question that he was as attracted to
her as she was to him. That was just as obvious as his re-
luctance to get involved.

So in order to avoid yearning for a relationship that was
obviously doomed, she'd ended up in one that had turned
out to be downright toxic.

The question was, who had framed her? Normally she'd
have assumed it was Corydon himself—he was fanatical
enough to fake evidence if he couldn't nail her any other
way.

The trouble with that theory was that Alerio was right.
Corydon simply didn't have the ability to construct a frame
tight enough to defeat the Chief's ability to pull it apart.

There had to be another mole somewhere in the organization.

But how could she prove it? Alerio had ordered her
comp to shut itself down when he'd locked her in here.
He'd even powered down her nanobot enhancements. She
had no doubt the Chief had also pulled her permissions to
access the Outpost comp for anything but ordering food
from the vendser. Which meant she couldn't hack her way
into the system to discover who had done this to her.

Dona rolled to her feet and began to pace in long, restless strides. Even as she strode back and forth, she kept a
careful distance from the cell doorway. She had no desire
to get hit by that repeller field.

Well, at least her incarceration had accomplished one thing. It had killed off the last of her inappropriate attraction to Chief Alerio Dyami.

There was no way in the Seven Hells she could love a man who could believe she'd work for the Xerans. Not after everything those monsters had done to her home world.

She was finally free of Alerio Dyami.

Nick opened his eyes to find a brilliant violet sky. Disoriented, he squinted up at the red sun riding high overhead.

A red sun in a violet sky? What the fuck?

He turned his head and saw a tumble of brilliant copper hair beside him. "Riane?"

"Hmm?" She stirred sleepily, then sat up abruptly to stare around them in astonishment. "How the fuck did we get to another planet?" She aimed a sharp look at him. "Did you do this? Where are we?"

He rose on one elbow and scrubbed a hand over his face. "We're on another planet?"

"Well, this sure as hell ain't Earth." She looked down at herself, registering the black leather pants and T-shirt she wore. "Huh. I'm dressed again." She eyed him. "So are you. When did that happen?"

She was right. He wore the same jeans and T-shirt he'd had on before. "I have no idea." Nick eyed her. "Does that computer of yours have any clue where we are?"

Riane cocked her head, as if listening to some voice he couldn't hear. "I'm not detecting any electromagnetic communication. At all." She frowned deeply, examining the sky. "Violet sky, red sun, no advanced civilization. Could be any number of worlds." She rolled easily to her feet, then aimed a look at him. "You sense anything?"

He, too, stood, peering around them. Underfoot lay a

carpet of thick green growth that reminded him of moss, though it was dotted here and there with colorful feathery structures similar to flowers.

Immense blue . . . things rose all around them, spearing toward the sky. He'd have called them trees, but they had no leaves. Instead, each branch ended in a big cluster of hard, glossy bulbs. Faint clicks and scrabbling noises sounded from the strange vegetation, suggesting some kind of life, though it was impossible to tell whether it was insects, animals, or birds. Or something else altogether.

Nick tried reaching out with his powers, searching for other intelligent minds. Riane was a strong, vivid presence next to him, but that was all. "Not sensing anything. Nothing sentient anyway. Lots of little . . . creatures, though."

"And some that are not so little." Riane nodded thoughtfully. "Nothing I recognize."

He blew out a worried breath. "Riane, how the hell are we going to get home?"

She looked around them again, pursing her lips as she fisted her hands on her hips. "That's a good question. I don't think we *can* get home, unless you can figure out a way to Jump us there."

"Even if I could, I need to know where the fuck we are before I can get us back."

Riane nodded, her gaze shrewd, decisive. "The first order of business is to figure out how we got here. If you didn't do it . . ."

". . . Somebody had to." Nick straightened his shoulders. "Maybe we should take a walk and see what we can see."

She shot him a look, lifting a red brow. "What, just wander around and hope we stumble on some form of transportation?"

"Got a better idea?"

Riane sighed. "Let's go."

* * *

Frieka trotted back into the suite of rooms he and Riane shared. Despite the clawing urgency he'd felt, he'd forced himself to head to the Outpost mess for food and water. He knew from experience that hacking a system could take hours of careful work. You'd have to be an idiot to attempt it on an empty stomach—or for that matter, without a bathroom break. He'd already taken care of both.

Serious hacking wasn't the kind of thing you charged into. That was a good way to get yourself killed triggering a Trojan or viral bomb, especially if you were trying to work without backup in a system that had obviously been compromised.

Mother Goddess, he missed Riane. She excelled at this kind of thing. He could do it, of course, but it was hardly one of his specialties.

Which didn't make a damn bit of difference, because he had to do it anyway.

His stomach coiled into a knot, but Frieka ignored it as he leaped up on the bed and settled down. He closed his eyes and opened a data channel to the Outpost mainframe.

This was going to be delicate work, because he'd just as soon not get caught at it. He knew the Chief and his team had worked to tighten the central computer's security system to prevent hacking. Obviously, the real traitor had found a way in anyway. Whoever it was had probably planted various defenses to keep someone from following his tracks.

Lethal defenses.

Carefully, Frieka began to search the network, probing for the evidence he was looking for. He started with the surveillance system, since he knew at least one recording had been tampered with. Unfortunately, as he scanned the recording of Dona's supposed crime yet again, he could find no evidence of direct interference in the image. Since he knew the recording was faulty, that had to mean that interference was deeply buried.

Luckily, he also knew there was a particular style in which each program was written. For a creature who was as much computer as Frieka was, variations in that style were as vivid and distinct as scent.

So Frieka went deeper, scanning through the underlying program script, seeking anomalies. It was a slow, tedious process that could not be done quickly. More than once he thought he'd found something, only to have the trail peter out.

He refused to give up.

Until, at last, Frieka caught a faint, distinctive pattern he knew from years spent in combat with Vardon's military space fleet. It was complex and impressive, somehow inhuman in its glittering intricacy.

And it was definitely Xeran.

Ha, you bastard, Frieka thought. *I've got you now.*

Carefully, wary of booby traps, the wolf began to probe the alien thread, working his way back along it, seeking to identify the traitor who had planted it.

He sensed something, a bit of code attached to the Xeran pattern. He probed harder.

Something dark and vicious and Xeran came raging through his com channel. An instant later his awareness was jerked out of his link to the mainframe.

He couldn't draw a breath.

Panicked, Frieka fought to suck in oxygen. The muscles of his chest ached savagely with desperate effort, but they didn't move. He tried to struggle to his feet, only to discover his body was completely paralyzed, his rib cage frozen.

Seven Hells, I've triggered a Trojan!

· 23 ·

❧❀❧

Nick walked beside Riane, staring around them in fascination. He was seeing more variety in the alien trees now—some of them were bright red, others a vibrant shade of purple. Their knobby outgrowths reminded him of coral.

He spotted a strange little creature perched on one of the globular clusters. It had six limbs and a long, narrow muzzle. Its eyes were huge, dark, and liquid, and it watched him warily before scampering away.

As a boy, he'd watched grainy old films of the moon landing, then bounced around the living room pretending to be an astronaut. Now he was actually walking on an alien planet, surrounded by alien life. "This is amazing."

"What?" Riane blinked at him as if trying to figure out why he looked so awed.

"All of this." Nick gestured around them. "This world, these trees and creatures. I can't believe I'm really here."

She shrugged. "It's a planet."

Nick smiled at her seen-one-you've-seen-'em-all tone. "Philistine."

"Hey, I'm more interested in getting home." Riane gave the area another wary look. "And avoiding anything that might want to kill us."

"You think something's going to . . ." He broke off at a sudden strong tug and a stabbing jolt in his biceps. Automatically, he set off in the direction the Stone indicated.

"Where are you going?" Riane hurried after him. "Wait a minute."

"There's somewhere I have to be." He lengthened his stride, driven by the sense of urgency that had suddenly started pounding in his brain.

"Where?" She sounded frustrated and worried. "Nick, dammit, you don't just go charging around a planet you don't know. That's a good way to get kacked by something."

"I can protect myself."

"Against the local equivalent of a T. rex?"

They rounded a stand of trees to see a towering, rocky black cliff rising in the midst of a rolling field of moss. Nick headed in that direction, knowing his destination when he saw it.

Riane made no further protest, instead padding along beside him watching their surroundings. She'd obviously appointed herself his bodyguard.

They reached the cliff, and Nick began to scramble up its face, hands and feet finding rocky handholds.

"Dammit, Nick!" Riane called up at him. He glanced down over his shoulder to see her climbing after him, exasperation on her pretty face.

Nick and Riane lay side by side on the motel room bed. Only their chests rose and fell.

Light flared in a blinding explosion. When the glow faded, the Victor stood beside the bed with His chief cohort of guards arrayed around Him. He had used a dampening field to keep the sonic boom of the mass Jump from wakening everyone in the motel—including their two targets.

Warrior Priest Gyor ge Tityus watched his god bend over the two. Given the low ceiling, the Victor had been forced to appear at less than His usual regal height.

Now He cocked his horned head, studying the Vardonese and the Demon with narrowed black eyes.

Gyor dared to look past the god's massive shoulder. The eyes of the Demon and his whore were open and glowing green from corner to corner, without whites at all. Yet the two appeared completely unaware of the Xerans. "Do they sleep?"

"It does not seem so." The Victor tilted His horned head, eyeing the couple with interest. For once, He did not use the Xeran priest tongue. "Their brains are as active as if they're awake. Even the whore's computer is active, yet there is no indication it senses us at all." He crouched to study the T'Lir clasped around the Demon's forearm. Green energy boiled around it. "Judging by the quantity of Coswold-Barre energy, this would seem to be a state induced by the T'Lir."

Gyor decided to risk another question. "Why would the Demon render himself vulnerable like this?"

The Victor shrugged His massive shoulders. "Who knows why the Demon does anything? If indeed it was his idea." He made a deep, rumbling sound in His throat and reached out until His hand hovered just above the snapping green gem. "I wonder," He mused, "what would happen if we cut off that arm?"

Riane climbed after Nick, frowning in worry. She hoped to hell he knew what he was doing.

Her misgivings only increased as she realized he was heading toward the entrance to a cave over their heads.

"Do sensors detect any sign of danger?" she asked.

"No life-forms are present in the cave," her comp said. *"There is no indication of energy or chemical booby traps. The atmosphere within the cave is breathable by humans, and the structure of the cave itself appears stable."*

Well, that was something anyway.

Nick reached the cave mouth, scrambled upright, and walked inside.

Blowing out a breath in frustration, Riane heaved herself over the cliff edge, rose to her feet, and strode in after him.

The Stone cast a bright green glow around the dark interior of the cave. Long shadows wavered where their bodies blocked the light.

Riane glowered at their surroundings. Was it her imagination, or did the walls look a bit too smooth to be a natural formation? And there was an opening in the back of the cavern that appeared to be a tunnel. It was pitch-black back there. She didn't like the looks of it at all. "Okay, Nick, we're here. Now what?"

"I have no—"

"Hello, Nick."

Nick turned toward the tunnel—and went pale. Startled, Riane jerked around. Her sensors hadn't warned her anyone else was present.

A woman dressed in jeans, running shoes, and a blue polo shirt stood in the dark opening of the tunnel. Though she looked much older than the woman Riane had seen just two weeks before, she was recognizably Charlotte Holt.

She was also transparent and glowing.

A chill crawled up Riane's spine. *"Is that a trid recording?"*

"Sensors do not detect any energy source. They also do not detect the image itself."

Oh, that wasn't good. Her sensors could detect any known form of energy, no matter how faint. She swallowed.

"Mother . . ." Nick took a step toward her, then hesitated.

Charlotte's foggy face smiled, a little sadly. "Yes, I'm dead."

Frieka was dying.

His vision flooded with dark spots, going gray as he fought to breathe. The Trojan had speared right through his antivirus protection program to attack his central nervous system.

Calm down, he told himself. *I've triggered Xeran Trojans before. I know what to do.*

Xeran attack programs always used a particular structure with certain predictable weaknesses.

Frieka looked for them, but the Trojan's structure was completely unlike anything he'd ever seen before.

The electronic contagion was spreading through his computer system with appalling speed, overloading the neuronet computer system that enhanced his intelligence to human levels.

There was no way to destroy the Trojan in time. There was only one thing left to do, but Sweet Mother, it was risky.

He had to shut down his neuronet computer completely before it could kill him. It was a strategy human cyborgs used when they encountered a virus they couldn't defeat, though as a last resort. It stripped them of access to their nanobot enhancements, leaving them easy prey for enemies.

But unlike a human, Frieka was nothing but an animal without his comp. Far more intelligent than any ordinary wolf, true, but still, a wolf. He'd lose the capacity to think, to reason, to communicate as humans did. He'd cease to be Frieka.

Unfortunately, it was that or die. If he shut his systems down, the Chief and his team would realize what had happened and be able to debug his comp.

So he gave the one command he'd never before given in his entire life.

"Deactivate."

In seconds. Frieka felt his mind begin to bleed away. It felt like dying.

His sensors shut down first, then the vocalizer that gave him the capacity to speak. Next his higher-level systems went, and his intelligence faded with terrifying speed. He wanted to panic, but there wasn't enough air.

Then his chest lifted, and there was a great inrush of cool, precious oxygen.

He could breathe again.

The wolf lay on the bunk, panting in great, desperate huffs.

Images flicked through his mind, sensations, fragments of conversation he could no longer understand.

And feelings.

Those he understood very well indeed.

A man, his face marked along one side with an intricate design, cuddling the wolf when he'd been only a puppy. There'd been warmth in the man's big hands, affection and kindness in his eyes.

And strength.

The wolf remembered fighting alongside the man. Fear, anger, the taste of blood in his mouth as he sank his teeth into enemies with metal horns on their heads.

A redheaded woman, putting a bowl in front of him, a smile on her face. Later, watching her grow round with child.

The child. The smallest human he'd ever seen, plump,

hairless, helpless, hands waving aimlessly, feet kicking, staring up at him with bright, curious eyes. A toothless smile.

Tiny fist buried in his fur as she held on to him, taking unsteady steps. Losing her balance and plopping down on her butt, only to grab his foreleg and struggle to her feet again.

A cloud of red curls topped a face with the tattooed man's eyes. The child lay curled around the wolf, crying because another child had hurt her. Helpless rage rose in the wolf's chest. *No one hurt his baby.*

A horned man carried her away, up into the sky. The wolf howled in panic, running after her. Finding her again, watching the tattooed man kill the horned one. Feeling her hands in his fur again. Joy too huge to be contained.

Waking up as the child crawled into his bunk, crying softly. Licking away her tears, tasting salt and lingering fear.

He lifted his head as fear stabbed through him.

Someone had taken the child again.

Silent as death, the wolf leaped off his child's bunk and slipped toward the door. It opened at his approach, and he started down the corridor. He was going to find the one who had taken her.

And he was going to kill.

Nick stared at the misty figure of his mother. "How . . . is this possible?"

"Just what I was wondering," Riane muttered, circling around to examine the back of the so-called ghost.

Charlotte turned to look at her. "No, this is not some kind of Xeran trick."

"You know, I'm not finding you all that believable." She curled her lip. "Can't imagine why."

"If you're my mother, what was the name of my favorite toy when I was six?" Nick demanded. His eyes had gone hard, suspicious.

"Charlotte" looked startled before her face softened in a smile. "It was a stuffed toy. You named it after the furry creature from that movie—*Return of the Jedi*. The Wookie. Damn, what was his name? Chewbacca! You slept with that thing every night. We lost it in a restaurant one time, and I damn near panicked. Had to go back and search for it."

His eyes widened. "Mother?"

"There's no such thing as ghosts," Riane told him firmly. "Scientists have been investigating haunted sites for centuries with the best tech we can develop. They've found absolutely nothing. Ghosts are only superstition."

Nick pointed at the wispy figure. "She's standing right there, Riane. How much proof do you need?"

"It could be an illusion created by a telepath for all you—"

"I didn't say I was a ghost," "Charlotte" interrupted calmly. "I said I was dead."

· 24 ·

"So what *are* you, then?" Riane challenged Nick's so-called mother. "And why are you taking advantage of this man's grief?"

"I'm not taking advantage of anything," the figure snapped with a trace of anger. "I *am* Charlotte Holt's spirit. When I died, my life force was captured by the T'Lir." She spread her arms. "Now here I am."

"But . . . why?" Nick asked. "How?"

"Charlotte" sighed. "Your T'Lir is one of the repositories of the spirits of dead Sela. It's their power that reinforces your own."

"*My* T'Lir? There are more?"

"Many more. Others are with the other Sela colonies, while—"

"You're buying this?" Riane rocked back on her heels to stare at him, incredulous. "Nick, this doesn't make any damn sense at all. Your gem is powered by the spirits of dead aliens? As my mother would say, 'Give me a break.'"

"We just woke up on an alien planet, but you didn't even blink. Why is that any less believable than this?" He folded his arms and glowered. "Shut up and let her talk."

Riane opened her mouth to snap back at him, but Charlotte forestalled her. "Perhaps it would help if I started at the beginning." The spirit sank down on the sandy floor of the cave, folding her transparent legs. Looking up at him, she patted the ground to either side. "Have a seat, children. Get comfortable. This is going to take a while."

Nick settled tailor-fashion next to his so-called mother. After a pause, Riane warily followed suit, ready to spring up at the first sign of a trap. *"Comp, alert me at any sign of danger."*

"Scanning."

Trouble was, she wasn't sure how much good it would do. Sensors apparently weren't much use when it came to ghosts.

Or whatever the Seven Hells "Charlotte" really was.

"This all started about ten billion years ago," Charlotte began, then smiled slightly, "on a planet far, far away."

"Do we really need to go that far back?" Riane asked drily.

"Patience, child." She gestured, and images filled the air before them, three-dimensional and vivid, of a violet world with wide swaths of land in blue and yellow. "It was a lush planet, with a wide variety of life-forms all fighting one another in ruthless competition for food, mates, and territory."

Riane snorted. "Just like on every other life-bearing planet we've ever discovered."

"True, but for some reason, this competition resulted in a biological arms race that was even more intense than usual. Not only did species grow steadily bigger and faster—developing claws, fangs, and horns—but three different species evolved intelligence. Separately and simultaneously."

Riane winced. "Ouch."

"Why ouch?" Nick asked.

"Because when evolving species develop intelligence at the same time, they become even more warlike and competitive against one another than a species that engages in tribal warfare," Riane told him. "So what you end up with are species that are really, really violent. Even more so than humans."

"Exactly." As they watched, a lizardlike race and two vaguely mammalian ones began to use tools, then create weapons. They fought bloodily, each species trying to wipe the others out, weaponry growing ever more complex as their intelligence grew. "Eventually the species we call the Sela succeeded in killing its rivals, then began a period of intraspecies warfare."

Riane blinked. "Those are Sela?" Instead of the cuddly six-legged aliens, they were brawny creatures that reminded her of six-limbed tigers. Their pelts were dark, striped, and they ran swiftly on two sets of powerful legs. Their arms were thinner, with long, agile fingers tipped with vicious claws. Their heads were vaguely feline, with pointed ears, large, intelligent eyes, and lots of sharp teeth.

Nick stared at the image with the same appalled fascination she felt. "I thought you said the Sela are pacifists."

"They are—now. Then, not so much," Charlotte explained. "With their rivals dead, the Sela had the leisure to continue developing ever more advanced technology and weapons. Soon they moved out into space."

"That is pretty much the pattern," Riane commented.

"True. But unlike humanity, the Sela home world was located close to the galactic core—Earth is out on one of the galaxy's arms—which meant their interstellar neighbors were much closer. And some of those neighbors had their own intelligent races."

Nick winced. "And given the Sela's charming personalities . . ."

"Exactly. They immediately embarked on wars of genocide against their neighbors, wiping them out and seizing their advanced technology. Each acquisition allowed the Sela to move farther and farther out into space in an expanding ring of conquest and bloodshed."

Images flashed through the air, portraying alien warships engaged in ferocious interstellar battles. Massive, exotic weapons stalked across burning worlds among ground-shaking explosions. In other images, the Sela fought hand to hand against creatures even stranger than they were. Killing. Dying.

"Didn't they ever get tired?" Nick asked. "I mean, humans eventually get sick of warfare and quit fighting."

His mother shook her ghostly head. "The Sela evolved to take joy in war, and their culture glorified warfare. They believed you only bought your way into the afterlife by death in battle."

"So how did they go from furry psychopaths to cuddly pacifists?" Riane asked.

"They finally encountered the one race that wouldn't fight back—because it didn't have to. The Di'jiri were ancient and unimaginably powerful, with the ability to alter the fabric of reality in ways not even today's Sela can. They had retreated from space, and were living a pastoral life when the Sela invaded their world."

"Bet that went well," Riane muttered.

Charlotte laughed. "Oh, very. Because the Di'jiri gave them psychic abilities on the spot."

Nick blinked. "Wait, *they're* the ones who gave the Sela powers? Why?"

"Think about it, son." Charlotte smiled. It wasn't a very

nice smile. "A race of violent killers who glorify murder suddenly given the ability to feel the pain of their victims—without the knowledge of how to block it out."

Riane snorted. "Damn, I wish somebody would do that to the Xerans."

Charlotte shook her head. "It is not a thing lightly done. It drove many irrevocably mad. Others fled in panic, but wherever they went, they spread their abilities to their fellow Sela." Now the images showed Sela screaming, killing themselves, being slain by their own kind. "The power spread like a pandemic. The Selan Empire collapsed, and their enemies took violent revenge. Billions died."

"Shit." Riane winced.

Charlotte nodded. "Now you see why the Sela did not do the same to the Xerans."

"How did they survive?" Nick watched the chaotic images with a queasy fascination.

"A few retreated into hiding while they attempted to learn to control their new abilities. They evolved a philosophy of pacifism and began to embrace their powers."

"Nothing keeps the Sela down, does it?" Riane asked, admiring.

"This came close." There was no amusement on the ghost's face. "The survivors began to realize the depths of their own murderous crimes. That was the most devastating punishment of all. So many slew themselves that they were on the verge of extinction."

Riane drew up her legs and rested her chin on her knees. "What saved them?"

"The invention of the T'Lirs. Many of the Sela's greatest warriors wished to atone for what they had done—but how does one atone for mass murder? It would take more than a lifetime. So it was they created the T'Lirs—a way to pass on the experience of the warrior generation to those that followed."

"How?" Nick demanded.

"The spirits of those who die are absorbed by the T'Lirs, then are passed on to those in the womb."

Riane recoiled. "What happens to the child's original spirit? Is it destroyed?"

Charlotte shook her head. "Souls don't die. The old spirit adds to the new. The children don't remember their ancestors' experiences at first—that does not happen until each has gained the maturity to deal with those memories. And much of the true grief is never remembered at all."

Nick's eyes widened. "You're waiting to be reborn."

She nodded. "Yes."

He leaned forward as a new thought occurred to him. "Am I the repository of one of those spirits?"

Charlotte spread her hands. "That I cannot tell you."

"Cannot or will not?" Riane demanded.

She merely smiled . . . and faded away like mist in the sun.

Nick bounded to his feet. "Mother! Dammit, don't leave! I need to know . . ." He turned to stare into the darkness before his shoulders finally slumped in defeat.

Riane rose and moved to rest a hand on his shoulder. "She's gone, Nick."

He gave her a look boiling with frustration. "But there was so much I wanted to ask her. Who was my father? Why didn't she tell me this stuff when she was alive? And where the hell are we?"

"And most of all, how do we get back?" Riane walked to the front of the cave and stared outside. "Maybe she'll—"

Something made a low, menacing sound.

"Warning!" her comp shrilled. *"Unidentified life-form approaching . . ."*

Riane whirled. "Nick, look ou—"

Something dark exploded from the tunnel in a rush of claws and teeth. It slammed into Nick like a starshuttle, knocking him flat. He yelped.

Nick! Riane started to leap toward them—and found her body wouldn't obey. She tried to shout, but she couldn't make a sound. She was completely paralyzed, frozen in place.

Struggling to force his attacker away, Nick bellowed in mingled rage and pain.

The wolf worked his way down the corridor, his nose to the floor as he sought the enemy who had stolen his child.

A cheerful female voice spoke in a waterfall of incomprehensible words. He caught his name, but he was too busy hunting to stop.

She said something else, half-laughing, but he simply kept going. He had to find the child thief.

Jessica Arvid watched Frieka pad down the corridor, nose to the floor, questing back and forth as he sought some scent. "What's his problem?" It was out of character for Frieka not to stop for an ear scratch and a joke.

"He's worried about Riane," Galar Arvid told her.

Jess looked up at her handsome new husband and lifted a brow. "What, he thinks he can track her by scent?"

"Frieka's a lot smarter than that." The Warlord stared thoughtfully after the big wolf. Galar wore his blond hair short and disdained the traditional tattoo, though, like Riane's, his father had been genetically engineered by House Arvid. "Looks like he's definitely trying to track something. Wonder why he isn't using sensors?"

"You could ask."

He snorted. "I don't think so. His temper is a little too short right now, and his teeth are a little too sharp."

* * *

The wolf stopped short in the corridor, breathing deeply. He could smell countless layers of scent, most of which he recognized.

But there was a trace of something else, too. Something faint and alien. A hint of Xeran reek, mixed with a scent he knew. His lips drew back from his teeth, and a deep growl rumbled in his chest.

He'd found the child thief.

· 25 ·

꧁꧂

The creature that had attacked Nick was a Sela,
but not the pacifistic, kittenish aliens Riane had described.
This thing was a primitive Sela, with fangs and slashing
claws on all six limbs. Its eyes shone a glowing, malevolent
green, and its thick fur, striped in black and blue, smelled
of alien forests.

And blood. Nick's blood.

It had caught him across the belly in its initial charge,
failing to disembowel him only because he had shielded
himself with every erg of power he could pull from the
Stone. Nick had gone for the knife he usually wore across
the small of his back. There was nothing there.

He had no weapons at all except for his strength and his
guts and the Stone. Even Riane was denied him. She stood
frozen at one end of the cavern, an expression of horror
paralyzed on her face. Only her eyes moved.

The alien had done something to her.

Now the Sela circled with him, moving in a low, feral slink, its tufted ears folded flat to its head.

"You are not worthy of the T'Lir, half-breed," its voice growled, not in his ears or even his mind, but in his very bones, his muscles and flesh. "I will kill you and take it as my right."

Nick peeled his lips back from his teeth. "Kiss my half-breed ass."

"I'd rather drink your blood." It charged him again, vicious and incredibly fast. He spun aside, avoiding another swipe of deadly claws by a hairbreadth.

The Sela whirled, displaying fangs the length of his hand. "Soft ape-thing. What are you without your weapons? Your guns, your knives. Helpless." It darted in again, rearing to slash with its four front limbs. He knocked one set of claws away with his forearm and spun into a kick, slamming a boot against the side of its head. The Sela roared in rage and leaped at him, jaws snapping.

Nick scrambled back, blocking its claws with a wave of force from the Stone. Something hot rolled down his forearm, and droplets of blood flew from his left foot, leaving a trail of scarlet on the cave floor. It had bitten him when he'd kicked it.

He was so fucked. The thought flew through his mind, was instantly suppressed as a potential self-fulfilling prophecy. That was the kind of shit you didn't think in a fight.

He had to find a way to beat this thing.

The only weapon he had was the Stone, but the Stone wouldn't allow its power to be used in direct attacks. Damned pacifists.

So where did this furry bastard come from?

The Sela charged in again, and Nick ducked—not quite fast enough. Vicious claws tore his flesh. He dodged an-

other lethal swipe and spun away like a bullfighter. Blood
rolled in a hot rush, pattering on the dust.

Too much blood.

The Victor hefted the quantum sword in his hand, eyeing Nick's T'Lir. Just as He was about to lift the energy
blade, He stopped, staring at the Demon's arm, which Gyor
held straight off the bed. "That is odd."

Gyor looked down at the half-breed's wrist. And started.
As he watched, six gashes appeared across the Demon's
forearm. Instantly, blood began to roll down it, bright scarlet.

Glancing over the Demon's body, Gyor noticed blood
flowing from a set of cuts over his belly. There was a third
set across the man's thigh, and one on his foot

"It is as if he does battle, Most Victorious," Gyor said
thoughtfully.

"With something that has claws. And it would seem he
loses." The Victor deactivated the sword and returned it to
Gyor. "I wish to observe further."

"Coward! Come and die with dignity," the Sela snarled.

"I have no intention of dying at all." Nick slammed a
spinning kick at its head, but it leaped away like the cat it
resembled.

"You haven't the will to use what you have, soft ape."
The Sela gaped its jaws in something that bore a chilling
resemblance to a grin. "I will kill you and eat the beating
heart out of your female."

And that was exactly the wrong thing to say. Fury surged
in Nick, bringing the familiar darkness he had learned to
fear—and use, when he had to. He'd never needed it more.

Nick let it come, surging through bone and blood, strengthening him, enhancing his speed, his agility.

But as he watched the creature stalk him, he realized it wouldn't be enough. The bastard was just too damn big.

His mind worked furiously. He couldn't blast it. He'd tried that before in earlier fights with the Xerans. The Stone just wouldn't allow its power to be used that way.

But it could enhance his strength, reinforce his bones and his skin into something more like armor . . .

The Sela barreled into him in that moment of distraction—*Idiot, you don't think in a fight! It's all training or nothing.* Its massive weight flattened him. Jaws opened wide, the Sela lunged for his throat . . .

Nick struck out in an act of raw instinct, a vicious open-handed swipe right across its eyes. The Sela screamed, convulsing away from him, blood flying from its muzzle.

He staggered to his feet, bleeding, automatically lifting both hands to block.

They were tipped in green, glowing claws.

He'd created them from the Stone's power. Which made sense. Though he couldn't use the power against enemies directly, the Stone would allow itself to be used to change his own body. What he decided to do with those changes was on his head.

You haven't the will, the Sela had said.

That was the key. Will. It was will that shaped the power. Nick looked at his hands again, and his claws lengthened, sharpened. His skin began to glow a soft fluorescent green.

He bared his teeth at the Sela as the dark joy of battle filled him again. "Now. Let's try that again."

Riane was a cyborg, and she had fought against and beside other cyborgs all her life. She was no stranger to superhuman speed and strength, no stranger to acts of agility that mocked gravity. Yet she had never seen anything like Nick's fight with the Sela.

She'd thought in those first horrified moments that she was going to have to watch him be ripped apart and eaten. He had no weapons at all, against a creature that was one big weapon. And she could do nothing to save him.

Riane's heart seemed to contract in her chest until it felt like a stone, cold and hard and aching.

Feeling helpless, she watched Nick do dogged battle, refusing to give up despite the odds against him. Her heart climbed into her throat as she watched him dodge, duck, and backpedal, somehow avoiding the Sela's vicious attempts to disembowel him.

But the outcome seemed inevitable—until the Sela threatened to kill her. Then claws sprang from Nick's hands, and it was the Sela who bled.

Just like that, his fighting style changed. He'd always been a graceful man, but now he began to attack with a ruthless speed and agility that seemed more than human. It was as if his spine was abnormally flexible, as if he had muscle where no human should have muscle. And there was a look in his eyes, a chilling, dark joy she'd never seen on his face before.

He began fighting like the Sela he fought.

Still, by all rights the alien should have torn Nick apart. After all, it had six sets of claws to his two, along with that mouthful of tearing teeth.

Yet every time it tried to tag him, his skin sparked and glowed green, blocking its strikes. She'd seen his ability to withstand blows that should have killed him, but this was an order of magnitude greater.

Yet the change was more than that. Nick fought with a kind of savagery he'd never shown before, his face contorted with a blend of rage and sadistic pleasure.

Sweet Mother, what the hell is happening to him?

It was agony, watching him fight, unable to help, unable even to speak.

Her mind kept flashing back to the way he touched her when they made love. The strength of his hands, the tenderness of his mouth, the soft moss green of his eyes. Now those eyes were hard, feral, more animal than man.

Yet that was better than watching him die. If she had to, she would find a way to bring back the man he'd been.

Somehow.

Nick fought in a bubble of mindless instinct. His every sense seemed heightened. He could hear the puff of dust under paws and boots despite the growls and grunts of effort and rage. He could smell the musk of fear.

As he watched the flicker of the Sela's huge eyes, he knew what the alien was going to do next. He could feel it in his own muscles, sense it like a scent in the air. He met each swipe of those great paws with a shield of power, blocking the strikes before they could sink into his flesh.

His own strikes sent alien blood flying in violet arcs.

For the first time in his life, he fought without fear, without doubt. Instead, there was only a savage delight in his own strength, his own invulnerability.

And the sight of his foe's violet blood. It splashed hot across his lips. Unconsciously, he tongued it away.

It tasted good.

Nick felt his lips curl in a vicious smile. His opponent's eyes widened.

Oh, yeah!

What the fuck am I doing? The thought stabbed through the battle madness, almost jerked him sober. *This isn't me.*

The Sela reared over him on two back legs, preparing to smash down on him with the other four. Nick dashed in beneath the creature and slashed his claws across its haunches, hamstringing it. The leg gave under its weight, and the Sela toppled.

Nick was on his foe before the alien had time to rise again on its good legs. Leaping astride its back, he grabbed its jaw and jerked its head back. Closed a clawed hand around its throat, preparing to rip and tear and kill.

Years of battling Xerans had taught him to kill quickly, without mercy, as a matter of simple necessity. A dead enemy could not come after you again.

The Sela struggled, trying to throw him off. Nick tightened the grip of his thighs, riding it. He could feel the alien's life pulsing in frantic throbs, its muscled sides heaving between his legs, the fur thick and fine.

He wanted to kill it. Ached to kill it, to feel the beat of its life slow beneath his hands.

Abruptly he remembered all those the Sela had killed in their quest to build their empire. Species rendered extinct, worlds destroyed, entire interstellar civilizations laid waste. He thought of the horrible guilt they'd felt when the Di'jiri had forced them to feel their victims' pain. How they'd turned their back on war because of it.

Now he felt the echo of that guilt in his own heart, the horror of stealing another intelligent being's most precious gift.

Life.

Stupid. Stupid to hesitate, when the Sela he fought could turn and kill him. And part of him wanted to kill. Hell, the craving for blood whispered in the depths of his mind like the devil tempting a sinner.

Killing the Sela would be so easy. So smart. And it would feel so *good*.

"Do it," the alien gasped, its voice thrumming in his bones. "Prove you are the fit heir to our blood after all."

"But maybe I don't want to be." He didn't have to kill. Not with the abilities he had. He could protect himself and

Riane without killing the Sela, even if the alien attacked him again.

He certainly shouldn't kill simply to feed that dark vampire craving in the hidden depths of his soul.

Nick released the Sela's throat and leaped away, not taking his eyes away from his foe. "Go. We've spilled enough blood."

The alien staggered to its feet, favoring the injured leg. Its outlines began to blur and shift. It shrank, its body taking on another shape, hard muscles softening, claws shrinking, tufted ears growing rounder, eyes larger. Wiser.

Kinder.

"You learn quickly," the Sela told him. "And your heart is open, despite the temptation of bloodlust. But you are not stupid. A good thing, in a Guardian. You *are* worthy of the T'Lir." It started to turn away toward the tunnel at the rear of the cavern.

"What the hell was this?" Riane exploded, jolting forward as if suddenly freed. "Another one of those damned tests you people are so fond of?"

But the Sela only kept going. Even as it padded away, it turned to mist and disappeared. Just as his mother had.

"What the Seven Hells was that all about?" Riane snarled in frustration.

"Educating me," Nick said, knowing it was true. All his life, he'd struggled with his darkness. This was the first time he'd ever felt that he'd really won. "Teaching me how to fight with the T'Lir. And when to stop fighting."

· 26 ·

"His wounds," Gyor said, staring down at the unconscious Demon in shock. "They heal!"

Green sparks danced across the sets of gashes that marred the Demon's body. The wounds closed with breathtaking speed.

The sparks flew faster, brighter. Flared suddenly with a searing intensity. The Xerans cursed, blinded by the glare.

With the light vanished, the Victor swore in a rolling growl of rage that made His priests drop to their bellies in obeisance.

The Demon and his Vardonese whore were gone.

The wolf trailed the thief who'd stolen his child, following the traitor's scent into a familiar room full of tables and people and the rich smell of food.

His enemy sat at a table with the wolf's friends. The

child thief had fooled them all, and that made the wolf's simmering rage leap even higher.

He moved across the room in a low, rapid slink, his eyes fixed on the child thief's smug face. The wolf could almost taste the traitor's blood.

He heard one of his friends call his name, but he had no way to answer. And didn't care. All that mattered was killing the child thief.

The wolf did not bother walking around the table. He simply leaped across it, his powerful muscles clearing its width in one easy bound. He slammed into the child thief's chest with his full weight. The thief screamed like a rabbit as his chair went over, dumping him on the floor as the wolf went for his throat.

The thief's arm blocked the way, and the wolf bit. Bone snapped, and the taste of hated blood filled his mouth. Another rabbit scream. People shouted, bellowed the wolf's name. He ignored them and lunged for the child thief's throat again.

Just before his teeth closed, strong hands closed in his ruff and lifted him like a puppy. Threw him halfway across the room. He landed, kept his feet, skidded on the slick floor, then found traction and charged forward again.

Tattooed not-Baran man blocked his way, shouted his name. Must have been the one who'd thrown him. Must have denied him the child thief's life. The wolf lowered his head and snarled a warning.

And leaped for tattooed man.

A hundred kilos of pissed-off wolf slammed into Alerio's chest. The Warlord fought not to go down, instead burying his hands in the big beast's ruff. He barely managed to keep those snapping teeth from his throat. "Frieka, back off, dammit! Stop!"

The wolf's only answer was a ripping snarl, another lunge, and the castanet snap of teeth. Alerio barely forced the wolf's jaws away from his throat.

Galar and three other Enforcers tackled Frieka and helped Alerio wrestle him to the floor. The huge animal twisted, snapping, claws ripping through the thin fabric of their uniforms as he scrabbled to escape them.

"Fuck, Chief!" Galar bellowed, slinging a leg across the wolf's back so he could sit on him. "Frieka's vocalizer is off!"

"I noticed!" And according to Alerio's sensors, so was the wolf's computer. Which meant all that was left was instinct, rage, and a whole lot of teeth and claws with no interest in listening to reason.

Alerio, who'd gone to *riaat*, managed to get both hands around the wolf's muzzle and force the snapping jaws closed. *"Chogan!"* he shouted over his com unit. *"Bring a regenerator tube to the mess—and enough tranq to take Frieka down. He just tried to kill Corydon. And he's not very happy with the rest of us either."*

Chogan cursed. *"On my way!"*

"How's Corydon?" Alerio yelled, straddling Frieka's neck as he struggled to control the wolf's head.

"Broken arm!" Jessica Arvid yelled back. "Okay otherwise."

"Good. I've got some questions for the son of a bitch."

"How . . . dare you!" Corydon gasped, his voice high with pain.

"Easily!" Alerio gritted back, struggling with the wolf. He was seriously tempted to let go and watch Frieka take another chunk out of the investigator.

Two endless minutes later, Chogan raced in, a medtech

team at her heels towing the regenerator. They headed for
Corydon.

"Come tranq Frieka!" Alerio barked. "I want to talk to
Corydon before he goes in the tube."

"You're the boss." Chogan snaked an arm in past Alerio's
hand and shoved a pressure injector against a throbbing
vein in the wolf's neck. Five seconds later, the big animal
went limp.

With a chorus of relieved groans, the Enforcers crawled
off him.

"Fuck," Galar said, "I don't think I've ever seen him so
pissed."

Alerio aimed a narrow stare at Corydon. "I wonder why."

Chogan caught his forearm before he could start toward
the moaning human. "You need that regenerator worse
than Corydon," the doctor told him. "How many times did
Frieka bite you anyway?"

"Don't know. Didn't feel it." Alerio stalked toward the
Senior Investigator, who lurched to his feet, his expression
panicky.

"Tell me when he lies," the Chief told his comp. Aloud
he asked Corydon, "Why did Frieka go after you, Corydon?"

"The same reason he attacked you," the human retorted,
cradling his broken arm. "Obviously he went mad."

"Obviously." Alerio gave him a slow and silky smile.
"Are you a Xeran agent, Corydon?"

The man's eyes widened and flickered in panic. "Of
course not! I'm a Senior Investigator with Counterintelli-
gence. How could you even make such an accusation?"

"Is he lying?"

"Negative."

"Wrong. He's lying like a rug. I can see it on his face."
Aloud the Chief said, "Outpost power system, code omega
sixty-eight fifty-four, Alerio authorization."

"Confirm code omega sixty-eight fifty-four?"

"Confirm code omega sixty-eight fifty-four."

Indicator lights began going dark around the room as the Outpost mainframe started shutting itself down.

"Deactivate your comps now, people," Alerio said.

Galar frowned, worry in his eyes. "You think the mainframe has been compromised?"

"Isn't it obvious?"

Galar sighed. "Considering that son of a bitch was lying like a rug and my comp said he wasn't—yeah, it's obvious."

"I most certainly am not lying! You are all leaping to conclusions." Corydon backed away as Alerio turned toward him. Sweat had broken out on his forehead, and he supported his broken arm with the other hand. "Doctor, give me something for pain, and I can clear this up."

Chogan gave him a toothy smile and twisted something on the tube of her injector. "I'd be happy to—except I've had to deactivate my injector's pharmcom. I don't dare inject drugs when the whole system's been infected with a virus."

The investigator's jaw dropped as he stared at her in horror. "This . . . You can't! This is a violation of my rights!"

Alerio gave him a vicious grin as Enforcers began surrounding the human like wolves. "Oh, I haven't even gotten started yet."

One minute Nick and Riane were standing in the cave. The next, a swirling green mist flooded in around them.

When it vanished, they found themselves surrounded by towering trees.

"Where the hell are we now?" Nick demanded.

"My comp says Earth. Twenty-first century." Riane looked around them, frowning. "More or less exactly when we left, except we're about two hundred miles to the north and west of our motel. Huh."

He rolled his shoulders at the nagging sensation he had somewhere to be. "What?"

"This is close to the area where the Outpost was."

"Was?"

"Yeah, the Outpost was located in these mountains in the fifteenth century. Not here now, though. Population density probably got too high."

"But you're from the future."

"Yeah, but the Outpost is located in the past. It's a central point. Easier to Jump through time from there."

"If you say so." Nick shook his head. "This time-travel stuff confuses the hell out of me."

"Join the club."

The Stone picked that moment to hit him with an unpleasant jolt of heat. Prodded, Nick started in the direction of the psychic tug. "Come on. We've got somewhere to be."

"Great," Riane grumbled, trailing him. "Now what?"

"Got no idea. But it's important."

"Somebody in danger?"

"Yeah. And I think it's us."

Riane and Nick moved quickly through the woods, leaves crackling and rustling underfoot. "At least your wounds healed," she observed.

He grunted, lengthening his stride. Before he quite knew what he was doing, he was running, spurred on by the sense of urgency clawing at the back of his brain.

Riane ran easily alongside of him. "People up ahead." She hesitated. "Or something."

She was right. He could hear the sound of a steady chopping in the distance, then a ringing bang, as of a hammer striking something metallic.

His imagination began to spin scenarios, each more grim than the last. An axe murderer attacking a Boy Scout camp? What the hell could be going on out here in the middle of nowhere?

Riane slid to a stop, yelling something, he didn't quite hear what, just as the ground dropped out from under his feet. Nick plunged twenty feet straight down.

He landed in a crouch, the Stone snapping sparks as it absorbed the force of his fall.

"I said," Riane called from somewhere above him, "look out for the drop!"

"Thanks," he growled.

Nick glanced around warily. He seemed to have landed squarely in the middle of an RV park, though what it was doing out here miles from any visible road was a very good question. About thirty of the vehicles were parked under the trees, ranging from camper trailers to things the approximate length of yachts. Campfires crackled merrily between them, surrounded by various people of assorted ages.

Laughter and conversation died as they turned to stare at him. They were a thoroughly ordinary crowd, garbed in T-shirts and jeans or shorts on this pleasant spring day. They all seemed to be involved in some kind of arts or crafts. One man used a hammer and chisel on a half-completed wooden sculpture. A woman looked up from massaging a lump of clay on a potter's wheel. Several others worked at easels or looms, while a metalworker hovered over the anvil on which she'd been hammering something.

Yet each and every one of them stopped what he or she was doing to start toward Nick, expressions of fascination on their faces. A rising murmur ran over the group, something in a language he didn't understand. It sounded a lot like astonished delight.

"Nick," Riane said suddenly, her voice urgent as she scrambled down the cliff to join him. "I don't think they're what they appear to be."

Right on cue, his vision wavered, misted, as if from a fading dream. Nick blinked hard, then took a startled step back.

Instead of a group of humans, the clearing was filled with Sela.

· 27 ·

For a moment Nick tensed, until he realized these Sela were the soft, furry pacifistic variety, not the psychopathic six-legged tiger kind.

Thank you, Jesus.

They gathered around him in a fluffy herd, their eyes wide as they gazed up at him, their round mouths a little open, in a way that gave the impression of stunned wonder. Small, oddly jointed hands began touching him, brushing his arms, his chest, his blue-jeaned legs. Nick tensed again, and they instantly stopped. One of them made an inquiring sound.

"Riane, what's going on?" His voice sounded hoarse to his own ears.

"Not sure." Riane swept a cautious gaze over the crowd. "I don't think they're hostile, though."

"Of course not," a female voice said tartly. "They're Sela. They couldn't be hostile if they tried."

A woman about his own age strode into the group of

Sela, who parted for her, murmuring soft comments in that
fluting alien language of theirs.

Nick recognized her instantly. Every molecule of air
rushed out of his lungs, and he choked.

It was his mother.

But this time she was definitely no ghost. Dressed in
cropped jeans and a loose jean jacket over a T-shirt, she wore
her hair in a loose, attractive style around her face. A face
that was much, much younger than he remembered. No,
this woman wasn't his mother.

Not yet anyway.

Warrior Priest Gyor ge Tityus knelt beside the priests of
his cohort, eyes lowered before the Victor's rage. He knew
he'd be most fortunate if his god did not slay them all for
their failure in letting the Demon and his whore escape.

"I had them!" The Victor paced, the cheap carpeting of
the motel room scorching under His feet. "Who dared
snatch My prey from Me? Now they go leaping through
time, and it will take Me days to track them . . ." His thunderous voice trailed off.

Gyor dared a quick glance upward, tensing at his own
daring.

To his vast relief, a slow smile spread across the god's
golden face. "No," the Victor breathed. "I still sense the
signal from the nanobot bead. They have remained in this
time after all! Ha!" His black eyes widened, incredulous.
"And there are *Sela* with them!"

He wheeled toward the cohort, glowing incandescent
in His ferocious triumph. "My plan succeeded after all.
The Demon has led Us to Our prize!"

"Just as You predicted," Gyor said carefully. "Their destruction is inevitable."

"Oh, indeed." The Victor was all but dancing in His joy.

"Let Us return to the Fortress and gather Our forces. This night we kill them all!"

"Riane," **Charlotte said,** giving her a civil nod, before turning to look Nick over as if he was a complete stranger. Which to her, he was. "Our friends say you're the Guardian," she told him, "though nobody can figure out how the hell you came to be human."

Nick shot a quick look at Riane, completely at a loss. She shrugged, apparently having no more idea of how to deal with the situation than he did.

I've just met my own mother before I was born. Can my life possibly get any weirder?

Charlotte studied Nick with a detached interest he found a little disturbing coming from his own mother. "We sensed you were in the area, but when you made no effort to contact us, we figured you must have your reasons."

"Yeah, as in I didn't know what the hell was going on," Nick told her carefully. "And I'm still not sure. What do you mean by 'Guardian'?"

"You do not remember anything," one of the Sela said in a soft, musical voice, its enormous eyes studying his face. "You have not recovered any of your memories of your life before'?"

"So I *am* a reincarnated Sela?" Instinctively, he turned toward his mother.

"Reincarnated?" Charlotte frowned thoughtfully. "Not in the human sense. You have inherited that part of the Guardian spirit that passed on."

"We have no clue what you're talking about," Riane told her. "What's this Guardian you're talking about?"

"The colony's protective spirit. He's the only Sela among this particular group who retained the ability to fight without going mad." Charlotte frowned and rocked back on her heels, propping her hands on her hips. "That probably doesn't make sense to you, if you don't know anything about us. Billions of years ago—"

"We've already heard that part," Nick interrupted. "About this Guardian—I think I met him."

"Met *him*?" the English-speaking Sela asked.

"Yeah," Riane told it drily. "He tried to kill us."

"That must have been a vision." Charlotte nibbled thoughtfully on one long red nail. She'd never had long nails when he'd known her . . . *Of course not. They wouldn't have survived her first fight.*

"Seemed pretty damned real to me," Nick said. "And I had the wounds to prove it. At least until they healed."

Charlotte tilted her head thoughtfully. "In that case, you must have encountered the Guardian within the T'Lir itself, because the spirit has no physical being."

He snorted. "I repeat—seemed pretty damned real to me."

"Well, it would. Otherwise the test would not have worked."

Riane raked her fingers through her hair absently, eyeing Charlotte and her furry friends. They stared back at her with annoying placidity. "What's this obsession you people have with tests?"

"How else would we teach you anything?" The Sela gave her an expression that looked astonishingly like a grin.

Riane glowered at her. And it was definitely a "her," because in comparison to her fellow Sela, she was either very fat or very pregnant. "Are you with child?"

"Oh, yes. And we've met, by the way. I am Vanja, and my baby is the heir of Ethini's spirit."

No wonder Riane didn't recognize her. The last time she'd seen her, she'd looked like a matronly fifty-year-old.

"Who's Ethini?" Nick asked.

"My dearest friend. One of the Xerans killed her two weeks ago." Vanja sighed, then turned to Charlotte. "Speaking of the Xerans—"

"I will attend to it." She turned away, gesturing at Riane and Nick to follow. "Come on, you two."

"What?" Nick demanded, striding after her. He didn't like the resignation in her tone one bit.

"A Xeran strike force is on the way here to steal our T'Lir and wipe us all out."

Nick and Riane stopped in their tracks and stared at her back. She calmly kept walking.

"Then why in the hell," he exploded when the shock faded, "are we sitting here waiting for them? Let's get out of here!"

His mother shrugged. "What happens, happens. Your friend could tell you that."

"She's right," Riane told him with a resigned shake of her head. "They probably couldn't avoid it now if they tried."

Nick would never understand these people in a hundred years. He hurried after Charlotte, who turned to wait for them in the shade of a camper trailer's overhang. "Yeah, well, obviously *you're* going to survive," he told Charlotte, "but what about the Sela?"

Charlotte—the entirely too young Charlotte—searched his face. "How do you know I'm going to survive? Vanja said she had a vision, but she refused to tell me the details."

Nick opened his mouth—*because I'm here*—and then carefully shut it again. Should he tell her?

"Because he's here," Riane said calmly, crossing her arms and watching the other woman closely. "And he wouldn't be if you died."

He stared. "Were we supposed to tell her that?"

"Obviously, since I just did."

"I thought you were the one who was so paranoid about affecting the time stream."

"No, I'm paranoid about leaving twenty-third-century tech lying around in the past because it's fucking *illegal*."

Charlotte was staring at him. She'd just gone pale as milk. "You . . . You're my *son*? They didn't tell me—" She broke off, grimacing. "But of course, they wouldn't."

Nick sighed. He might as well spill the whole thing. "I was born in 1979. You raised me alone. I didn't even know about the Sela until the last couple of days. Hell, I didn't even know I was half-Xeran. Why didn't you tell me, dammit?"

"*That* would be why," Riane said drily. "You just told her she didn't tell you."

Oh. He rubbed his forehead, suspecting a headache was on the way. "But what if I *hadn't* told her?"

"But you did."

"But . . . Hell. Never mind. The important thing is, what are we supposed to do about the freaking Xerans?"

"Ulir has bought us some time," Charlotte told him absently, her expression abstracted. She was obviously struggling with her own set of realizations. "The strike team would have already arrived, except he managed to bend their warp field so it will deposit them five hours from now."

Which would give the Sela plenty of time to leave, if they weren't so damned stubborn. Or fatalistic. Or whatever the hell they were. "So what are we supposed to do with those five hours? Since we're not going to do the intelligent thing and run like hell?"

Charlotte didn't answer. Instead, she stared into his face, obviously fascinated, examining him as if looking for traces she recognized.

"Charlotte?" Riane prompted gently.

"Oh." The woman started, then cleared her throat and turned to Riane. "As I said, Vanja had a vision about this. She said you're going to need the ability to use the T'Lir."

"Me?" Riane stared at her.

"You."

"And you're going to teach me that nifty little trick in the next five hours?"

"Not . . . exactly. Simply attempting to teach you those techniques wouldn't work. You'd need the cerebral structures to wield that kind of power. That's why I had to give Jessica some of my blood. The blood altered her genetic code and grew new connections within her brain."

"Blood doesn't do that," Nick objected, rubbing at the knot of tension growing between his brows. His headache was definitely getting worse. "In fact, if you get the wrong type of blood, it can kill you."

"It wasn't that much blood. And at any rate, the blood was simply a matrix to transfer the DNA changes."

"But it took days for Jessica's brain to make those alterations," Riane pointed out. "We've only got a few hours."

"The T'Lir can accelerate the process." Concern lit her eyes. "Though I've got to warn you, it won't be much fun for you."

"Neither is getting my ass kicked by Xeran fanatics. Speaking of whom, how many Xerans are we talking about anyway?"

"Doesn't matter," Nick growled. "Considering that only the three of us can fight, we're going to be seriously outnumbered anyway."

Riane sighed. "Which means I've definitely got to have any powers I can get. Okay, let's do it, Charlotte."

"Me?" She held up both hands as if to ward the other woman off. "Sorry, you're beyond my pay grade at the moment."

"And Jess wasn't?"

"The Sela gave me the ability to change Jess." Charlotte jerked a thumb at Nick. "*He's* the one who has to change *you.*"

· 28 ·

"Wait a minute." Nick crossed his arms and glow- ered at Charlotte, utterly confused. "You're saying I've got to give Riane some kind of blood transfusion?"

His mother shook her head. "No blood exchange is necessary. You're the Guardian. You can simply create whatever cell structures she needs."

He dropped his arms and recoiled. "I don't think so. I have no idea how to do that. I know nothing about the human brain, much less whatever the hell hers is, with all that genetic engineering and computer stuff."

Riane grinned at him. "Computer stuff?"

"Oh, shut up," he snapped, thoroughly annoyed. "You're not seriously contemplating this, are you?"

Riane hesitated, considering the question, then shook her head. "Am I happy about it? Hell, no. But I've seen enough of these guys to know if they say to do something, you need to do it."

Nick rubbed his knuckles along his jaw, eyeing her.

"Aren't you the one who went batshit when I suggested a simple mind link? Now they want me to do things to your brain, and you're okay with that?"

"Yeah, I know." She stepped over to him and rested her hands on his chest as she looked up into his eyes. "Look, I've been watching you deal with some weird shit in the last couple of days. And if it's weird by my standards, it should thoroughly freak out a man from the twenty-first century. But somehow, you've handled it all."

"Haven't you noticed? I *am* freaked."

"Well, yeah." She smiled. "But you also manage to do whatever you need to do. Fight Her-Gla mercenaries, pass bloody tests conducted by nightmare Sela primitives, stick a knife through a Tevan's combat armor. Whatever it is, you pull it off, every single time."

"Yeah, but we're talking about your *brain*."

"Nick, I trust you. Guardian, half-breed Xeran, twenty-first-century human. Whatever you are, whatever you have to do, you always deliver."

"You're in love with him." Charlotte flushed as they turned to blink at her in surprise. She lifted her chin, almost defiantly. "That's a good thing for a woman to know about her future son. That somebody will love him."

"I'm not . . ." Riane began, only to stop, a stunned look on her face. She pivoted to stare at Nick.

He stared back, feeling his jaw drop. He swallowed. "I . . . still don't know what I'm supposed to do. About the brain thing, I mean." *Lame, Nick. Really lame.*

But what the hell was he supposed to say? *I love you, too*? Because he did. Maybe he'd loved her since he was fourteen years old. The idea of her, if nothing else.

And now that he really knew her, had fought beside her, made love to her . . .

Oh, yeah. He was so gone.

Too bad she wouldn't stay. And with him being this

"Guardian" of the Sela—who, God knew, needed a Guardian, especially with the Xerans dedicating themselves to wiping them out—well, he couldn't exactly go haring off to the future after her.

Which made him basically fucked.

"I can show you what to do." Charlotte paused, her lips twitching in amusement. "I mean, about the brain thing."

Implication being that the issue of his love life was, all too obviously, as beyond her as it was him. *Thanks, Ma.*

"Great," he said with a sigh. "Show me what to do."

"I . . . think this is the kind of thing that needs a little more privacy. In here, you two." She climbed the steps to the camper trailer. The flimsy metal stairs creaked underfoot as she pushed open the door and stepped inside.

Nick followed, thinking it was going to be cramped with the three of them in that one half-rusted little camper . . .

But the minute he stepped through the doorway, he realized it could hold not only all three of them, but the entire lineup of the Carolina Panthers. The interior was huge, an airy, echoing space, all white curving walls that looked almost organic.

At one end lay a sprawling bed covered in a bright red spread and a tumble of sunny yellow pillows. A table stood beside an immense window that took up most of one wall, showing a view of the green spring woods beyond.

There wasn't a straight line to be seen. Everything seemed to grow organically out of the floor—tables, chairs, even the sprawling, overstuffed cream couch.

"Is this some kind of illusion?" Riane demanded. Glancing over, Nick saw she looked as bewildered as he felt. "Or was the exterior the illusion?"

"Oh, no," Charlotte told them. "This is my part of the ship."

Nick stared at her. "What ship?"

"The spaceship the Sela arrived in."

"All those boxy vehicles are part of your ship?" Riane began to circle the enormous room, running her fingertips along the table and the backs of chairs.

"Basically." Charlotte nodded, though she was gazing at Nick again.

Riane turned to her. "So the RVs are not really separate? They just look like it?"

"Oh, they're separate. They all contain parts of the ship."

"I've seen mathematical theories that it's possible to create folded spaces like this, but nobody's actually figured out how to do it." Riane sat down on the couch and stretched her long legs out in front of her. "This is amazing."

"And the Victor would kill for the knowledge of how to do it, too. If He obtains it, or the other knowledge of the Sela . . . the Galactic Union will fall." Charlotte tucked her hands into the back pockets of her pants, her expression brooding. "You have no idea what life would be like under a Xeran theocracy. I do. I grew up on that planet. My father taught me the Victor was God—mostly by beating belief into me. It was . . . hell."

"My grandfather abused you?" Torn between horror at the idea and fascination at learning more about his mysterious mother, Nick moved closer.

"Oh, yes. It was his duty, you see. Women are weak. Unworthy." Her smile was bitter.

Riane snorted and laced her fingers behind her head. "Any culture which throws away half its intelligence pool deserves exactly what it gets. No wonder Vardon kicked their asses."

"Don't underestimate the Victor, Riane. He is powerful, and He holds a grudge. If He gets his hands on the T'Lir . . ." She spread her hands. "Vardon will be His first target. You may count on it."

"Yeah, I figured." Riane's expression turned brooding. "That's one reason I'm willing to do this."

"And since there is not much time, I should let you get to it." Charlotte crossed to Nick and took his face between her hands. Mystified, he allowed her to pull his head down. Her mouth touched his forehead for a soft, maternal kiss.

He sucked in a breath as complex and alien knowledge swirled into his mind. Suddenly he knew exactly what he needed to know to make the changes he had to make. He could see the brain structure in his mind, vivid as a memory. It was so clear, so obvious.

But just as powerful as that knowledge was the realization that his mother was touching him for the first time since he was fourteen.

Abruptly this surreal experience became painfully real, and Nick caught her shoulders, instinctively trying to prolong the contact.

Charlotte looked up at him, surprised. He felt his eyes sting.

Green eyes, so similar to his own, widened. "I'm dead in your time, aren't I?"

He winced. "Mom . . . Charlotte . . ."

She closed her eyes, her face going still and grim. "I suspected as much. The expression on your face when you saw me the first time . . . You looked like you were seeing a ghost."

"I love you." There was so much he'd wanted to say to her. All those words seemed to pile up on his tongue now, choking him. He forced them out anyway. "You were . . . You *will be* an amazing mother. You taught me everything I needed to know about courage, about love. About protecting the helpless. The man I am I became because of you." Running down, he added lamely, "I just wanted to tell you that."

Charlotte rested her forehead against his. "Thank you. I am honored."

Before he could say anything more, she broke away from him and hurried to the door. He opened his mouth to call her back, but she had already slipped out and closed the door behind her.

"Fuck," Nick muttered, suddenly furious with himself. "I shouldn't have told her that she's going to die. What a moron!"

Riane rose from the couch and walked over to drape one arm around his waist. "Everybody dies, babe. And the other things you told her were a hell of a lot more important." She gently urged him around to face her. "I need to have one of those conversations with my mother."

"You aren't close?"

"Oh, we're extremely close." Riane's expression turned thoughtful, and she shook her head. "Thing is, I tend to obsess over my father. What he thinks, what he's done. But my mother has been every bit as important in shaping me, and I've never really told her that." She forced a smile. "But we've got other fish to fry right now. Let's go get started."

"Uh. Sure." Looking down into her rich chocolate eyes, Nick hoped his utter terror didn't show on his face.

It was one thing to know what to do. It was another to actually do it.

· 29 ·

Nick's green eyes were enormous with an expression of pure panic Riane had never seen in them before. Despite her own carefully hidden fear, she found herself smiling. "You know what your problem is?"

His lips twitched. "I don't know what the fuck I'm doing?"

"No." She took his hand and towed him toward the couch. "You're thinking too much. When it comes to the Stone, you do your best work when there's not a thought in your head."

"Gee, thanks."

She dropped onto the couch, and pulled him down beside her. "Look, they said the Guardian lives inside of you, right? I've noticed that whenever you're pissed off or worried about saving my ass, that's when you cut loose."

"Well, yeah. Because I'm pissed off or worried about you."

"No, because you quit thinking so damned much, and

you give the Guardian room to work." Riane threaded one hand in his silken hair and pulled him in for a kiss. "So we need to give the Guardian room to work."

She put everything she had into that kiss, first sipping delicately at the warm velvet of his lips, then sliding her tongue into his mouth in slow, suggestive thrusts.

He felt stiff against her at first—and not in a good way—still too damned conscious of the challenge ahead.

So Riane began tracing the tips of her fingers along his cheeks, following the jut of bone, the strong angle of his jaw, the cleft of his chin. And all the while, she kissed him, slow licks and tender thrusts of the tongue, mixed with gentle bites. All designed to seduce. "Let go," she whispered against his mouth. "Let the power roll. Let it come."

A spark leaped from his lips to hers, bright, hot, carrying a psychic snap that made them both jump.

"Yeah," Riane purred. "Oh, yeah. That's right. More."

Nick pulled back a fraction. His irises had gone a gently glowing green. It spooked her a little, so she fisted her hand in his hair and pulled him in again, kissing, tasting.

His lips felt feverish. Another spark jumped into her mouth with a sharp pop, but it didn't hurt this time.

It felt good.

A sweet tingle ran up her spine and into the base of her brain. And back down again, bringing every sensual nerve in her body to life.

Nick cupped her head in big hands so warm they almost burned. Heat that wasn't really heat spread through her like the blaze of passion growing between them. Minutes spun by as he kissed her, endless and glittering. Riane felt lost in the rise of passion, in the slow thrust of his tongue and the roll of his hips.

"Warning!" her comp squawked suddenly. *"Unusual cellular activity occurring in areas of the brain that should not be experiencing—"*

"Comp, deactivate," Riane interrupted.

"This is not advised given the current—"

"Comp, obey command."

It produced a strange, high-pitched yelp and went silent. Leaving her blessedly alone with Nick. Nick, who drew away from her, breathing hard, his hands stroking her breasts through the fabric of her shirt.

His eyes were a solid sheet of green from corner to corner. Even the whites were gone.

Riane closed her eyes as he kissed her again. Sparks seemed to flood her mouth with every slow lick and kiss. She squirmed at the surging heat spiraling up her spine.

Nick slipped a hand beneath her shirt, found her breast. His fingers were still burning hot, yet they felt good to her. Urging her back on the couch, he settled on top of her, kissing his way down the pulse of her throat.

Riane opened dazed eyes. A rose bloomed, floating in midair just past his shoulder. She blinked, and it was gone. She inhaled sharply. The scent of roses was so vivid, she instinctively looked around for them.

But there was nothing there.

Long fingers plucked, stroked the nipple that peaked hard for his attention. Nick swept her shirt up and pulled one lacy cup of her bra down. Riane sighed, her head swimming, and let herself float on a river of sensation and swirling light.

Power rolled through Nick in intoxicating waves that surged into his hands and out through his burning fingertips.

He could feel Riane changing under him. Feel the Power of the Stone respond to her, sending sparks dancing around them as if caught in a strong wind.

And he could feel *her*. The core of her, hot and strong and deliciously female. He could sense her love of him, delicate and blooming bright in her most secret heart, half-denied even to herself. She might consider that love doomed—hell, he did, too—but that did not make it any less real.

And deep inside her, he also sensed the furtive dream of finding a way to be with him. Somehow, despite the Sela and the Xerans and the Enforcers. Despite everything working against them.

Feeling half-drunk, Nick suckled her sweet breasts, wanting to give her the same pleasure she gave him just by loving him. He reached down, unsnapped and unzipped her pants, slid a palm between her thighs.

Wet. So very wet. He moaned against her mouth, eager as she surged under him. He slid a finger inside her, and she threw her head back. Red hair danced and shifted around her face like gleaming silk. "Nick!"

"Yeah. God, yeah!" He had to be inside her. Now, with power leaping around them like an electrical storm, wild and crackling.

He stripped her pants down her thighs, then was forced to stop and fumble with those damn clunky boots of hers.

Riane whimpered and tugged at his shirt, her usually graceful hands oddly uncoordinated. "Naked." It was a demand, even if only half-coherent.

Nick grinned at her and pulled off his shirt and jeans, pausing only long enough to toe off his running shoes.

She still wore her top and bra, though both were pulled up to bare those beautiful breasts. He didn't bother with undressing her further.

Riane reached for him, her eyes glowing green, mixed with sparks of hot Warfem red. He went into her arms like coming home, settled over her as she wrapped her legs around his hips. They both sang moans as he drove deep.

Light swirled around them as they strained against each other, power rising with every delicious thrust. Riane answered each strong dig of his cock with a liquid pulse of her sex, so seductively tight it was all he could do to hold on.

Wet. Sweet God, she was wet, and tighter than anything he'd ever felt. Groaning in his ear, plunging up against him, meeting his strength with her own. Her nails dug into his back, and her heels ground against his ass, spurring him on. Maddened, he plunged and plunged and plunged.

She arched under him with a yowl, and came in long, rippling contractions that sucked and pulled at him in silent, luscious demand.

Nick shouted, and released his own desperate hold on control. As he came, green comets exploded through the room, lighting up everything, spilling showers of sparks.

"Jesus," he muttered, gazing around them in wonder. "That never happened before."

Then he realized they were floating a foot above the couch.

"Shit," he muttered.

They started to fall. Nick caught them in mid-drop—he didn't want the entire weight of his body stabbing his cock into Riane. He lowered them more carefully, until her back and his knees settled into the couch cushions again.

"As quickies went," Nick said, lifting his head to grin down into her face, "that one was really . . ."

He stopped. Riane's eyes were open, her lips parted. He had the chilling impression she wasn't aware of him at all. "Riane?"

She made no answer.

Quickly, he pulled free of her body, grabbed her, and sat back down on the couch, pulling her across his lap. She was as limp as a rag doll. "Riane, wake up!"

"Frieka," she moaned. "Frieka needs me. He's gone wolf. Deactivated. Corydon . . ."

Ice crept the length of Nick's spine. "Frieka's not here, Riane. We're at the Sela's encampment, remember?"

"Hunting the thief." Her head rolled back and forth against his shoulders. "He's hunting the thief."

"Holy shit." Nick laid her down on the couch, grabbed his jeans, and dragged them on.

He started to race for the door, then stopped short, realizing Riane looked a little too obviously like he'd just banged her brains out. He turned back long enough to pull her bra and shirt into place, then horsed her jeans back onto those long legs. She fought him weakly, moaning about her wolf.

"Mother!" he shouted, adding a telepathic bellow for good measure.

"The Victor," Riane whimpered. "He's infected the Outpost. Infected my hair."

Shit. She was completely off her head. "There's nothing wrong with your hair, baby."

"Bugs in my hair." Riane reached up and began to yank at her braid, so hard he knew it had to hurt.

He grabbed her wrist. "Riane, don't do that, honey."

"Nick?" Charlotte hurried in, followed by a large Sela with sable brown fur. "What's wrong?"

He sighed in relief at the sight of them. Hopefully they'd know what to do. "She's hallucinating! What's wrong with her?"

"Yeo?" Charlotte nodded at the Sela, who started forward. "This is Yeo. He's a healer."

"But does he know anything about humans?"

"I know whatever I need to know." The Sela padded over to the couch and reared to examine Riane with those long, inhuman fingers. He—she? it? Nick couldn't tell gender with these people—made a humming sound of satisfaction. "The new neural complex is coming in nicely. Very fast growth, too."

"Frieka!" Riane shouted in alarm. "Don't hurt the Chief!"

"I don't care about the neural complex!" Nick snarled,

tightening his grip on her as she batted weakly at the air. "Why is she off her head?"

"Oh, she's not. Her powers are just coming in. Because the growth is occurring so rapidly, she's more conscious of her visions than her immediate surroundings."

"Traitor," Riane muttered. "Fucking Temporal Enforcement sent us a traitor to investigate treason. Fox in the henhouse. Dickholes."

"Is she going to be all right?" Nick demanded.

Yeo looked up at him with huge, kind eyes and patted his knee. "She'll be fine."

"Will she be finished with the transition by the time the Xerans arrive?" Charlotte asked.

The Sela cocked its head, considering Riane's anguished face. "Now that, I can't tell you. It will be very close."

"Can you speed the process?" Charlotte demanded.

"I don't think so." Nick glowered and gathered Riane closer protectively. "This is rough enough on her as it is."

"It'll be rougher if the Xerans arrive and she's helpless," Charlotte growled back. "We need her in good enough shape to fight. The three of us are outnumbered as it is."

He winced. "Good point."

"But irrelevant, because there is no way to make the process any faster," Yeo told them. "Call me if she takes a turn for the worse." The healer dropped to the floor again and turned to go.

Nick seriously considered grabbing him by the scruff to stop him. "Wait a minute. Where are you going?"

Yeo shot him a look that strongly resembled amusement. "You don't need me, boy. And we must make preparations for our guests."

"What guests?"

"He's talking about the Xerans." Charlotte rested a comforting hand on his shoulder. "Calm down, son. Sit and talk to me."

She aimed a look at the floor nearby. A second couch sprang up, reminding him of a time-lapse image of a mushroom growing after a spring rain. Settling down on the couch, she cocked her head and studied him. "You do love your pretty Warfem a great deal. Don't you?"

"There's a lot to love," Nick told her absently, watching Riane mutter and jerk in his arms. Sparks flashed around her, reacting to her growing power. "Besides, she reminds me of you. Strong. Principled." He smiled slightly. "Stubborn as hell." Glancing up, he found Charlotte staring at him in utter fascination. "What?"

"It's just . . . I never expected to have children. Not after . . ." She waved a hand around at their surroundings, indicating her involvement with the Sela. "I didn't think I'd be any good at it. Xerans don't exactly value kids, other than as future warriors, mothers of warriors, and servants of the Victor."

"Sounds like a pretty dysfunctional culture."

"You have no idea."

"He's mad," Riane whispered. "Powerful and mad. Coming here. No!" Her head jerked back and forth, hair sliding across Nick's arms.

Charlotte's lips took on a bitter twist. "Sounds like she's talking about the Victor."

"He really is crazy?"

"Oh, yes. Even the Xerans know it. But as Riane said, He's also really powerful, and nobody wants to piss Him off."

Absently stroking Riane's hair, Nick studied his mother. "What if we killed Him?"

"Nobody would be happier than the Xerans. Of course, the whole flipping culture would plunge into chaos as competing factions tried to take control." She considered whatever mental image that statement summoned before shaking her head regretfully. "Unfortunately, I'm not sure He can be killed."

"If He's alive, He can die."

"But that's what I'm saying. He's immortal. How can you kill an immortal?"

"That's got to be a myth," Nick protested. "Not even the Sela are immortal."

"True. No living thing is immortal." She shrugged. "But the Victor is not a living thing."

· 30 ·

Alerio opened his eyes and sat up on his bunk. For a moment, he just sat there, trying to get his bearings. His eyes felt gluey, and his mouth had a nasty aftertaste he associated with a long antivirus session. *"Computer, are you activated?"*

"Affirmative."

"Any sign of continuing unauthorized Trojan activity?"

"Negative. All systems are functioning properly."

He blew out a breath and fell back on his elbows in relief. It had taken him hours to identify and destroy the Trojan, but he'd finally succeeded. Now it was time to check on his fellow Enforcers. He'd ordered the agents to work in pairs, assigning one fourth of them to take the first shift while the second group watched over them. Then the first crew would watch over the second. After those two groups were back online, the third and fourth teams would alternate. It would be slow work, but this was not the kind of thing you could rush, not with an infection this massive and invasive.

He frowned, glancing around his cabin. Speaking of which, where the hell was Galar, who had been serving as his spotter? The Master Enforcer was nowhere around, though he'd been here when Alerio went under. *"Comp, contact Master Enforcer Galar Arvid."*

The comp's pause went on just a little too long. *"No response."*

Alerio's frown deepened. Galar would never have left him alone under these circumstances. Unless, that is, something had gone badly wrong while he was out.

He rolled off his bunk and moved through his quarters, conducting a fast but thorough search by eye and sensor. There was no sign of the big Warlord. Not that there were many places to hide in here.

Frowning darkly, Alerio moved for the door, keyed it open, and stepped outside. And froze in horror.

Galar lay sprawled on the deck just outside his door, his eyes staring sightlessly at the ceiling. Blood pooled around his body in a lake of red. His throat had been slashed.

"Galar!" Going cold with shock, Alerio dropped to one knee beside his friend and searched for the pulse that should beat beneath the agent's jaw. *"Dr. Chogan, man down outside my quarters!"*

Even as he made the call, he knew it was too late. Galar's body was cold. Chogan could do a great deal, but she couldn't bring back someone who had been dead that long.

"No response from the infirmary," his comp said.

What the hell?

"Activate all Enforcer emergency response teams," Alerio snapped. Something was badly wrong, and he damn well wanted to know what was going on. *"I want at least two teams down here, and two more to check the infirmary.*

Everyone else conduct a thorough deck-to-deck search of the Outpost, including the concourse and civilian Jump stations. I want a full status report on anything unusual."

The next pause was so long, there was ample time for a chill to start crawling up his spine. *"There is no response to the call."*

What the fuck was going on? *"Send evidence collection 'bots to this location."* There was nothing he could do for Galar now except find his killer. But his most immediate concern was the living members of the Outpost, both agents and civilians.

With a last apologetic glance at his friend—oh, hell, he was going to have to tell Jess her husband of two weeks had been murdered—Alerio rose and started down the corridor.

He found the next body lying in the corridor. Wulf was a short, massively powerful heavy-worlder who had always been more than a match for anything he encountered. Someone had stabbed him over and over again. His blood splashed the bulkheads, deck, and ceiling in a three-meter radius. He had obviously fought hard for his life.

And Alerio had failed him. Hadn't foreseen this. Hadn't prevented this.

By the time the Chief found the fourth mutilated body, he was running. He didn't even break step. If there was anyone left alive, it was his job to save whoever it was.

Too late for the rest.

He needed his weapons. His armor, his knives, a shard pistol at the very least.

Had to be Xerans. Had to find the sons of bitches. And kill them. He'd grieve once his enemies had paid for what they'd done.

Alerio charged into the armory, fury, grief, and guilt boiling inside him like a toxic stew.

Just inside the door, he slid to a stop as shock rolled over him like an ice-water bath.

Ivar Terje looked up at him from Dona Astryr's butchered body. The traitor was covered in blood. "I told you I'd kill her."

Alerio's scream of anguish rang in his own ears, tore at his throat . . .

Alerio opened his eyes and sat up on his bunk. For a moment, he just sat there, trying to get his bearings. His eyes felt gluey, and his mouth had a nasty aftertaste he associated with a long antivirus session. *"Computer, are you activated?"*

"Affirmative."

"Any sign of continuing unauthorized Trojan activity?"

"Negative. All systems are functioning properly."

Chief Alerio Dyami finally collapsed back in his restraints, his massive body going still, panting, his wide eyes staring blankly at the infirmary ceiling. At least he wasn't howling anymore. Those deep-throated bellows of horror had ripped at Dona's soul like a point-blank blast from a shard pistol.

His last shout had been her name. It had sounded like a death scream.

But even as he fell silent, Galar Arvid began to bellow his wife's name from the next bunk, fighting the field restraints that barely kept him from tearing his way free. Jessica hovered by his side, stroking his face in a desperate attempt to calm him. "I'm here, baby, I'm here," she chanted. "I'm fine. It's an illusion, baby . . ."

"Jess!" he roared. "Jess, no!"

Dona looked away, pain knifing her chest.

Ten more bunks filled the room, all occupied by the Outpost's senior officers. The agents muttered, swore, raged, then fell into a comatose stillness before beginning the process all over again.

Chogan hurried past, red medical robes flaring wide around her legs.

"Any luck?" Dona called desperately.

The doctor paused for a weary moment. She looked like hell, her mouth pinched in a white face, her eyes haunted with worry for her patients. "No, dammit. The nearest we can figure, these agents were able to debug their computers just like the rest of the Outpost, but that seems to have triggered some kind of secondary infection. I deactivated their comps, but it didn't even slow the thing down. Apparently whatever it is has somehow infected their brains, but my sensors can't even detect it. I have no fucking idea what we're dealing with."

"Sweet Goddess," Dona whispered.

"Yeah. That goddess of yours—you might want to do some praying to her." As if unable to stand still another moment, Chogan strode away again.

"I don't think I can take much more of this." Moving like a sleepwalker, Jess joined Dona beside Alerio's bed. She had picked up a cup of stimchai in shaking hands. The liquid had grown cold, judging by the lack of steam. "I feel like I'm about to start screaming. Why was everyone except the senior staff able to get rid of the Trojan? These are the most experienced agents on the Outpost—they should have been able to defeat this thing if anybody could."

"That's a really good question." Dona took the cup of stimchai away from Jess and dropped it into one of the bedside recyclers. "Why don't we go"—she peeled her lips back from her teeth—"*ask* the only guy who knows? I don't know about you, but I'm thoroughly sick of watching these men suffer."

Jess looked startled for a moment before an answering grin lit her face that was every bit as carnivorous as Dona's.

"Yeah, I have a couple of questions for Alex Corydon my-self."

Though after they finished with the traitor, he might be in no shape to talk to anybody else for a good long time.

"If the Victor's not a living thing, what the hell is He?" Nick demanded over Riane's low moans of distress. Strok-ing her hair, he tried to soothe her restless twisting. He felt sick, helpless. It was not a sensation he was used to—or liked one bit.

Charlotte spread her hands. "That's a difficult question. He . . ."

"Chief!" Riane suddenly rolled off the couch and sprinted for the door.

"Shit! Riane!" Nick bolted off the couch after her, but she was already through the door. He hit it right after her, leaping into the RV clearing.

The Sela glanced around at them in confusion, having evidently returned to their human guises. "Dammit," he roared, "somebody grab her!" They only blinked at him, standing frozen over their various artistic projects.

Actually, he supposed he couldn't blame them. Riane bounded along like a deer, and he suspected if any of the Sela had tried to stop her, she'd have plowed right over them.

Nick put his head down and lengthened his stride, des-perate to get to her before she disappeared into the woods.

Which was when two men stepped out of empty air and caught her, arresting her frantic flight. She yowled in fear and swung a wild fist, but one of them grabbed it.

Nick's instant relief turned to horror when he realized the men wore the black and red armor of the Xer. She screamed again, struggling against their armored hands, but she was too disoriented to fight with any effectiveness.

"Let her go!" Nick bellowed. The Stone flared hot green against his upper arm, spilling sparks around his feet.

"I think not." Another figure winked into view—naked, nine feet tall, and glowing golden, His bald head crowned with a set of horns that would have done a longhorn bull proud, a third spiral horn jutting between them. He snatched Riane from her captors as easily as if she were a toddler.

She howled and struggled, but His massive arms crushed tight around her, subduing her helpless writhing.

"Now," the Victor said over Riane's gleaming copper hair, "it seems each of us has something the other wants. Hand over the T'Lir . . . *now*. Otherwise . . ."

More Xerans popped into view, moving rapidly in among the Sela, quantum swords chiming. The Sela cowered away from them, fear and bewilderment plain on their illusionary human faces.

The so-called god grinned. ". . . Well, let's say things are apt to become quite bloody."

Dona and Jess strode toward the brig at a pace barely short of a run. "I hope that bastard knows something useful," Jess growled.

"Would the bastard in question be Corydon? Because if so, I want to help."

The two women looked around to see Frieka trotting after them. His vocalizer indicator lights flashed blue amid the thick black fur around his neck. Alerio had managed to debug the wolf's computer system before starting the disastrous work on his own.

"I'm not sure that's such a good idea, Fuzzy," Jess told him cautiously. "His guards—"

"Aren't any more crazy about this situation than we are," Dona interrupted. "Besides, having been on the receiving end of Frieka's teeth, I'll bet Corydon would find them a very effective threat."

"Good point."

"I've always thought so." Frieka bared the fangs in question. "Just tell me what part of him you want me to bite first. Speaking of which, what *is* the plan?"

Dona veered down the corridor that led to the brig. "We're going to make the fucker talk."

"Simple, ruthless, and effective, considering how gutless the little weasel is. I like it."

"I do try."

"Which is one of the things I like about you. How are the Chief and Galar?"

"Still raving."

"Galar keeps remembering having to shoot that bitch ex-lover of his, the one who tried to kill him years ago." A fine muscle worked in Jess's delicate jaw as she stared down the corridor with bitter eyes. "But when she falls dead, her face turns into mine. He keeps seeing that over and over in an endless nightmare loop."

"How do you know that?" The wolf cocked his dark head up at her as he trotted along by her side.

"I see the dream in his mind. He's a really strong broadcaster. The grief and guilt are driving him crazy. And I can't seem to punch through all that crap and convince him it's not real." Jess curled her lip in a snarl of rage. "We've *got* to make Corydon tell us what he did—and how to fix it."

· 31 ·

"You're right there," Frieka told Jess as the three of them strode toward the brig. "But fixing whatever Corydon's done is not going to be easy. I've encountered all kinds of viruses, Trojans, and assorted other ugly cyber attacks. This is the worst I've ever seen."

"Which brings up a really good point." Jess dropped her hand to his head to give him an absent ear scratch. "If Corydon is the computer illiterate you all say, how did he manage to infect Galar and Chief Dyami? Neither of them would be easy targets."

"Obviously, he got it from the Xerans," Frieka said. "They've always been light-years ahead of everybody else when it comes to crafting that kind of crap. As to the vector he used—well, we're just going to have to ask him."

They rounded the corner to see Wulf and Tonn Eso standing guard in front of one of the cells. The two Enforcers looked around at their approach, brows lifting.

"Any change?" Wulf asked, concern in his striking turquoise eyes.

"No," Dona said shortly. "Why don't you two take a break? Frieka and I will keep an eye on the prisoner."

Tonn and Wulf exchanged an uneasy glance. "I don't think that's such a good—"

"Don't you dare leave me with those two lunatics!" Corydon called through the repeller field. "And where's my lawyer? I have rights!"

Wulf turned to glare at him through the doorway. "Nobody is Jumping in or out of the Outpost until we're absolutely sure the cyber attacks you planted have been contained."

"You have no proof I planted a damn thing!"

"Except for your confession," Tonn rumbled. He was a big, jovial blond, broad and handsome, well known for his wicked sense of humor. He didn't look at all amused now.

"A false confession, coerced by your commanding officer. Who will be drummed out of the service by the time I'm through with him!"

All five of them glowered at the traitor. "You know, I feel the need for a big, steaming cup of stimchai that will take a long, *long* time to drink," Wulf told his partner. "How about you?"

"Just what I was thinking." Tonn looked down at Dona, Frieka, and Jess from his towering height. "You'll keep an eye on the prisoner while we're gone, right?"

Frieka bared his teeth. "Oh, we'd be delighted."

The Victor held Riane dangling three feet off the ground, one massive hand wrapped around her vulnerable throat. Her eyes rolled, staring around wildly at some vision only she could see. She didn't appear conscious of her real situation at all.

"Since when do gods hide behind a woman?" Nick growled, hoping his utter fear for her didn't show.

"Hide?" The Victor laughed, a thoroughly chilling sound. It had a metallic undertone, like a machine trying to imitate a human emotion it didn't feel. "I merely make your position clear to you, Demon. I hold all the advantages. You can either surrender—or watch us kill everyone here."

Nick threw a quick look around. The Xerans had methodically surrounded the Sela, quantum swords chiming a chilling note. He spotted Ivar among them—the cocky bastard had his visor up. Yet the big redhead's face was oddly expressionless, his eyes a little blank, as if nobody was home.

The Sela shrank away from the invaders, huddling together, fear and misery plain on their illusionary human faces.

How the fuck was Nick going to get out of this one without getting all those poor aliens slaughtered? Not to mention Riane and himself. Charlotte was the only one likely to make it out of this mess alive, and that only because she was fated to give birth to him. He figured she'd end up Jumping back to 1979 one bounce ahead of a Xeran hit squad.

"I think your lover's attention is slipping," the Victor purred in Riane's ear. She just hung there, obviously so far out of it she had no idea what was going on. "Perhaps we need to remedy that." His gaze locked on Nick's, He ran his tongue along her cheek in one long, slow, repulsive swipe.

"Very brave." *Dammit, Nick, think of something!* "Grabbing a disoriented woman and threatening a bunch of pacifists you know can't even fight back."

The Victor only grinned. "It's not my fault you let yourself be outflanked."

That lick had done something to Riane, and it wasn't

good. She'd looked worried before, obsessed with whatever she saw in her visions. Now all the blood slowly drained from her face, leaving her dead white, her dark eyes pools of horror. She began to struggle in the Victor's hold, but without her usual fighter's skill. Her voice spiraled into a scream. "Nick! Frieka!"

"That's the thing about cyborgs." The Victor slanted her a clinical look even as He controlled her frantic struggles with no effort whatsoever. "They have such exquisite control over their own bodies. But that wonderful neuronet is also the perfect means to control them. Someone like me can just slip down those pathways into their vulnerable brains and do all kinds of entertaining things." He turned that chilling black gaze on Nick. "I can kill her just as easily as I can torture her. Now, unless you enjoy listening to her howl, I suggest you stop stalling and turn over the T'Lir."

"You wouldn't dare let that creature attack me!" Corydon sidled away from Frieka as the wolf stalked him stifflegged across his cell.

"I wouldn't bet my ass on that if I were you," Dona drawled. Crossing her arms, she leaned against the wall next to Jess, who watched with silent intensity.

"If you touch me," he spat at the wolf, "I'll see you drummed out of the service! I am innocent of these charges, and I'm going to prove it!"

"That would be quite a trick," Frieka said, his lips rippling in a vicious snarl, "considering that once I cleaned your doctored recording, it plainly shows you using a code breaker to enter Riane's locker. Then you removed her T-suit and Jumped away with it. The next day, that same suit malfunctioned, stranding her in time. Even the stupidest jury will be able to connect the dots."

"Where'd you send her, Alex?" Dona asked in a deceptively conversational tone.

"Did you kill her, Corydon?" Frieka lunged forward with a savage snap of gleaming white fangs.

Corydon jumped back, his shoulders slapping against the bulkhead behind him, his eyes widening in panic. "No!"

"Then what did you do with her?" the wolf demanded, his ruff rising, his eyes icy blue slits.

"I did nothing!"

"He's lying," Jess said, her voice calm and deadly. "I can sense it."

Frieka snorted. "Hell, I can *smell* it. He reeks of lies." He took another step forward, until his nose almost touched Corydon's belly. The man shrank away, sidling backward along the wall. Frieka followed, his head low, his ears flat.

"She's safe!" Corydon gasped. "She's in the past and safe."

"Where in the past?" Dona fired back.

"Twenty-first century. There's a man there the Victor is obsessed with, in some little town in South Carolina. Millhouse or Mill Village or something. There was this police report. He'd saved some woman from being raped on . . ." He trailed off, as if it had belatedly occurred to him he was saying too much.

"*When?*" Frieka snarled.

"May 23, 2009!"

"What was his name?" Dona demanded, moving closer until she loomed over the shorter man.

"I don't rem—"

"*What was his name?*" Frieka's snarling muzzle was now barely a centimeter from Corydon's crotch. The wolf opened his jaws . . .

"Nick Wyatt!"

"What did you do to Galar and the others?" Jess asked in a low, deadly voice.

Corydon looked up, about to make a denial. He paled as he saw the unearthly green glow in the depths of her eyes. "Nothing!"

"You're lying again, Alex." Jess advanced on him, the glow brightening. "Don't bother. The Sela gave me psychic abilities, and I can sense every lie you think."

He curled a scornful lip, but fear gleamed in his eyes. "That's kakshit. Humans don't have psychic abilities."

"We used to think that," Frieka said. "But then, we also used to think you could change history. We were wrong, weren't we, Alex?"

Jess peeled her lips off her teeth. The green glow brightened to the intensity of a laser torch. *"What did you do to my husband?"*

Corydon's eyes widened until the whites showed all around them. "I had no choice! The Victor told me He'd kill me if I didn't follow instructions!"

Dona leaned a fist against the wall beside his head. "And what were those instructions, Alex?"

"Nanobot infections. He gave me patches with nanobots and a list of targets." Corydon licked his lips, sweat beading on his dark blue skin as he eyed Frieka, who rumbled in menace. "I just put the patch on my hand and then touched each target. The nanobots would invade whoever or whatever it was. First the mainframe, then senior officers. Didn't take much. A handshake was enough."

"Why did you choose Riane to strand in the past?" the wolf growled. "Was she on that Xeran list?"

"They weren't that specific. It just had to be someone who had met Charlotte and the Sela so she could point Nick in the right direction. I suggested . . ."

"You *suggested* Riane?" Frieka roared.

"Yes!" Corydon exploded, as if finally goaded into defiance. "You and that father of hers ruined my career! I shouldn't be toiling in some minor office after thirty years as an Enforcer! I should—"

"Be serving time in a penal colony on treason charges," Dona said coldly. "And I intend to make sure you end up precisely where you belong."

Riane struggled in the Victor's hold, her face twisted in grief, tears sliding down her cheeks. Her suffering seemed to tear bloody chunks from Nick's heart.

His first instinct was to use the Stone to drag her out of the illusion, but it was coldly obvious the Victor would start killing everyone if Nick turned his attention away long enough.

Handing the T'Lir over was no option at all. Nick was damned if he was going to give that kind of power to some Xeran lunatic who already thought He was a god.

Too, Charlotte's spirit was held within the Stone, along with those of all the dead Sela waiting to be reborn. He damn well wasn't going to leave them trapped at the Victor's mercy. The false "god" would destroy them all if He could figure out a way to do it.

Nick flicked his gaze around the clearing. Charlotte stared back at him across the huddling Sela, her expression cool, watchful. Obviously waiting for his signal to fight. Unfortunately, he counted a hundred Xeran priests in the clearing, plus the Victor. Those odds were ridiculous, even with the T'Lir.

Their only chance was to take all these bastards off-balance.

His claws! Hope rose as Nick remembered the energy weapons he'd created for his battle against the primitive Sela.

No. His heart sank again. Even that kind of weaponry wouldn't be enough. He needed something more.

Too bad that primitive Sela was an illusion created by the Stone. They could have used him . . .

He wasn't an illusion, Nick. Charlotte's voice rang in his mind. Startled, his gaze met hers across the crowd of Xeran warriors. *I told you before. You're the heir to the Guardian's spirit. He's you.*

· 32 ·

Nick sprawled in a twisted, bloody heap, his green eyes wide and glassy in death, his waxy face twisted in an expression of horror. Frieka lay next to him, his black fur matted with gore, pink ribbons of intestines spilling onto the deck.

The wolf's blue eyes rolled to look up at Riane as she crashed to her knees beside them. "Nick! Frieka!"

"We depended on you," the wolf said, the blue lights of his vocalizer flashing dimly, giving his computer-generated voice a deceptive steadiness. "You failed us. You left us to die. Not fast enough. Not strong enough. They were right—you're not the warrior your father was."

"I'm sorry, Frieka! I shouldn't have brought you with me." Tears stung her eyes as she touched the wolf's matted fur. Her gaze slipped to Nick's face, and pain shot through her. She wanted to howl.

Hand trembling, Riane reached toward Nick's bloody face. Dead. He was dead. And she was responsible . . .

He'd always believed in her. And she'd failed him.

"I always knew it would end like this." Frieka moaned. "You were a failure in the military, and you're a failure as an Enforcer. Now you've killed us both." The wolf's head dropped, his eyes going glassy. "Failure . . ." His computerized voice trailed away into a dying buzz.

Riane stared at the wolf, shocked. He'd never said anything like that in all the years she'd known him. Even when she'd screwed up as a child, he'd never attacked her self-confidence. In fact, the only time Frieka had ever really chewed her out was for doubting her own abilities.

He'd even given her Femmat commander a royal verbal reaming when Riane had resigned the service. *That girl is every bit the warrior her father is,* the wolf had snarled at the astonished woman, who looked as if no one had ever dared question her before. *If there's a problem, it's in your lack of leadership skills.*

"Riane . . ." It was her father's voice, choked, gasping in pain and anguish. "Mother Goddess, child, what have you done?"

She turned, numb as a sleepwalker. Baran stood in the Outpost corridor staring at them in horror.

Riane lifted a shaking hand in pleading. "I'm sorry, Father! I didn't mean . . ."

"You've always been a disappointment," Baran rasped, moving like a robot to tower over her. "But I had hoped for better than this. I never really believed you'd fail us so utterly. I trusted you not to get him killed. My dearest friend . . ."

Riane looked from her father's devastated face to Nick's death-glazed green eyes. *Why can't I remember how they died? If I got them killed, why can't I remember what I did?*

Realization slashed through the stew of guilt and

dazed grief. *My father would never call me a failure, even if I had gotten Frieka killed. He has always believed in me.*

Like Nick. Nick, with his steadfast faith. A powerful and intelligent man who had no need to believe in her. Yet he did. And loved her.

He wouldn't have believed in a failure.

Riane stared up at the image of her father. And an image was all it was. *This isn't real. It's a cyber attack. Just like the illusions I saw tormenting the Chief and Galar.* "Get the fuck out of my head."

She raised her hands, and green light poured from her fingers with a thunderous boom, blasting the false Baran. He roared, a sound of anger more than pain, melting into a stinking black sludge that tried to ooze away like some kind of primitive amoeba. *Seven Hells, it's a mass of nanobots!*

This was no mere virus, no Trojan. Someone had infected her with nanobots, like the one her vision had revealed spying on her from her braid.

Fury rose through her stunned guilt and grief, washing away her sense of helplessness. Riane called more power, burning the sludge out of her mind with Nick's Stone.

Her vision flashed a blinding green. When it cleared, she was hanging in the air, something hot and choking wrapped around her throat. She was surrounded by Xerans armed with quantum swords. There had to be a hundred of them at least.

What was worse, they had hostages. A bunch of twenty-first-century civilians stood among them, looking frightened.

No, not civilians, she realized, recognizing some of the faces from their arrival in the RV park. It was the Sela.

Nick stared at her across the crowd, his face pale and

grim. A priest held a quantum sword centimeters from his throat. The energy blade chimed like a bell.

What the hell was holding her up in the air? She jerked her head around and met the Victor's mad black gaze.

Oh, Mother Goddess, Riane thought. *We're screwed.*

"I'm getting bored," the Victor said, glowing golden fingers tightening around Riane's throat. She gagged, her face darkening.

The chiming of the priests' swords picked up a menacing, urgent note that rang around the clearing. Huddling together like frightened children, the Sela looked around at them nervously.

Fuck, Nick thought. *I've just run out of time. Whatever I'm going to do, I've got to do it now.*

Riane had said it before, when he'd been panicking over the thought of trying to alter her brain: *They said the Guardian lives inside of you, right? I've noticed that whenever you're pissed off or worried about saving my ass, that's when you cut loose.*

Well, yeah. Because I'm pissed off or worried about you.

No, because you quit thinking so damned much, and you give the Guardian room to work.

Nick needed the Guardian now, in all its savagery and power. He remembered his battle with it, the size, the ferocity. And he remembered his own joy in the combat, in conquest, and in the taste of blood.

He'd felt that before.

It was the darkness in himself he'd always feared and worked to control. *That's him,* Nick realized. *That's the part of me that's him.*

"You've just run out of time," the Victor snapped, and

gestured to the Xeran standing next to him. "Gyor, kill that Sela."

The warrior pivoted, lifting his blade over the head of a hugely pregnant little blonde whose eyes widened in terror. Vanja, Nick realized. It was the Sela pregnant with her friend's spirit.

Nick acted between one desperate heartbeat and the next. He reached down, down to that dark part of himself that craved battle and blood and the death of those who hurt him. The part he'd worked so hard to hide, even from himself.

And he let it roar, detonating in an explosion of rage and power, ripping cells wide in a furious blast of booming green light.

He howled.

The Xeran who'd been about to swing on Vanja instead whirled toward him, startled at the explosion of energy.

A huge clawed paw lashed out, slamming against the priest's helmet. He smashed backward into several of his fellows, fell to the ground, and did not get up.

"Now," the Guardian growled, *"I will let thy blood."* He spoke in the Xeran priest tongue, a language Nick had never spoken.

But then, he was no longer Nick.

At first Riane thought Nick had Jumped, between the explosion of light and the thundering sonic boom of displacing air. But then the light had faded, and something huge stood where he'd been.

A Sela. It looked like the primitive version he'd fought, except it was at least twice as big, and it glowed a molten green. Its roar made the bones of her chest vibrate. Even the Xerans froze in terrified amazement.

That was a fatal mistake. The towering Sela leaped among the priests with a tiger's deadly grace. Warriors screamed like children.

The next slice of huge claws ripped through one Xeran's armor as if it were rice paper. Blood sprayed as the warrior howled and toppled, curling in agony around his torn belly.

Quantum swords chimed and flashed. Riane gasped, knowing those blades could slice right through combat armor.

They glanced off the Guardian's glowing hide as if it was harder than a starship's hull. The creature whirled and bit a priest's helmeted head right off his shoulders. The decapitated head went rolling as the Guardian leaped on a new target.

The Sela were screaming in high, helpless squeals.

"I think," the Victor said in her ear, "I've seen enough."

The world pinwheeled around Riane as He tossed her aside like a discarded doll. She hit the ground rolling. For a stunned moment, she simply lay there, unable to believe what she'd seen.

Get up, dammit. Banishing her astonished paralysis, she rolled to her feet, looking around desperately.

The Victor charged across the clearing toward the Guardian, massive arms outspread. The big Sela's roar of challenge made her blood run cold.

But Riane had problems of her own. One of the priests leaped at her with a bellow of rage, blade lifted, apparently intending to take his fear and fury out on her.

Luckily, when she saw Nick transform, she'd gone to *riaat.* Now Riane danced back and whipped into a kick, slamming the heel of her foot into the side of the warrior's head. Apparently expecting a helpless target, he lost his grip on his sword. She snatched it out of the air, braced, and used it to behead him in one ruthless sweep.

From the corner of one eye, Riane spotted another figure racing toward her. She wheeled, blade lifted to strike, only to arrest the stroke in mid-motion when she realized it was Charlotte.

"We've got to get the Sela out of here," the woman panted. "All this death—they can't take it. And if these priests quit trying to take down Nick and turn on them . . ."

Riane grimaced, knowing exactly what she meant. The Sela were mentally linked. When one died, the rest went into a howling grief that inflicted a ferocious psychic feedback on any unprotected human mind. The Xerans had invented a way to block the effect through their helmets, but Riane and Charlotte were unprotected.

Riane had taken the full brunt of one such psychic feedback attack a couple of weeks ago. She'd only been able to recover by ordering her comp to cut off all emotion so she could fight. But Charlotte didn't have a comp.

"The ship," Riane said. "Let's get them into one of the RVs. Is there a way to lock the Xerans out?"

Charlotte nodded. "Yeah, I can close the ship's dimensional bubble off once we've got them inside. Good idea."

"You get them moving. I'll cover your retreat." She frowned across the clearing. The Guardian blazed like a green star, surrounded by a cautious ring of Xeran warriors. He lunged toward one of them, a huge paw blurring. His target screamed in agony.

Spotting an opening, the Victor surged forward, striking out with clawed hands. The Guardian whirled and reared to meet Him. The two huge figures grappled as the watching warriors roared, surging around them with waving swords.

"Fuck," Riane breathed. No matter what he looked like now, Nick was in there somewhere. And he was badly outnumbered. She had to help him, but there was virtually nothing she could do alone.

Unless . . . She remembered how Nick had sent a vision three hundred years into the future to save her when she was a child. If she could do the same . . .

Drawing a deep breath, Riane reached for the Power of the Stone. It felt as if she plunged into a storm of violent emotion, of rage, savagery, and bloodlust.

Mother Goddess, is that Nick? Despite her dismay, she drove her will into that roiling cauldron of energy. If she could only reach Jessica with a vision . . .

The power did not respond.

Jess strode down the corridor beside Dona and Frieka as the three headed for the infirmary.

"I can't believe that little weasel has been slinking around the Outpost for two weeks now, leaving a slime trail of Xeran nanobots on everybody he touched," Dona growled.

"Which is why we could never clear the Trojan out of the Outpost mainframe." Frieka flicked an ear in disgust. "Each time we got rid of it, the nanobots would reinfect the system and keep us from sensing that Corydon was a lying sack of shit."

"And the same thing happened to Galar and the others?" Jess asked, still trying understand the idea of computer viruses that attacked humans.

"Right." Dona gave her an approving nod. "Even though Chogan supposedly deactivated their comps, the nanobots could still use the agents' neuronetworks as a pathway to induce whatever delusions they chose."

"Will Chogan be able to get rid of the nanobots now?"

"Yeah, once we clean the infection out of the mainframe, which in turn must have infected her medical comps. Otherwise, she'd have detected the nanobots at once. It's a pretty exotic attack, but not unknown."

"Well, that's good," Jess said in relief. "Now if we can just find Riane . . ."

"We'll find her," Frieka growled. "All we have to do is get the system back online."

· 33 ·

He knew nothing except the crunch of bone in his ears and the sweet taste of alien blood on his tongue. Their swords glanced off his armored hide like stalks of red-wheat parting around a harvester's legs. He danced among them to the music of their screams.

Only the false god was a proper opponent, though He had grown cautious after feeling the bite of the Guardian's teeth and claws.

But the Guardian had grown cautious of Him, too. Those great horns were far more than ornament. That was as it should be. There was no sport in hunting prey that could not make one bleed in turn.

As the people said, "One only lives on the edge of death."

An enemy priest glanced toward the children being herded away into the ship. The Guardian lunged, hooked the alien with his claws, and flipped him to land twenty lengths away. His shriek cut off in a juicy crunch.

There. None of the aliens would dare look at anything but the Guardian now. His children could complete their escape in peace.

The sooner the better. They no longer heard the music in the screams of the enemy, and their pain made his soul ache.

A dangerous distraction.

The false god lunged at the Guardian, striking out with claws as sharp as his own, slicing through the shield of his energies to the vulnerable flesh at his core. Nick writhed in his emerald cocoon. The Guardian diverted power to heal himself and sank his teeth into the false god's belly. He grimaced at the taste. Not flesh, but a stinking mass of tiny, oily nanobots that writhed away from his teeth like maggots.

But still the god bellowed, in outrage as much as pain.

Despite the taste, the Guardian smiled and took another bite . . .

Nick looked through a sea of green, flying. It was as though he wore the Sela like a suit of armor made of energy.

Or *it* wore him.

Each time one of the Xerans fell to his claws, he felt a savage joy, primal and alien. Even the pain of his own wounds was a dark pleasure, and his body's fear carried an exhilarating jolt.

But some of his wounds weren't healing.

Most disturbing of all was the sense of other thoughts just below the surface of his mind, in a language he could almost understand. Dark thoughts, ancient and terrible. And very alien.

The Xerans, he thought, *have fucked with the wrong Sela.*

* * *

The Victor snarled in frustrated rage. Dozens of His priests lay dead, and the Demon had inflicted great wounds in His own glowing golden flesh. Yet nothing they did even slowed the creature down.

And it was the T'Lir that made it all possible.

To the Victor's senses, the creature was a swirl of Coswold-Barre energies—a blinding green warp in the fabric of space time.

A god in truth.

The Victor wanted to howl with frustration. That a primitive half-breed should command such power was an offense against Him. He wanted to kill the Demon for that sacrilege alone.

And yet the beast refused to acknowledge His superiority, refused to hand the T'Lir over to Him, though it was obviously His by right.

If anyone should command such power, it was the Victor.

Curse him! The Victor snarled. He would rip the T'Lir from the Demon's bleeding corpse if it was the last thing He did. He struck out. To His satisfaction, He felt His claws rip through those energies to find vulnerable human flesh.

Ha! I made you bleed that time!

He slashed again, but this time, the Demon twisted aside, avoiding the stroke. A massive paw swiped, sending another priest staggering away, screaming.

Luckily His men were too disciplined—and fearful of Him—to flee. Still, these were His elite forces. He'd spent decades training them, indoctrinating them, teaching them to fear and worship Him. The loss of so many experienced priests would cripple His command structure.

Yet in His rage, He found He didn't care. All that

mattered was the T'Lir. Once He had its power, the rest would not matter.

Riane stood outside the largest of the RVs guarding the Sela as they scrambled to safety. They were concealed from the central clearing by another of the Sela's vehicles, so the Xerans had failed to notice their prey escaping inside.

Which was no surprise, considering the way Nick was ripping into them. He'd even inflicted wounds on the Victor. Bites and claw marks marred the so-called god's glowing skin as blackened shadows, like sunspots on a star.

Unfortunately, none of them had even slowed the bastard down. He just kept going after Nick, ripping into that glowing Sela skin.

Which raised the sickening question of what those claws were doing to Nick's merely human body.

Mother Goddess, Riane hated standing here just watching. Unfortunately, she knew better than to try to wade in. If she'd had her armor, she would have been tempted, but without it, she was nothing more than a potential hostage.

And Frieka raised me better than that, thank you.

A strong hand clamped down on her shoulder. Riane whirled, fist raised, only to stop short when she realized it was Charlotte. The woman was pale as a ghost. "We've got to stop him, Riane!"

"Who, Nick?" She glanced back over her shoulder at the glowing figure.

"Yes, Nick!" Charlotte snapped. "He's killing them! Well, actually they're already dead, but if he doesn't stop now, they're not coming back!" She shoved past and started toward the brawl.

"Wait!" Riane grabbed for her arm. "What the hell are you talking about?"

"He's draining the T'Lir!"

Riane's jaw dropped. "What? How is that even possible?"

"The T'Lir's power comes from the life force of those held within it. Normally, they recharge over time, but this form he's taken is pulling too much energy. Vanja says if he keeps it up, he'll begin draining the spirits past the point they can recover."

"Which means what?" Riane demanded, very much afraid she knew.

"They won't come back!"

Shit! Nick's mother was in there. Riane whirled and drew on the power of the T'lir for a mental bellow.

Nick! You've got to stop! You're killing the T'Lir!

He and the Victor came together with a thundering boom and crackle of clashing energy. Sparks rained around them, green and golden. Xeran priests ducked away from flying clawed arms and feet.

Riane, straining to reach Nick's mind, sensed only a savage pleasure in the sensation of fangs sinking into flesh.

"He's not listening," Charlotte said grimly. "I can't get through to him either."

"Dammit," Riane snarled. She drew the two quantum swords she'd tucked into her belt and activated them. Their blades began to chime in menacing unison. "Guess I'll have to fight my way in there and get his attention."

Charlotte nodded. "I'm with you."

They broke into a wary jog around the nearest RV and into the clearing. Riane's belly coiled into a knot. She could see Nick rearing over the heads of a pack of priests. His roar shook the trees. "Sweet Mother Goddess, Nick," she whispered, awed. "No wonder you're draining the T'Lir."

And what the hell made her think he'd listen to her? Was he even human anymore? His thoughts sure didn't sound like it.

But this was Nick—the man who'd held her, made love

to her so tenderly, saved her life more times than she could count. If he ended up destroying his mother's soul while in the grip of some alien delusional state, he'd never get over the guilt. She couldn't let him do that to himself.

"Let's go." Riane took a deep breath, blew it out, and began to run, Charlotte racing at her heels. Together they sprinted toward Nick and the knot of brawling Xerans. His earsplitting roars made her stomach clench tighter with dread.

One of the priests saw them coming and bellowed something, pivoting to face them. Riane threw herself at him, her sword chiming a furious note. It clashed with his blade, ringing like a carillon. Another priest's sword swung toward her face, but Charlotte parried it before it could take off her head. Riane disengaged her blade from the first priest's, drove her elbow into his faceplate, and ran him through when he staggered. She ducked a wild sword swing, parried yet another blade, and bellowed, "Nick! Nick, dammit!"

He reared over the crowd, then crashed down on the Victor like a breaking wave. Something black and liquid went flying.

"You do realize this stunt's going to get us killed, right?" Charlotte yelled.

"Yeah, well, nobody's immortal." She parried a stabbing thrust at her chest, spotted another blade coming straight down at her face, and shoved forward with all her *riaat*-powered strength to avoid it.

Riane broke out into empty space, staggered. Something bright and green loomed in front of her. She looked up. And up. And up.

Nick/Sela reared over her, glowing green muzzle contorted to reveal fangs the length of her whole hand, his eyes narrow with savagery. Paws bigger than her head cast a blinding light down on her face.

He was about to come down right on top of her.

"Nick!" She screamed it, using both her lungs and every erg of power she could draw from the Stone.

He fell on her like a breaking wave. She was engulfed in light, blinded, deafened by his furious roar . . .

"Riane, what the fuck do you think you're doing? Are you trying to get yourself killed?"

She opened her eyes—to her shame, she realized she must have closed them—and found herself surrounded in a cocoon of green. And Nick's arms, strong and human, were tight around her.

Mother Goddess, I'm inside the Sela with him.

The sight of Riane staggering into the middle of the combat circle had damn near stopped Nick's heart. Especially when the Victor's cold black eyes had fallen on her with murderous frustration.

The ice-water shock of adrenaline blasted right through the Sela's blood frenzy, snapping Nick back to full awareness. Good thing, too. He'd barely managed to drag her into the energy construct in time to save her ass. *"The Victor almost disemboweled you, you little twit!"* he snapped. *"You scared the shit out of me!"*

"Charlotte's out there!" she yelped, more wild-eyed than he'd ever seen her.

"She backed off when she saw me grab you. Ran back across the clearing with a priest in pursuit."

"Shit."

He looked over the crowd to watch his mother whirl on the man and run him through with her sword. He blew out a breath in relief. *"Don't worry, she's already kacking him. Mom's tough."*

"Not that tough. Nick, Vanja said you're draining the T'Lir. Killing the spirits. You've got to break this off now, or they won't be able to come back."

"What?" Nick reached for the energy of the T'Lir—
and realized it was fading. He went cold. *We've got to stop!*
He punched the thought through to the Guardian's feral
consciousness. *They're growing too weak!*

Nick felt the creature give the Sela equivalent of a shrug.
They are willing to die to save my children.

But I'm not willing to kill them!

You, it said, *are not in charge.*

· 34 ·

✤

"Didn't you teach me I didn't have to kill? Yet you're killing Xerans—and spending the spirits of our people to do it!" Nick snarled.

"I will not allow my children to become extinct, boy. Yes, when the battle madness lifts, I will bear the pain of what I do. But the living will survive. The dead would be the first to say they've had their lives."

Despite what the Guardian said, Nick thought he could stop him. He could certainly try. But then what? He'd be at the Victor's nonexistent mercy with no way to defend himself. And so would Riane. She wouldn't have a chance. He couldn't give her up to those bastards.

And what if the T'Lir fell into the Victor's hands on his death?

The Sela would be only the first to die.

He couldn't risk it, not even to save his mother's spirit.

Besides, it was a risk she wouldn't want him to take. She'd willingly given up her own life to keep the T'Lir away from the Victor. He couldn't make that sacrifice meaningless.

"What the hell's going on out there?" Riane asked suddenly, jolting Nick out of his preoccupation.

He saw at once what she meant. The priests were no longer pressing in close to the Guardian, trying to get their blades into his glowing hide. Instead, they'd retreated into a loose and wary ring, leaving the Victor and the Guardian facing off.

"Look at him, my priests!" the Victor barked, backing away to circle the Guardian, who turned to keep Him in view. "See how the Demon's glow weakens. Victory is in our grasp—he dies!"

"Fuck," Riane snarled.

Nick's heart sank as he realized the bastard was right. The Guardian's construct no longer blazed as bright and solid as it had. Which meant the spirits must be very close to death. And when they were gone . . .

The Victor coiled into a crouch, a smirk on His face, despite the wounds that marred His own glow. "Watch closely as I finish him, my sons."

And He would. Unless . . . *Can you draw from me instead?* Nick asked the Guardian. *Save the spirits?*

It would kill you, boy.

But could you do it?

Yes. You might even survive long enough for me to kill that creature. The Guardian's deep mental voice sounded grim. *Very well. Prepare yourself—he attacks.*

Nick curled his arms tighter around Riane's slender body and braced her as they floated inside the Guardian's thinning construct.

The Victor charged, horned head lowered to gore, clawed hands reaching.

Now, the Guardian said.

Pain ripped through Nick like a blade of solid ice. Everything in him cringed, but instead of fighting it, he opened his mind, embraced the bitter, spreading numbness. A thick green cord of light flashed into being, feeding into the Guardian's head, into each clawed arm and leg. The glow of the construct brightened even as Nick grew colder, paler.

Riane wrapped her arms around him. Warm, fierce, her spirit blazed bright in his mind, beating back the cold of death. *"I'm here,"* she breathed.

"What are you doing?"

"Lending you my strength through the T'Lir." Keeping *you alive.*

Distantly he felt a vibrating shock as the Victor hit the Guardian. "You die for nothing," the Victor hissed in the Guardian's glowing ear. "Fighting you, drinking the blood of your energy, has told me what I needed to know about creating a Coswold-Barre warp. I don't need your bauble anymore."

The Guardian's lips drew back from his glowing fangs. "You will not live long enough to use what you have learned." He lunged for the Victor's throat.

Gritting his teeth, Nick fed more of himself to the Guardian. The green cord thickened.

Riane curled her long legs around his waist, her skin like hot silk against his chilling flesh. Her lips kissed the weakening pulse under his ear, and it strengthened. Her hand touched the center of his chest, and his heartbeat's flagging rhythm steadied.

"Don't you dare die," she breathed. *"Don't leave me alone, Nick Wyatt. I need you."*

He moaned and found her mouth with his, and she filled his chest with her warm breath. *"I love you,"* he whispered.

The Guardian's jaws clamped onto the Victor's shoulder. He toppled backward, dragging the startled god with him—into the reach of all four clawed legs.

The Guardian began to rip at the false god, tearing chest,

belly, and groin with those dagger-blade claws. The Victor howled and tried to jerk free, but He couldn't break the Sela's grip.

Great dark rents appeared in his golden glow, spreading, darkening.

His priests shouted in horror, a babble of confused voices. The Guardian ignored them, still tearing at his writhing captive.

The Victor shrieked, a high, inhuman sound, and exploded into a rain of oily dropplets. The Guardian roared in displeasure, blinded by the sticky black goo.

"What the fuck is that?" Riane snapped. *"Blood?"*

Nick gasped, unable to answer. His head was spinning, vision darkening. Cold rolled through like a black tide. He dragged Riane desperately close, craving her warmth.

The Guardian rolled onto all six legs, shaking his head furiously, looking around for his foe. But the Victor was gone. All that was left was the black liquid, which rolled rapidly away toward the priests.

They scrambled around the clearing, grabbing for it. The liquid climbed their hands, their legs, crawling up onto their bodies to coat their T-suits in an oily sheen.

The Guardian roared and leaped at the nearest warrior, who yelped and Jumped in a blinding flash of light and a rolling sonic boom.

The Sela wheeled, but the others were vanishing, too, taking the remnants of their god with them. In moments, the clearing was empty.

The Guardian roared in victory. The ground shook under his paws the instant before he vanished.

Riane hit the ground with a bone-jolting thump as the Guardian's energy construct disappeared from around her and Nick. "What the hell?"

She sat up, staring around her in dismay. Even the RVs were gone from the clearing. The Sela had apparently made good their escape while everyone's attention was diverted. "The least they could have done is left us a ride ho—"

Glancing down at Nick lying next to her, Riane froze. His eyes were closed, dark lashes stark against skin that was more gray than pale. "Nick!" Alarmed, she grabbed for him. Automatically, she glanced at his T'Lir. The armband's stone was dark, with none of its normal healthy green glow. *"Comp, is he alive?"*

"Heartbeat very faint. He is in deep shock. His life signs are fading. He needs immediate medical attention."

"And where the hell do you suggest he get it?"

"Riane!"

She looked up in relief at the sound of Charlotte's voice. The woman raced across the clearing toward her. "I thought you'd left!"

"Vanja said you were going to need me." She dropped to one knee by Nick's side. "I'll have to Jump you back to your Outpost if he's going to make it."

"Well, why in the hell didn't you do that earlier?"

"Because the Sela wouldn't let me, dammit!" she exploded. "Nick and the Guardian had to take a chunk out of the Victor."

Meaning they'd known the clash was fated to happen. And they made damn sure it had. "Son of a bitch!"

"Yeah, for pacifists the Sela are really ruthless." She grabbed Riane's shoulder and laid a hand on the center of Nick's chest.

They materialized in the center of the infirmary, startling Chogan so badly the woman spilled her cup of stim-chai all over the front of her medical robes.

Luckily, Charlotte's version of a Jump lacked the usual sonic boom and energy discharge, or it would have damaged a whole lot of delicate medical equipment.

"Riane!" the doctor gasped, brushing at the liquid. "Where the hell did you—"

"Never mind!" Riane interrupted desperately. "This man is dying!"

Chogan took one look at him and forgot her questions. "Techs! Somebody get me a regenerator tube!"

Watching the tube's transparent lid seal over her lover's face as a pink mist flooded the chamber, Riane sighed. And promptly wondered if her relief was premature. This was Sela business after all. Who knew whether mere twenty-third-century medicine would be enough to repair whatever damage the Guardian had done?

"Is he going to be all right?" she asked anxiously.

Chogan studied the tube's readouts. "He seems to be stabilizing. What happened to him anyway? And . . ." She frowned. "Did you know he's half-Xeran?"

Riane dropped into the nearest chair and began, helplessly, to laugh.

"She knows." Charlotte folded her arms and settled against the wall to wait.

Riane briefed Chief Dyami about her experiences while sitting in a chair next to Nick's infirmary bed. As she spoke, she absently stroked Frieka's big head, which was planted solidly on her knee as if he had no intention of letting her out of his sight.

Ever again.

Charlotte sat next to her, adding any details she could— or would, given the Sela's instructions to her.

"So let me get this straight. Your friend here," Dyami gestured at Nick, who was now deeply asleep rather than comatose, "fought the Victor while in the energy-construct guise of a giant primitive alien?"

Riane scratched her nose. It did sound pretty ridiculous, if you hadn't actually seen it. The reality, on the other hand, had been sheer terror. "Well, yeah. Apparently the normal laws of physics don't really apply to the Sela."

"And this construct beat the Victor so badly, he exploded into some kind of goo?"

Riane nodded. "Apparently the Victor is actually a really large nanobot colony."

"It's rumored on Xer," Charlotte said distantly, "that the Victor was a great military leader back in the first days of the colony, a couple centuries ago. They say He was a cyborg. As time went on and He began to age out, He replaced more and more of his body with nanobots. Now . . ."

"All that's left are the 'bots." Dyami grimaced, plainly not taken with the theory. "I think I saw a triddie about that once. It wasn't a very good triddie either."

"Well, the Victor is definitely not fictional," Riane told him tartly.

"So what about Nick?" Charlotte demanded, leaning forward in her chair. "Vanja said he needs to stay here."

Dyami gave her a narrow-eyed look. "Why?"

"You're going to need him. The Victor isn't going to stay goo for long. And when He recovers . . ."

"He told the Guardian he had learned how the T'Lir works from fighting him," Riane said. "Assuming he wasn't lying, the Galactic Union is going to need all the help we can get."

"That may be, but legally Nick's situation is complicated," Dyami pointed out. "He is a temporal native."

Frieka lifted his head. "I checked, Chief. He disappeared from the historical record without a trace."

"Yeah, and the Mother Goddess knows that Xeran DNA doesn't belong in the past." Dyami sighed. "You'll have to go before a Temporal Enforcement judge, but I doubt you'll have any real trouble getting him permission to stay in this century."

Riane blew out a breath. "Thanks, Chief."

"No, thank *you* for getting back here in one piece to tell us about the shit storm headed our way." He rose to his feet and dropped a hand on her shoulder. "Glad to have you back."

Frowning, Riane watched him duck out of Nick's medical bubble. "Was it just me, or did the Chief seem really subdued?"

"He locked Dona in the brig on suspicion of treason," Frieka told her bluntly. "Now that she's been cleared, she's still not real happy with him."

Riane winced. "Ouch."

"Riane?" Nick's voice sounded faint, cracked. He stopped and cleared his throat. "Riane?"

She sat up in pleasure. "Hey! You're finally awake. How do you feel?"

"Like I got run over by a train. Which then backed over me a couple of times." He licked dry lips. "Is there any water?"

She turned to the bedside vendser to get it just as Frieka reared beside the bed.

Nick gave him a smile. "Frieka. Hey."

The wolf gaped his jaws in a lupine smile. "Riane says you showed me where to find her when that dickhole Xeran kidnapped her when she was twelve."

"Yeah." He reached eagerly for the cup. Riane steadied it as he drank thirstily.

"So that leaves just one question." The wolf's eyes narrowed. "Just what are your intentions toward my little girl?"

· 35 ·

"Frieka!" Riane yelped, horrified.

Nick choked on his water and began to laugh.

The wolf eyed him. "I don't think this is a subject for humor."

Nick wiped his mouth. "Actually . . ." He stopped to cough. "I don't think so either." Sobering, he looked Frieka right in the eye. "I love her. My intentions are to be a part of her life, for as long as she'll have me, in whatever capacity." He looked up to see Riane's dark eyes going wide and round, her soft lips parting. Unable to resist, he caught the back of her head and dragged her down for a kiss. She tasted so sweet, it was all he could do not to moan.

"Pheromones!" the wolf said, and pretended to cough. "A huge, choking cloud of pheromones!" But there was satisfaction in his blue eyes.

He waited until they came up for air. "But for the record"—he leaned in close and showed his impressive teeth—"if you hurt my kid, I'll rip out your heart and eat it."

Nick blinked at him. "That's fair."

They left Nick alone to get dressed in a dark green civilian tunic and pants Riane had obtained from a unit in the wall. Everything fit like a glove and sealed with something like Velcro, except without the Velcro—he'd have loved to know how that worked. After sliding his feet into a pair of soft black boots, Nick stepped out of the dome to look for Riane, her wolf, and Charlotte.

He found them waiting just outside.

"I wish I could stay," Charlotte told him without preamble, "but I need to get going." She looked tense, anxious, a little grim.

"Back to the Sela?" Nick reached for her hand. Her skin felt too cool, and he frowned at her in worry.

"No." She lifted her chin, her gaze level and determined. "I need to find your father."

Nick tensed. "Vanja told you who he is?"

Charlotte's smile was so slight as to be almost invisible, but her gaze was warm. "No, but I figure he's a tall, handsome devil. Like his son." Her smile turned a bit sad. "Not a bad one-night stand."

"Charlotte . . . Mother . . ."

Her hand tightened around his. "Listen to me, Nick. I'm proud to know I'll become your mother. I can think of no finer accomplishment. And I know my life with you will give me a great deal of pleasure and pride."

He dragged her into his arms for a fierce hug. She held him close, then pressed her lips to his cheek and stepped away. His eyes stung.

Riane promptly pulled her into a warm embrace. "Thank you for him."

Charlotte's eyes widened in surprise, then she hugged the taller woman back. "And thank you for loving him." When Riane released her, she took a deep breath.

"But what about the T'Lir?" Nick frowned down at the still-darkened gem that hugged his upper arm, wondering if he was supposed to give it to her—and what use it would be if he did.

Charlotte pulled up the loose sleeve of her shirt. An identical armband clasped her upper arm, though considerably brighter, its metal lacking the scratches of his own. Green sparks danced in its depths. "Vanja gave me this before I left. Apparently it just changed shape all on its own." Catching his confused frown, she explained, "It used to look like a snow globe. It's the earlier version of yours."

Nick touched his, frowning. "What *about* mine? Did the spirits . . . ?"

"Vanja said that you saved them when you let the Guardian draw on your life force. They're really weak, though, so you need to avoid using the T'Lir for a while. It's going to take them time to recover."

He sighed in relief. So her future self survived still, inside the Stone, waiting to be reborn. Some of his grief lifted. "Good."

Charlotte took a deep breath and blew it out. "Well, I'd better get going, or I'll never want to leave."

A green glow flooded the corridor, and she was gone.

Frieka looked up at them. "Which officially makes me the third wheel here. Since judging by the pheromones"— he sneezed explosively—"mating will soon commence, I'm out of here. I think I'll go find Dona and cheer her up."

As they watched, he trotted out of sight.

* * *

Frieka was right. They almost didn't make it back to Riane's quarters.

Nick and Riane were in each other's arms before the door slid completely closed. It was a hard kiss, flavored with joy, fierce relief, and a lingering sadness for Charlotte's sacrifice.

Tasting that last, Riane instantly resolved to make Nick forget his losses. At least for a while.

She stripped his tunic off over his head and bent to give one of his pecs a promising nibble. He chuckled in pleasure and anticipation, threading his hands through her hair. "God, I love you."

Riane lifted her head to grin up at him. "And I love you." Her eyes stung suddenly, and she cleared her throat, a little surprised at the sudden fierce intensity of the emotion. "More than I can say."

Nick bent and hauled her up into his arms. Chuckling, Riane wrapped her legs around his waist and dove into another kiss. Tongues stroked, teased, swirled hungry circles around each other. By the time they drew apart, they were both panting.

"I hope there's a bed in here somewhere," Nick told her, a glitter in his eyes. "Or one of us is about to end up buttdown on the floor."

Riane laughed. "Right behind you."

He glanced over his shoulder. "Ahh. There it is." He turned and carried her over to the bunk, then tumbled both of them onto it.

They got busy for a while, dragging off clothes and boots, laughing as various items went flying. Finally, they were both blessedly naked.

Riane sighed in pleasure at the feeling of his warm bare skin against hers, hard-muscled and strong.

And so deliciously *alive.*

"For a while there," she told him, "I was afraid we weren't going to make it."

Green eyes narrowed. "Well, we did. And we're going to stay that way. I'll kill any fucker that tries to take you away from me."

His mouth crushed down on hers again, hot and fierce with promise. Fingers tangled in her hair dragged her head back, and he began nibbling his way down the length of her neck. Paused to swirl his tongue over the jut of her collarbone, then give it a quick nip before continuing downward.

Feeling decadent in her pleasure, Riane let him work his way to her breasts. "You have," he told her between teasing licks and nibbles, "the most delicious nipples I've ever had the pleasure to taste."

"What a coincidence." Riane sat up on her elbows to watch. His dark hair felt like silk as it fell across her breasts. "I like your jutty bits, too."

He looked up, a grin dancing around his mouth. "Jutty bits? Jutty *bits*? Any part of mine that juts is *not* a 'bit'!"

She smirked. "Jutty kielbasa? Jutty man snake? Jutty . . ."

He dug his long fingers into her ribs, and she shrieked out a laugh. "Watch it, you! A little respect for the intercontinental ballistic missile of passion!"

Riane stared at him. "Two things. You call your dick an ICBM? And second, if you can even *pronounce* 'intercontinental ballistic missile' right now, your blood supply is not where it's supposed to be."

"Blood supply?" An expression of mock outrage on his face, he sat up and grabbed his cock. Which, judging by its length, breadth, and rosy rigidity, was more than up to the task she had in mind. "I'll show you blood supply!"

Quick as a blink, Riane planted a hand in the middle of his chest and shoved. He toppled over on his back with a shout of laughter as she pounced. A hand curled around his cock, and she swooped in to engulf as much of that delicious length as she possibly could.

Riane's mouth felt so hot, wet, and staggeringly delicious that he almost came on the spot. "Wait a minute!" he protested, managing, with a effort of will, to pull his cock free. It definitely wasn't happy to leave her mouth.

She glared at him in grumpy frustration. "What do you mean?"

"Sixty-nine!" he gasped, and rearranged himself. Riane wasted no time straddling his face while she scooped his cock up and popped it into her mouth again.

The sensation of that clever tongue dancing over the head of his erection made his eyes roll back in his head. God, she was good at that.

Determined to give her every bit as much pleasure, Nick parted her delicate nether lips and lifted his head for a long, slow lick. To his satisfaction, she jerked against him and moaned.

As if challenged, she took him deeper, her throat working around his length in mind-blowing ripples. Her long fingers found his balls, rolled them tenderly, cupped, and stroked. Each movement of that talented hand coiled his building orgasm another fraction tighter.

He slipped a finger into her depths and began to stroke as he licked slow circles around her clit. Riane quivered, loving the pleasure that jolted through her with each thrust, the wet delight in every flick of his tongue.

She took him down again, enjoying the way he jerked in luscious reaction. The soft hair on his chest teased her hard nipples, adding another sweet flourish of delight. Riane closed her eyes, savoring the salty, slightly bitter taste of his pre-cum, the clean male scent of his body.

Her exotic warrior, with all his power and hidden vulnerabilities . . .

And *hers*. As she was his. Body and soul and heart.

The climax took her by surprise, roaring up out of that hungry part of her soul that had been lonely too long, despite the best efforts of family and friends and Frieka. Long, rippling pulses of orgasm, pumping hard through her core. She lost her grip on his cock as she threw back her head to scream.

Suddenly she was flat on her back, and he was rearing over her, his green eyes wild. He drove into her in one long thrust, sweet and ruthless, filling her so completely she yowled.

"God, Riane!" he gasped, and began to pump. Riding hard between her legs in deep, powerful drives.

"Nick, I love you!" She cried out in pleasure and wrapped arms and legs around him, drawing him close, wanting to touch every inch of him with every inch of herself. "Mother Goddess, I love you!"

"Love you . . ." he panted. "Love you . . ."

Shuddering, convulsing at the sharp, fierce bursts of delight that jolted through them with every thrust, they surged and rolled together.

And came simultaneously with one long, chorusing scream.

Panting and exhausted, Riane and Nick lay in a deliciously sweaty heap. Listening to his heartbeat slow, she picked up a long curl of his hair and stroked it absently between her fingers.

They had a long road ahead of them, she knew. He had three centuries to catch up on now—he didn't even speak Galactic Standard after all. Knew nothing about life in the twenty-third century. Luckily, all that could be taken care of easily enough. A few educational data implants, and he'd know everything he needed to learn in a few hours.

Learning to use all that knowledge would take longer, but he was more than up to the job. He'd already learned to do something similar with the help of the Stone after all. He . . .

"Riane . . ." he began, his tone hesitant.

"Mmm?"

"I realize I've got a long way to go before I can pull my own weight in this time . . ."

Riane snorted. "Judging by what Charlotte said about the coming trouble with the Victor, I suspect you'll be more than pulling before long."

"Which brings up another problem. There's going to be war, and it's probably going to be ugly."

"Wars usually are."

He took a deep breath. "Marry me anyway."

She froze, breath held. "What?"

"Uhhh . . ." He met her gaze, his own worried. "Do you even have marriage in this time?"

"Oh." She blinked, stunned. "Yeah, we get married."

"Good. So." He licked his lips, vulnerability in his eyes. Swallowed. "Will you marry me, Riane Arvid?"

The grin that spread across her face was so broad, it almost hurt her cheeks. "Yes!" She whooped and threw both arms around his chest. "Yes, yes, yes!"

"Good." He closed his eyes in relief, gathering her close. "That's very good."

The kiss went on a long, long time.

Turn the page for a special preview of

KISSING MIDNIGHT

By Emma Holly

Coming June 2009 from Berkley Sensation!

Paddington Station, 1933

Graham Fitz Clare was a secret agent.

He had to repeat that to himself sometimes, because the situation seemed too ludicrous otherwise. He was ordinary, he thought, no one more so, but he fit a profile apparently. Eton. Oxford. No nascent Bolshevik tendencies. MI5 had recruited him two years ago, soon after he'd accepted a job as personal assistant to an American manufacturer. Arnold Anderson traveled the world on business, and Graham—who had a knack for languages—served as his translator and dogsbody.

He supposed it was the built-in cover that shined him up for spy work, though he couldn't see as he'd done anything important yet. He hadn't pilfered any secret papers, hadn't seduced an enemy agent—which wasn't to suggest he thought he could! For the most part, he'd simply reported back on factories he and his employer had visited, along with writing up impressions of their associated owners and officials.

Tonight, in fact, was the most spylike experience he'd had to date.

His instructions had been tucked into the copy of *The Times* he'd bought at the newsagent down the street from his home.

"Paddington Station," the note had said in curt, telegraphic style. "At 11:45 tonight. Come by Underground and carry this paper under your left arm."

Graham stood at the station now, carrying the paper and feeling vaguely foolish. The platform was empty and far darker than during the day. The cast-iron arches of the roof curved gloomily above his head, the musty smell of soot stinging his nose. A single train, unlit and silent except for the occasional sigh of escaping steam, sat on the track to the right of him. One bored porter had eyed him when he arrived, shaken his head, and then retired to presumably cozier environs.

Possibly the porter had been bribed to disappear. All Graham knew for sure was that he'd been waiting here fifteen minutes while his feet froze to the concrete floor, without the slightest sign of whoever he was supposed to meet. Doubly vexed to hear a church clock striking midnight, he tried not to shiver in the icy November damp. His overcoat was new, at least—a present from the professor on Graham's twenty-fifth birthday.

That memory made him smile despite his discomfort. His guardian was notoriously shy about giving gifts. They were always generous, always exactly what the person wanted—as if Edmund had plucked the wish from their minds. He always acted as if he'd presumed by wanting to give whatever it was to them. The habit, and so many others, endeared him to his adopted brood more than any parent by blood could have. The professor seemed to think it a privilege to have been allowed to care for them.

All of them, even flighty little Sally, knew the privilege was theirs.

Though Graham was old enough to occasionally be embarrassed by the fact, there really was no mystery as to why Edmund's charges remained at home. Graham's lips pressed together at the thought of causing Edmund concern. If tonight's business kept him waiting long enough to have to lie to the professor about where he'd been, he was not going to be amused.

Metal creaked, drawing his eyes to the darkened train. Evidently, it wasn't empty. One of the doors had opened, and a dainty Oriental woman was stepping down the stairs of the central car. Her skintight emerald dress looked straight out of wardrobe for a Charlie Chan picture. Actually, she looked straight out of one, too, so exotically gorgeous that Graham's tongue was practically sticking to the roof of his mouth.

He forced himself to swallow as her eyes raked him up and down.

"Hm," she said, flicking a length of night black hair behind one slender shoulder. "You're tall at least, and you look healthy."

Graham flushed at her dismissive tone, and again— even harder—when she turned her back on him to reascend the stairs. Holy hell, her rear view was smashing, her waist nipped in, her bum round and firm. Graham knew he wasn't the sort of man women swooned over, not like his younger brother Ben, or even the professor, whose much-younger female students occasionally followed him home. No, Graham had a plain English face, not ugly but forgettable. Normally, this didn't bother him—or not much. It just seemed a bit humiliating to find the woman who'd insulted him so very attractive herself.

That green dress was tight enough to show the cleft

between the halves of her arse. His groin grew heavy, his shaft beginning to swell. The sight of her lack of underclothes was so inspiring he forgot he was supposed to move.

"Don't just stand there," she said impatiently over her shoulder. "Follow me."

Shoving *The Times* into his pocket, he followed her, dumbstruck, into a private compartment. She yanked down the shades before flicking on two dim sconces.

"Sit," she said, pointing to the black leather seat opposite her own. Her hand was slim and pale, her nails lacquered red as blood.

Graham sat with difficulty. He was erect and aching and too polite to shift the cause of the trouble to a different position. Hoping his condition wasn't obvious to her, he wrapped his hands around his knees and waited.

The woman stared at him unblinking—taking his stock, he guessed. She resembled a painted statue, or maybe a mannequin in a store window. In spite of his attraction to her, Graham's irritation rose. This woman had kept him hanging long enough.

"What's this about?" he asked.

She leaned back and crossed a pair of incredibly shapely legs, a move that seemed too practiced to be casual. Her dress was shorter than the current fashion, ending just below her knee. Graham wasn't certain, but from the hissing sound her calves made, she might be wearing real silk stockings.

"We're giving you a new assignment," she said.

"A new assignment."

"If we decide you're up for it."

"Look," Graham said, "you people came to me. It's hardly cricket to suggest that *you're* doing *me* favors."

The woman smiled, her teeth a gleaming flash of white behind ruby lips. Graham noticed her incisors were unusually sharp. "I think you'll find this assignment more in-triguing than your previous one. It does, however, require a higher level of vetting." She leaned forward, her slender forearm resting gracefully on one thigh. The way her small breasts shifted behind her dress told him her top half had no more undergarments than her bottom. Graham's collar began to feel as tight as his pants. The space between their seats wasn't nearly great enough.

"Tell me, Graham," she said, her index finger almost brushing his, "what do you know about X Section?"

"Never heard of it," he said, because as far as he knew, MI5 sections only went up to F.

"What if I told you it hunts things?"

"*Things?*"

"Unnatural things. Dangerous things. Beasts who shouldn't exist in the human realm."

Her face was suddenly very close to his. Her eyes were as dark as coffee, mysterious golden lights seeming to flicker behind the irises. Graham felt dizzy staring into them, his heart thumping far too fast. He didn't recall seeing her move, but she was kneeling on the floor of the compartment in the space that gaped between his knees. Her pale, strong hands were sliding up his thighs. His cock lurched like it could hasten their possible meeting.

"We need information," she whispered, her breath as cool and sweet as mint pastilles. "So we can destroy these monsters. And we need you to get it for us."

"You're crazy." He had to gasp it; his breath was coming so fast.

"No, I'm not, Graham. I'm the sanest person you've ever met."

Her fingers had reached the bend between his legs and torso, her thumbs sliding inward over the giant arch of his erection. She scratched him gently with the edge of her bloodred nails.

"Christ," Graham choked out. The feathery touch blazed through him like a welder's torch. His nerves were on fire, his penis weeping with desire. He shifted on the seat in helpless reaction. Her mouth was following her thumbs, her exhalations whispering over his grossly stretched trousers.

"I'm going to give you clearance," she said. "I'm going to make sure we can trust you."

He cried out when she undid his zip fastener, and again when her small, cool fingers dug into his smalls to lift out his engorged cock. Blimey, he was big, his skin stretched like it would split. She stroked the whole shuddering length of him, causing his spine to arch uncontrollably.

"Watch me," she ordered as his head lolled back. "Watch me suck you into my mouth."

Graham was no monk. He watched her and felt her and thought his soul was going to spill out of his body where her lips drew strong and tight on him.

He didn't want to admit this was the first time a woman had performed this particular act on him. He could see why men liked it. The sensations were incredible, streaking in hot, sharp tingles from the tip of his throbbing penis to the arching soles of his feet. She was smearing her ruby lipstick up and down his shaft, humming at the swell of him, taking him into her throat, it felt like. Her tongue was rubbing him every place he craved.

The fact that she was barking mad completely slipped his mind.

"Oh, God," he breathed, lightly touching her hair where she'd tucked it neatly behind her ears. The strands were silk under his fingertips, so smooth they seemed unreal. "Oh, Christ. Don't stop."

She didn't stop. She sucked and sucked until his seed exploded from his balls in a fiery rush. He cried out hoarsely, sorry and elated at the same time. And then she did something he couldn't quite believe.

She bit him.

Her teeth sank into him halfway down his shaft, those sharp incisors even sharper than he'd thought. The pain was as piercing as the pleasure had been a second earlier. He grabbed her ears, wondering if he dared to pull her off. Her clever tongue fluttered against him, wet, strong . . . and then she drew his blood from him.

He moaned, his world abruptly turned inside out. Ecstasy washed through him in drowning waves. She was drinking from him in a whole new way, swallowing, licking, moaning herself like a starving puppy suckling at a teat. All his senses went golden and soft. *So good. So sweet.* Like floating on a current of pure well-being.

He didn't know how long it lasted, but he was sorry when her head came up.

"You're mine now," she said.

He blinked sleepily into her glowing eyes. Was it queer that they were lit up? Right at that moment, he couldn't decide.

"I'm yours," he said, though he wasn't certain he meant it.

"You're not going to remember me biting you."

"No," he agreed. "That would be awkward."

"When I give you instructions, you'll follow them."

"I expect I will," he said.

She narrowed her eyes at him, her winglike little brows furrowing.

"I will," he repeated, because she seemed to require it.

She rose, licking one last smear of blood from her upper lip. As soon as it disappeared, he forgot that it had been there.

"Zip yourself," she said.

He obeyed and got to his feet as well. It seemed wrong to be towering over his handler, though he couldn't really claim to mind. She handed him a slip of paper with a meeting place in Hampstead Heath. As had been the case with the note tucked into his paper, the directions were neatly typed—no bobbles or mistakes. He had the idle thought that Estelle would have approved.

"Tomorrow night," the woman said. "Eleven sharp. You'll know when you've seen what we need you to."

"Will you be there?"

He thought this was a natural question. Any male with blood in his veins would want to repeat the pleasures of this night, if only to return the favor she'd shown him. But perhaps he wasn't supposed to ask. She wrinkled her brow again.

"*I* won't be," she said, "but chances are our enemy will."